"Ruby, please, I haven't seen you in twenty years."

He heard the edge in his voice. Fear? He wasn't sure what scared him, couldn't put it into words. Yet at the same time relief traveled through every cell, as if all along he'd been expecting this and the moment had finally come.

"I'm just glad to see you." He emptied his lungs and whispered, "To know you're okay."

Ruby's eyes filled again and she lowered her head.

"Oh, no, Ruby. I don't want to upset you. I'm sorry. I just can't believe you're here."

She held up her hand in a clear signal to stop. "I'm okay, Mike. Really. I don't want to worry your little boy. I don't even know what's brought on these tears."

She didn't? He knew exactly what his jumble of emotions was all about. He'd never loved anyone the way he'd loved her. Now he had to know what had brought her back to Bluestone River.

Dear Reader,

Thanks for joining me in Bluestone River, a fictional prairie town in Illinois. Although I grew up in Chicago, a great city built on the Midwestern prairie, my parents took us on memorable road trips to explore small towns in Illinois and Iowa. Some of those places look a lot like Bluestone River, and a few even have cherished covered bridges. The covered bridge spanning the river in *A Family for Jason* has a special place in the hearts of Ruby Driscoll and Mike Abbot—it's where they carved their names and sealed their promise to love each other forever.

At its heart, *A Family for Jason*, book one of my new Back to Bluestone River series, is a reunion story. But Mike and Ruby can have their second chance only if they're willing to confront—and heal—the past.

Thanks for coming along on this trip to Bluestone River. Enjoy getting to know characters trying to breathe new life into their hometown as they struggle with the past and nurture their hopes for the future. Be sure to sign up for my mailing list and visit me on Facebook and Twitter: virginiamccullough.com; Twitter, @VEMcCullough; and Facebook, Facebook.com/virginia.mccullough.7.

To happy endings,

Virginia

HEARTWARMING

A Family for Jason

———

Virginia McCullough

◆ **HARLEQUIN**® HEARTWARMING™

Recycling programs
for this product may
not exist in your area.

ISBN-13: 978-1-335-51079-2

A Family for Jason

Copyright © 2019 by Virginia McCullough

Printed in U.S.A.

www.Harlequin.com

Virginia McCullough grew up in Chicago, but she's enjoyed living in many places, including the coast of Maine, western North Carolina and now northeastern Wisconsin. She started her career writing magazine articles but soon turned to coauthoring and ghostwriting nonfiction books. When fictional characters started whispering in her ear, she tried her hand at writing their stories. Now, many books later, Back to Bluestone River is her second series for Harlequin Heartwarming readers. When she's not writing, Virginia eagerly reads other authors' books, hangs out with family and friends, and plans another road trip.

Books by Virginia McCullough

Harlequin Heartwarming

Girl in the Spotlight
Something to Treasure
Love, Unexpected

Visit the Author Profile page
at Harlequin.com for more titles.

To adults and children who courageously work to recover from life-changing traumatic events and crises, with a nod of gratitude to the professionals and volunteers who step up to help them heal.

CHAPTER ONE

RUBY DRISCOLL BLINKED back tears at the sight of Emma standing on her porch on this golden late September afternoon. Emma had warned her about what to expect, but the sight of her best friend bent over with her hands clutching a walker still put a lump in Ruby's throat.

Ruby hurried up the porch stairs and gingerly wrapped her arms around Emma's shoulders. "I'm so sorry about this."

Emma smiled faintly and patted the walker. "No pity party for me. This contraption is only temporary until the op next week, Rubes."

Rubes. Only a handful of people had ever been allowed to call her that, and they were all from deep in her past. Her dad. Emma, her first friend, and Mike, her first love.

Seeing pain pinching Emma's face, images of a tall, spunky girl raced through Ruby's mind like movie clips. This was *Emma*, who once did twenty perfect and unforgettable cartwheels in a row, beating her nearest competitor by eight. Emma, always the first to call out "Hey, Rubes, I dare you to swim all the way to the raft." Then Emma would take off like a shot, leaving Ruby struggling to keep up.

Now Ruby couldn't help but stare at her almost thirty-eight-year-old friend gripping the walker, her knuckles white. She'd exchanged slim-legged jeans for baggy drawstring pants. Her long, dark brown hair was gone, replaced with a no-fuss pixie.

"Come in," Emma said. "Let's get you settled."

"I'll get Miss Peach. She's been cooped up in the car for hours. I'll walk her around the yard before I bring her in."

Emma rolled her big brown eyes. "Only you would end up with a dog named Miss Peach. You, who never wanted the bother of a house plant, let alone a pet."

Ruby smiled and went back down the stairs to her car. "Things happen," she replied, looking back over her shoulder. "But you'll see. Peach has lovely manners."

Adjusting to living in someone else's house, even Emma's, was part of the reality she'd signed up for. But it wasn't Ruby's fault Emma was a cat person. No one had pressed Ruby to rescue a cat. Peach—Ruby dropped the Miss part most of the time—was a lovely golden retriever who'd more or less shown up at her door. Ruby lifted the hatchback to let the dog jump to the ground. "Time for introductions, Peach. You need to be on your best behavior."

Ruby clipped on the leash and wandered into the field of prairie flowers and grasses adjacent to the house. She lifted her face to the sun and closed her eyes, needing a minute to settle the uneasy stirring in her belly. Arriving on Emma's doorstep was mixed up with so much more than simply adjusting to sharing someone else's space for a couple of months. Only two weeks ago, Emma had called and asked her to come back to Bluestone River to help her through a back surgery. The procedure was a step of last resort and with any luck it could resolve the damage caused by an old injury once and for all.

No need for Emma to point out the obvious: Ruby had nothing to lose by walking away from her life in Florida. In fact, Emma had been the first person Ruby called after the superintendent of the Morton School District told her to clean out her desk and leave the building. Only two years earlier, Ruby had embraced her job as the head of special programming for the school system with her whole heart, living and breathing her innovative antibullying program as if nothing else mattered. Now, her reason for staying in Florida had vanished with her job.

Ruby was brash in assuring her mom and her sister, Dee, that she'd quickly regroup and find a new, even better position where her efforts would be appreciated and fully supported. Maybe she'd even change fields. Wouldn't that be something? In the meantime, Ruby feigned a breezy attitude during phone conversations with Emma, as if to say "don't be silly, being unemployed was no big deal." She had no regrets, she glibly claimed. Like she could fool Emma any more than she could fool herself.

Twenty years ago Ruby fled Bluestone River and vowed never to come back. Leaving was her choice, but that hadn't prevented her from feeling driven out by a tragedy that exploded every dream she'd ever had. The idea of returning to Bluestone River for any reason had been unthinkable, at least until Emma called. Ruby never could say no to her best friend.

Now, the autumn breeze caressed her cheeks and fallen leaves swirled around Emma's front yard and called up bittersweet memories of carefree days with Mike and Emma and all their friends.

Ruby called the dog back to her side. "I couldn't leave you behind in Florida, no matter what." At the moment, the retriever was far more interested in the smells on the unfamiliar ground than the sound of Ruby's voice, but Peach didn't resist being led back to the house. "Don't worry, girl, you'll grow on Emma, just like you grew on me." Ruby gave Peach an affectionate pat before going back up the stairs and letting herself in the house.

"This place is fantastic, even better than the photos," Ruby called out as she glanced around the great room and the open kitchen and dining room.

The log home sat on twenty-five acres on the edge of town and only a half mile or so from Bluestone River's landmark covered bridge. Emma's late husband had designed this grand house with its stone fireplace and large windows, but Neil died not long after he and Emma had moved in. Everything inside, from the simple lines of the modern teak dining-room table and chairs, to the vintage needlepoint pillows on the couch, reflected Emma's flair for blending old and new and making it all look chic. And uniquely Emma. Ruby saw no sign that Neil had ever lived there. Not surprising.

Thinking about Neil always brought on a bout of sadness. She knew way too much about Neil and Emma's unhappy years spent trying to make their marriage at least tolerable. They'd not let their private troubles seep out into the world, though. According to Emma, most people in town assumed she and Neil were happy high-school sweethearts, a lucky pair building their dream home. But Ruby was no outsider, so she knew the truth. Ruby pushed away those dark thoughts. None of it mattered now, anyway.

The air was filled with the aromas of chocolate and ginger, and a sweet yeasty scent, like baking bread. "Em, please, don't tell me you've been baking."

Emma flashed a pointed look. "Seriously? I can't stand long enough to bake. That's why I hired Brenda. She lost her job and needs a little income, so she does light cleaning and shopping, mostly for older people." She smirked. "And people like me. She made a bakery run earlier. I don't want us to run short on goodies."

Emma stood at the counter, her walker set aside for the moment. She pointed to sliding doors that opened to the deck. "That's the magic spot. The place I take most of the tons of pictures that turn up on your phone."

"Almost daily," Ruby said with a snicker. In the last couple of years, Emma's emails and texts included shots of the deer regularly roaming the land, probably coming up from the direction of the river. Flocks of geese from the bird sanctuary visited the sloping field behind the house. About half of Emma's acres were wooded. The rest was a field of prairie grasses and wildflowers whose shades of purples and reds and yellows were fading now.

"It's an incredible place, Em. I see why

you love it so." Luckily, it was plenty big enough to offer a separate space for her and Peach. She looked down at the dog, who'd stretched out in front of the patio doors. "See? I told you the dog was quiet. She's being a little shy now."

Nodding to acknowledge Peach, Emma said, "Let me take you to your room before we have coffee. And yes, there's lots of space for your cute retriever." She shot Ruby a pointed look. "Okay, I admit, she's a gorgeous dog. But I'm still surprised. Even as a kid you showed no interest in four-legged anything. No dogs or cats or gerbils. And you weren't one of the horse girls."

Ruby shrugged. What started as Ruby keeping the dog for a couple of days as a favor turned into taking in Peach for good. Even her mother and Dee thought it was another sign of Ruby never letting a crisis, hers or someone else's, go unmarked. Naturally, Dee had quipped, Ruby would end up with a dog whose eighty-something-year-old owner died suddenly.

With Emma going down the short hallway at a snail's pace, Ruby stayed well behind and timed her steps to the clunking of the walker hitting the hardwood floor. Once inside the room, though, Emma sat on a bench at an antique dressing table with a beveled oval mirror and inlaid designs in the wood.

Ruby took in the cheerful pale sage-and-white bedroom, larger than it looked in photos and even more inviting. The closet doors alone took up half of one wall. The small writing desk and reading chair were positioned next to another set of patio doors looking out on the field of flowers. Touched by the obvious attempt to make her comfortable, Ruby remarked, "You said this was really a suite that has everything. And it's true. The closet has more room than I could possibly need for what few things I brought."

Emma frowned. "On the phone the other day you said everything you own fit into your car. Is that really true?"

"Almost. That's how I wanted it and I managed to make it work." Leaving Florida had been the easy part of all that had happened. Determined to take only what she could jam into the trunk, Ruby had packed up her apartment right down to the coffeepot and dish towels. Volunteers from the women's shelter arrived one morning with a truck and hauled away her things— sofa, bed, sheets, even the vacuum cleaner. Watching the practical items of her life disappear, Ruby *almost* convinced herself it was all for the best. She *needed* a change, anyway. Right?

She took a couple of steps to stand behind Emma and fluffed up the deep brown hair framing her face. "I love your short cut. And your hair is so shiny, like it always was. All you have to do is run your fingers through it and you're done." She smiled at Emma in the mirror. "But you could shave half of your head and you'd still be beautiful."

Emma responded with an "oh, please" groan.

"Playing around with your hair brings back lots of memories. Remember how we used to put it all in giant rollers in useless attempts to make it curly?" Ruby laughed. "Now you're lucky it's straight and nice and thick."

Emma responded with a quick nod. "Not having my hair hanging down my back took some getting used to, but don't become too attached to this pixie look." She stood and gripped her walker. "As soon as I'm mobile and active, like I used to be, I'm growing it back."

Ruby drew her head back at the rise in Em's voice as she spoke each word. "Yes, ma'am. You can do as you please."

"I didn't mean to sound harsh." Emma let out a soft chuckle. "My mind wasn't really on my hair. I was recalling Neil demanding to know why I insisted we put up the drywall and finish this room right away. And why such a pale sage? I told him it was the color of your bedroom growing up, and you'd chosen it yourself. It was like I knew one day you'd be back." She paused. "Maybe even for good."

Ruby's throat closed. Not that it mattered, since she had no sarcastic comeback to Emma's remark. She'd committed to staying for whatever amount of time Emma needed her. In some ways, it was a two-way street. As long as she and Peach stayed in this peaceful room in Emma's house, Ruby could cut her expenses and make her savings last until she figured out where to go and what to do next. But long-term? Ruby couldn't conjure up any circumstance that would keep her in Bluestone River.

"Rubes? Don't go all silent on me. I didn't mean to upset you," Emma said in a low voice. "I was just talking off the top of my head. Like wishful thinking."

"It's okay." Ruby gave her friend's shoulder a friendly pat. "Maybe if I could stay in this room and never leave, it would be okay. But even if I found a job in the schools or with a crisis line, which is unlikely, I can't get past the minefield of memories." Ruby stared at the floor. "Sometimes, the sweetest of them are as unbearable as the worst."

"I know, I know. You've said as much for twenty years now."

Emma turned her walker to face the doorway. "But Ruby, not everyone in town remembers or, to be blunt, cares what happened to your family. Meanwhile, you've let a twenty-year-old tragedy rule your life."

"Well, so sorry," Ruby snapped, keeping her distance behind Emma, who'd started down the hall. "No lectures, please."

"Up 'til now, I've always happily visited you wherever you happened to be," Emma said, not breaking her pace until she reached the table and eased into a chair. "I accepted your refusal to visit me here. To be more precise, I *preferred* it. You know that. Taking off to see you was a good excuse to get away from Neil and our problems."

"You and I had some great trips over the years," Ruby said, hoping to steer the subject away from her family history.

"Didn't we ever," Emma said with exaggerated nostalgia. "Now that you're back in town, though, I think you'll finally get it, Ruby. Your memories are like ghosts that follow you around. You can't run fast enough to get ahead of them."

Ruby held her tongue and tried to cool the heat rising within her. The last thing she wanted was to lash out at Emma, but earlier, when she'd driven past the Welcome to Bluestone River sign on the way into town, every muscle had gone rigid. She'd gripped the wheel and forced herself to keep her foot on the accelerator and not the brake. She didn't need Emma challenging her now. She leaned over and calmed herself by burying her hand in Peach's fur and patting her back.

"Let's not talk about this now, Em. Not any of it." Unable to resist, she added, "I

promise we can examine all my question-
able choices another time."

Emma nodded. "Okay, but consider
this—nothing is as you left it. Sadly, this
town not only isn't growing, it's shrinking.
Our population is barely seven thousand.
It was nearly ten thousand when we were
kids." Emma grimaced. "When we go down
to River Street, you'll see all the boarded-
up businesses. And since Mike's dad gave
up the resort buildings and land at Hidden
Lake, we attract fewer and fewer tourists."

The immediate jolt in Ruby's body threw
her off balance. All it had taken was the out-
of-the-blue mention of Mike. She managed
a response. "At least a bird sanctuary is an
actual Abbot family legacy." When she'd
looked him up online a couple of years ago,
Ruby learned Mike worked for a law firm
in Cincinnati. Apparently, his dad had followed him there and had since died. That
was the extent of her knowledge of what
had happened to Mike Abbot in the last two
decades.

"Before long only a few people will even
remember the town once had a resort on
the lake," Emma mused. "No member of

the Abbot family has any ties to Bluestone River."

Like me and my family. But she'd long wondered if Mike's grown-up life had come close to matching their old high-school dreams. Hers sure hadn't measured up, but maybe Mike had made better choices.

"At least you don't have to worry about running into Mike," Emma said. "Although wouldn't it be good to finally…"

Ruby raised her hand. "*Stop.* I don't want to talk about Mike. Let's just stay out of the past, at least for now." Ruby paused. "I just got here."

Emma raised her hands in surrender. "Okay, if you say so."

Yes, I say so. Ruby turned away and busied her hands pouring their coffee.

EVERY TIME MIKE ABBOT walked inside the Bluestone River Elementary School he was yanked back into his childhood with rocket speed. Maybe it was the familiar smells of paint and clay from the art room, or the aroma of butter cookies floating in the air through the halls that caused the memories to come rushing back. Even the buzz of little kids talking and laughing as they scurried out of their classrooms hadn't changed. Only the sleek laptops replacing clunky monitors on the teachers' desks marked the passage of time. When Mike learned one of his favorite teachers, Elaine Cermak, would be his son's teacher now, the school seemed to fling open its doors to welcome him home.

He stood a few feet from the classroom door and watched the kids head down the hall, their minibackpacks bouncing. He spotted Jason holding a picture as he came through the door, the last child out.

"Hey, buddy," Mike said, crouching down and ruffling his son's curly brown hair, exactly like his own. "Can I see what you made?"

Jason responded with a solemn nod. The same way he responded to most questions, except when the answer was no and he shook his head.

Mike took the picture from Jason's outstretched hand and smiled at the dots and slashes of orange and yellow on the trees and the ground. It looked like fall in the drawing and matched what Jason saw outside. He'd made small figures with round heads and curved lines. *Geese flying across the sky*, Mike thought, just like the birds that flew over the lake at their house. "Lots of geese, huh? And I like your leaves."

As Mrs. Cermak approached him, she said, "Your boy is quite the artist, Mr. Abbot."

Mike didn't even try to muffle his self-conscious laugh. "Please, call me Mike."

"I'm not supposed to." Mrs. Cermak spoke with a conspiratorial lilt in her voice. "But I carry around a distinct memory of you sitting in the front row of my classroom for both second and third grades. You'll always be just Mike to me."

Shifting her gaze to Jason, she rested her hand lightly on his shoulder and led him back into the classroom. "Jason, why don't you choose a book from the shelf and sit on the pillows with it for a few minutes. I need to talk with your dad. We won't be long."

Jason looked up at him as if questioning if that was okay. "Go ahead, Jason, I'll be right here." Mike watched his son obediently go to the bookshelf near the teacher's desk and plop down on the cushion in front of the books.

"Has there been any change?" Mike asked when Jason was out of earshot. He stiffened his shoulders to brace himself for the answer. This was only the middle of Jason's fourth week in school, after all. Change this soon was almost too much to hope for.

His former teacher offered an apologetic smile. "I'm sorry, Mike, but no. I wish I had a better report. But he's still completely silent."

Mike looked at the drawing he held. "But he's doing first-grade work. Right?"

"Absolutely. That's why I wanted to talk with you." Mrs. Cermak tapped her temple. "Your boy is smart, really sharp. When he's ready to speak again, I'm sure he'll easily transition into a regular classroom. He doesn't need to be in a special-ed class because of any learning disability." She tilted her head and smiled. "But you already knew that."

True enough. But his six-year-old, a boy Mike had taken custody of only a few months ago, was held back in any classroom by what two different child psychologists in Cincinnati called mutism. His inability—more accurately, unwillingness—to talk was Jason's response to the trauma of not only losing his mother, but also seeing her die in the same fire that left burns on his lower arms. Mike knew that kind of horrific, sudden loss too well. But he'd been eighteen, not six, when his mother had been killed in a car accident. It was hard for Mike to put into words, but he understood his son's need to stay silent. At that same time, every morning Mike climbed out of bed hoping this would be the day he'd hear Jason's voice again. He went to sleep at night with the words *maybe tomorrow* looping through his head.

Mike had attacked Jason's problems head-on, first learning all he could about post-traumatic stress disorder. Fortunately, Jason's situation wasn't all bad news. Regular play therapy and the stability of living with Mike had dramatically eased some of the signs of Jason's chronic anxiety, even with the move from Ohio to Illinois. Jason's second move in less than six months. Still, the conclusion was the same: the six-year-old would eventually speak, but on his own schedule, and only when *he* decided it was time.

Mike nodded toward Jason, who was in his line of vision. He'd set aside his book and now stood at the nature table arranging wooden farm animals in a straight line. "At home, he's been spending a lot of time outdoors, exploring, collecting leaves and sorting them into separate piles by color and size. Very orderly," Mike said, smiling. He knew exactly where that trait had come from. "Living at the lake has been a novelty for him. I've told him we're here to stay, but he probably doesn't understand what that really means."

"No, likely not, but keep talking to him, reading stories," Mrs. Cermak said, "and let him draw all he wants." She leaned in closer. "One piece of advice, Mike. Why don't you start waiting for Jason outside the school? You don't need to hover. He's been here nearly four weeks now and Jason can make it to the front of the building on his own."

Mike knew that...sort of. But his worries were stronger than the facts. "It's just I'm afraid kids will make fun of the scars on his arms." Fortunately, they'd faded and weren't quite so obvious now. "I know they'll heal more. But what about his silence? Even friendlier, outgoing children won't get why he doesn't talk—or laugh. Why would they? I'm afraid that someday, some little kid, even a well-meaning one, will try to goad him into speaking. Or a mean child will harass him."

Mrs. Cermak stared at Jason, who was still playing at the nature table, before turning to Mike. "I'll be honest. Every school has a few students who are mean to other kids, but it doesn't go on in my classroom. You can probably guess that my students are particularly vulnerable. So I keep an eye out for any name calling or jeering, and protect the kids as best I can," Mrs. Cermak said, gesturing around her. "Our teacher aides stand outside and watch for the first sign of trouble."

Maybe because he'd grown up in the school himself, it bothered Mike to hear about *any* bullying problem. Nevertheless, he tried to find Elaine Cermak's words reassuring.

The teacher formed a circle with her arms in front of her. "I keep my kids in a close-knit group as much as possible. Remember, these eighteen children all have some issues or they wouldn't be in my classroom in the first place."

Mike nodded, admitting to himself his first instinct was to be overprotective. He almost laughed out loud. That was a huge understatement.

"How's it going with *you*, Mike?" Mrs. Cermak asked. "Have you found office space yet?"

Glad for the quick change of topic, Mike offered an update. "It took a long time to get my big old barn of a home aired out and cleaned after so many years of being shuttered like an old haunted house. I just started looking for a space on River Street. I'm working with a Realtor and finding I have lots of choices." He shook his head. "Many more than I expected."

Mike told Mrs. Cermak about hiring Heather Stevens, a woman who offered after-school day care for about half a dozen kids, including his Realtor's little girl. "I need Jason to get used to being with a sitter. Better he adjust now than wait until my law practice gets going." He snickered. "Assuming it ever does."

"It will, Mike." Mrs. Cermak tightened her mouth. "It hurts to say this, but you shouldn't have any trouble getting a good deal on an office."

"So I've seen." At the beginning of the most beautiful season in north central Illinois, Bluestone River looked neglected. Forgotten. "It was kind of a shock to see so many empty storefronts."

Mrs. Cermak agreed and then called to Jason to tell him his dad was ready to take him home. Always looking for positive signs, Mike was pleased with the shy smile Jason gave his teacher when she said she'd see him tomorrow. Mike held out his hand and Jason immediately took it. Even with all the challenges confronting him, Mike paid attention to how much he enjoyed the feel of Jason's small, warm hand in his.

After the short—and silent—ride home, they split a peanut-butter-and-jelly sandwich, something Mike enjoyed as much as Jason. Then Mike led the way down the front yard to the lake and pushed the rowboat across the short sandy beach to the water's edge. He buckled Jason into his life jacket and lifted him onto the seat in the bow. "Whaddya say we go all the way around today?" he asked as he pushed off and climbed in himself.

Jason nodded. Enthusiastically, as Mike expected. From his first trip out on the lake, Jason seemed content to watch the ducks in the water and listen to the geese honking when they took flight from their nesting places in the marsh grasses. Mike wished a pair of swans would visit and nest, like they had done when he was a kid. So far, though, only ducks and geese hung around.

Mike stayed close to the shore and rowed at a leisurely pace. He had no place else to be. Since he'd been back in the house he grew up in, Mike had taken Jason out on the lake almost every day. He reminded himself of his own dad, who'd died a few years ago. When Mike was a little boy like Jason, he'd spent a lot of time on the lake with his father learning how to row and handle a boat. Mike planned to pass on those same skills to his son.

Today, though, Mike's routine followed the guidelines that Gloria Vance, Jason's therapist, and Mrs. Cermak encouraged in order to provide the stability and safety that would lead to Jason's recovery. That need for consistency led him back to his home on the peaceful lake. From the minute he got the call telling him Zoe had died, it seemed inevitable that Mike would bring his son to a new life in Bluestone River.

He'd have to find a different routine when rainy fall days became days so cold the lake froze over. Soon enough he'd have to drag the boat into the storage building, a seasonal chore he grew up with. Mike spent his childhood on this small lake, swimming its length and hanging out on the raft that was tethered in the center. The resort had once been filled with guests and Mike and his gaggle of friends. Mike had spent many hours rowing around the egg-shaped lake as a teenager with Ruby by his side.

He was silent as he maneuvered toward the goose beach, as he'd started calling it for Jason's sake, pausing only to wave at Millie Kress, the retired science teacher who ran the bird sanctuary now. The place drew a number of tourists in the summer and fall. Well, sort of. Since he'd been back, he'd never seen more than a couple of cars in the parking lot he passed before turning down the road to the house. Most days Millie's SUV was the only vehicle parked there.

When his dad closed the resort over ten years ago, Bluestone River lost a major tourist hook. Deeding the land to the bird sanctuary was supposed to draw in different kinds of visitors. Even Mike thought it would attract the twentysomething crowd concerned about wildlife, or long-time residents who wanted to preserve several hundred acres of land. From what he could see, the sanctuary lacked any kind of PR program and only a few grade-school classes arranged visits.

"It's just us and the birds, huh, Jason?" The birds mostly had the whole place to themselves. Mike suspected Millie liked it that way, but it didn't bode well for the sanctuary's future. He didn't even know who paid Millie's salary, supposedly more token than real. A gloomy thought.

Mike pulled himself back to the present and grinned at Jason. "When I was your age, Bluestone River was a much busier place. So was this lake." He waved in the direction of the shore, where some boarded-up housekeeping cabins were barely visible through the trees. "My mom hired high-school kids to clean cabins on Saturday morning to get them ready for new people coming in that afternoon. I worked here, too, just like a regular employee."

Mike had probably never worked harder than he had cleaning those cabins until everything looked fresh and they smelled like disinfectant and furniture polish. Reassuring smells in the not-so-fancy resort business, at least that's what his mother liked to claim.

"Lots of my friends had summer jobs here—we liked working the snack bar best."

Just talking about the past to Jason opened a floodgate of memories, especially of his mom hiring Ruby. She handled customer service, an overblown title for delivering extra towels and glasses to guests or rolling a crib into a cabin. "But we all got our turn to scoop ice cream." Mike laughed. "I made hundreds of ice-cream cones every summer. Just like the kind I make you— sometimes two big scoops."

Jason had been paying attention all along, but his eyes lit up at the mention of ice cream.

Mike often thought about how much fun he and Ruby had working the evening shift. She'd pile her long, dark red hair under the white baseball-style caps his mom made them wear. Then, when it was nearing dark, they'd check off every box in the closing-up routine and finally shutter the serving window. Ruby would wait until she was outside again to take off her cap and let her wavy hair tumble down her back.

Sometimes they rode their bikes out to the covered bridge to hang out with their friends. Other nights, especially when the sky was clear and the moon cast its light on the lake, they'd put one of the resort's boats in the water and row out to the tiny cove, the same place he was taking Jason now. The first Abbot owners named it Hidden Lake because it was surrounded by woods and off an old farm road on the edge of town. He and Rubes had a running joke about wishing his great-grandparents had bought a lake with more protected coves or curves or trees on the shore to give them places to hide. As it was, no matter where they went, Mike's mom and dad could always keep an eye on them.

His chest tightening at the emotion of each image, Mike pulled the oars inside the boat and let it drift in the light breeze while he turned his attention back to his son. "It's quiet here, isn't it? No motorboats allowed because it's only forty-five acres. We used to have kayaks and a couple of little sailboats, though."

With that, Mike ran out of things to say. He couldn't talk to anyone about what really weighed on his mind. *Ruby*—not only his first love, but, as it turned out, also his only love. He'd never tried to describe to anyone what he'd felt for Ruby or the tragedy that separated them. Teenage love or puppy love, even first love, were all the wrong words when it came to labeling how he felt about Ruby. Not even close.

Distracting himself, Mike reached out and patted Jason's knee. "I'm glad you like it here. We've got more places to explore along Bluestone River." So far, he'd avoided the covered bridge, another place he'd hung out growing up. There was plenty of time for that. He studied his son's face, a combination of himself and Zoe. Her dark blue-gray eyes, his curly brown hair. Mike could even identify the straight nose that reminded him of his mother.

Jason was five years old when Mike first heard his name. He hadn't known Zoe was pregnant when she left Cincinnati to take a new position in a law firm closer to her hometown in Pennsylvania. Later, he overheard a couple of women at the firm talking about Zoe having a baby boy, and given the suspicious timing, Mike contacted her to find out if there was any possibility the baby was his. Their fling had been brief. And stupid for two lawyers in the same firm to think they could date without anyone noticing. Mike had regrets over that show of bad judgment, but that was nothing compared to his raw nerves when he called Zoe, knowing he had to find out if he had a child.

When Zoe assured him he wasn't Jason's dad, Mike had forgotten all about it. A late-night call a year or so ago changed everything. It turned out Jason's presumed father began to have doubts and suddenly demanded a DNA test. When it ruled him out, that left Mike. Zoe delivered the news in stark terms, and more or less told him he didn't have to get involved. She was fine with raising Jason alone.

Mike wasn't fine. No way could he take a walk. This was a far cry from the way Mike imagined starting the family he'd always hoped for. So what? What he'd wanted was irrelevant. He'd resolved to be a real dad to a boy who'd never seen him or heard his name. No matter what it took to make it work. Mike started visiting and got to know Jason, at least as much as the miles between them allowed.

Then one night last June, Zoe's father called to say she'd died in a fire in their family's cabin. Jason had survived with burns on both hands and arms. As terrible as that was, Mike soon learned those physical injuries were the least of it. The emotional fallout hadn't faded like the scars on his son's skin. From the time Mike saw Jason in the hospital up to this moment rowing on the lake, Jason had not spoken a single word. Mike heard his son's voice only when he cried out during one of his nightmares. At first those awful dreams happened almost every night and continued when Mike took Jason home to his apartment in Cincin-

nati, but since moving to the lake in Bluestone River, they'd gradually become less
frequent, until now the agonizing cries oc-
curred only once or twice a week.

Sometimes Mike found it hard to grasp
how much *he'd* changed—almost overnight.
Not just the circumstances of his life, but
what he thought about and how felt inside
his own skin. He'd gone from a guy who
stopped for a beer and burger with his co-
workers after hours to a dad who reminded
himself to put Jason's rain jacket in the car.
He taught his boy to count out the money
for his weekly lunch pass and, in the most
dadlike of jobs, checked Jason's pockets for
crayons or puzzle pieces before throwing his
jeans in the wash.

From the time he'd started at the firm
in Cincinnati, he'd made good money and
added to his retirement fund every month,
paid off his student loans early and built up a
respectable investment account. He'd never
imagined he'd end up counting on what he'd
put aside to support his child while he tried
to make a brand-new law practice a success
in a stagnating town.

"On warm sunny days like this, I'm glad

we live out in the country and not in Cincinnati," he said to Jason, really as a way to remind himself why he'd quit his job and moved to Bluestone River. Mike had tried to make life seamless in the city, but in the end he followed his gut and left his secure job behind. Overriding his jumbled mix of feelings, he'd brought Jason to the emotional shelter that was the Abbot family home on the lake. It still stood, rambling and neglected. Not knowing why, Mike had argued with his dad about holding on to the house and the lake in the deal that turned everything else over to the sanctuary. In the end, Mike won the argument, without really understanding why it was so important to him. He understood now. *Thanks again, Dad, for letting me win that one.*

He watched Jason stare at more noisy ducks paddling over for a look at the boat. Seeing his son's faint, peaceful smile gave Mike the boost of confidence he needed about his decision to reconfigure his life, challenges and all.

"We've always had lots of ducks at the lake. My mom used to say the ducks were *ubiquitous*. U-bi-qui-tous," he repeated slowly, with a laugh. "I remember when she used that word and then told me it meant the ducks were *all over the place*."

Smiling to himself, he recalled how often his mom had used unusual words, as if slipping a vocabulary lesson into their everyday small talk. When he was young he'd groan whenever she did it, but by high school he laughed with his friends about the words that he could pull out for any occasion. *A panoply of words*, Mike thought, one of his mom's favorites.

Enough of this. No more mulling over the past, not with Jason sitting in front of him. Like every other day, Mike had plenty to think about in the present. Like dinner. "Hey, buddy, how about we head home? I'll fix us some mac 'n' cheese for dinner. Then we'll break out the ice cream—the kind with the chocolate and peanuts."

Jason nodded eagerly, but he kept his eyes on the ducks, who paddled alongside the rowboat all the way back to the beach. What was Jason thinking? Mike asked himself that question dozens of times a day. In moments like this, he yearned to hear Jason's voice. But there was nothing he could do to make that happen. Except be there with him. And wait.

CHAPTER TWO

WITH PEACH AT her side, Ruby broke into a slow jog from Emma's house to the unpaved farm road that led to the covered bridge and the park on the other side of the river. She'd been with Emma a few days now and they'd settled into a comfortable routine.

They had yet to venture beyond the house, but they didn't have to. Not with Brenda around to take Emma's grocery list to the store and come back with bags of food. They had everything they'd need for the coming week and beyond, right down to Emma's favorite jelly donuts from Sweet Comforts, a new bakery in town. As if they'd never heard of calories or carbs, the owners specialized in old-fashioned doughy pastries. Emma remarked it was about the only new addition to Bluestone River worth mentioning since Ruby left.

The surgery loomed in Ruby's mind in a

somber sort of way. As much as she wanted to be like Emma, wildly optimistic about the outcome, Ruby knew her friend had been on a roller coaster of high hopes of a full recovery only to be let down and disappointed too many times. But she was careful to hide her doubts, especially because Emma was like a horse at the gate waiting to get going. Emma counted on reclaiming her confident stride. She lived for the day that walker would be history.

Too restless to sleep much last night, her friend had finally fallen into a deep slumber stretched out on the couch after lunch. Ruby took that as her chance to slip out with Peach and take the dog beyond Emma's acres. "We both need to work our leg muscles," Ruby said to Peach as she picked up the pace. Ruby was no marathoner, but she liked her long walks and two- or three-mile runs a couple of times a week. That's how she kept herself—and Peach—in shape.

"Time to visit the river, and the bridge, too," she said, breathing a little more heavily as she increased her speed. They soon passed another field of goldenrod and the last of the Queen Anne's lace swaying in the light breeze. "Once upon a time, the old bridge was my favorite place in town." She glanced down at the dog and grinned. "Like you care."

On her way into town she'd seen signs on the highway for the semifamous covered bridge, a landmark meant to lure people to see one of the last of its kind in the state. In the past, most people found the bridge and Bluestone River itself when they were on their way somewhere else, like the state park to the east and a couple of historic towns on the Mississippi River to the west. By the time she and Emma were teenagers, the bridge had turned into a trendy photo-op spot.

Ruby could hear the water rushing over the rocks, the closest thing to rapids Bluestone River offered, before she made the turn on the road and the red wooden structure came into view. She stopped abruptly a safe distance away, while the air buzzed around her head and her ears pulsed a warning from her heart. Did she really want to risk the pain of reliving memories already surfacing? She could turn back and pretend there was no bridge, no river, no park.

Peach strained at the leash and Ruby forced herself to keep going, as she knew she should. She couldn't sleep night after night in Emma's lovely sage-green room and pretend she'd never been young and happy in this town. She couldn't act like she hadn't fallen in love with a boy named Mike. She'd take it a piece at a time, she decided, as she walked through the covered bridge looking straight ahead. No need to pay attention to the colorful spray-painted hearts drawn around names and initials painted and carved on the inside walls.

Mike had carved their names inside one of the smaller hearts on an almost empty spot in a lower corner. She'd drawn the heart herself and painted the borders in bold magenta. Probably faded by now. It didn't matter. Her grown-up heart wasn't ready to look at their names, anyway.

Emerging into the sunlight again, she stopped at the railing to watch foamy whitecaps downriver, which was wider and deeper than the rocky section where the water seemed to rush under the bridge. "So, Peach, I spent hundreds or hours here when I was growing up. What do you think of that?" She glanced at the dog, whose nose was busy exploring the patchy grass. "Not much, huh?"

Always amused by her one-sided conversations with Peach, Ruby felt a little lighter when she wandered into the park. Clouds were forming rapidly in the west and casting shadows over the riverbank and the woods behind the playground. A few bikers were riding on the trail running adjacent to the water and a handful of kids were on the swings and climbing the ladders to the top of the two slides. Peach pulled on the leash, urging Ruby to move a little closer to the children and the woman supervising them.

"Shush," she said when the dog let out a low bark. "No barking, no chasing kids, even though you like them." Ruby walked around the edge of the playground and sat on a bench and stretched her legs out in front of her. Peach, her tail wagging at maximum speed, pressed her side against Ruby's leg as she kept the kids in her sights. Ruby knew little of her dog's history, except that she'd lived with her elderly owner in an apartment across the landing from hers. From the first day Ruby had agreed to look after Peach, the dog's tail always picked up speed when children were around.

Emma liked to tease Ruby about finally getting a pet when she always insisted she would never have one. Early one morning the dog's yelping and scratching from inside the apartment door signaled something was wrong. Ruby called 911, and paramedics soon discovered Peach's owner, who'd apparently died in her sleep the previous night. Ruby agreed to watch the dog until her neighbor's adult children arrived. Then she agreed to keep Peach for a couple of days while the funeral arrangements were made. And sure, she wouldn't mind taking care of Peach until the apartment was emptied and closed up. And so it went. One day, her neighbor's son came right out and asked if there was any chance she'd take the dog off their hands permanently. By that time, Peach, bewildered and quiet, had wormed her way into Ruby's heart. She couldn't have said no.

Ruby rubbed the fur on Peach's neck, thinking how peaceful it was to watch the kids play. This playground had been added to the Bluestone River Park when Ruby was about the same age as these children. Her gaze settled on one little boy staring at her and Peach from one of the swings. He was moving back and forth in a lackluster way, dragging his feet across the protective rubber mat under the swing. When he got off the swing and began walking toward them, Ruby took hold of Peach's collar and told her to sit. "Good girl," she said when Peach settled on her haunches. "Now stay. And no barking."

When the boy was still a few yards away, caution led Ruby to greet him. "Hi there. My dog is friendly, but she doesn't know you." She indicated that he should come to her left side, opposite the dog, who sat at her right. "You're welcome to say hello."

The boy nodded solemnly, but then a faint smile appeared. As he inched ahead, Peach's tail swished across the ground.

"Her name is Peach. I'm Ruby."

The boy didn't say anything, but the smile stayed.

"Here comes somebody you know." Ruby nodded toward a woman hurrying across the gravel with a toddler planted on her hip.

"I think your little boy likes my dog," Ruby

said. "She's very gentle, so it's okay if he comes a little closer."

"Do you want to do that, Jason?" the woman asked.

That was all the encouragement the boy needed in order to come close enough for Peach to start sniffing his shoes.

"This is Jason. He's one of the kids I watch after school." She patted the toddler's leg. "This is my little one, Molly."

"Well, if it's okay with you, Jason can pet the dog. Peach is pretty sweet."

Jason's big blue-gray eyes opened wide as his smile spread across his face. He moved closer and stroked Peach's back.

"You've made a friend, Jason."

The boy glanced Ruby's way, but still didn't speak.

"He's kind of quiet." The woman patted the top of the boy's head. "That's okay. You'll talk when you're ready." She flashed Ruby a pointed look.

She was trying to communicate something, but Ruby didn't know what. Not exactly. But the thin pale lines and telltale puckering of burn scars on the boy's forearms might have something to do with his silence.

"How many children do you take care of?" Ruby asked, keeping her eye on Jason.

"Two all day, and three or four after school. It varies some. Plus my Molly." She gave the toddler's foot a little shake. "This is only Jason's second day with me. We're having a good time, but we better get back home. Your daddy is coming for you soon, Jason."

Ruby got to her feet and turned to the little boy. "I need to leave, too, but I'm glad you got to meet Peach. Maybe I'll see you another day, Jason."

Jason gave Peach a final pat before running off. But when he looked back and waved, Ruby waved back. He might be silent, but he sure wasn't withdrawn. Jason occupied her mind on the walk home and while she heated up beef stew for dinner. Even when she said good-night to Emma her thoughts veered back to the boy in the park. There was something about him. Not a familiarity exactly, but she found herself relating to the boy in some way she couldn't define. Hmm...puzzling.

ON SUNDAY MORNING, Mike kept up the breakfast table patter as he put their dishes in the sink. "Lots to do today," he said. "How about if we go to the park first and then we'll go to the supermarket in Clayton?" He had to laugh at his tone, as if trying to make a trip to the grocery store into an exciting adventure. Who was he kidding? Twelve miles east, Clayton was a bigger town, and from what Mike could see, the businesses that once served Bluestone River had mostly either closed up altogether, or had relocated to Clayton.

When Jason nodded, Mike thought he saw his eyes lighting up a little at the mention of the park. Heather said Jason enjoyed it, and had even approached a dog and its owner cautiously. She assured him she'd kept a close eye on him. Mike was pleased Jason hadn't been too afraid or shy to run off to have a look at the dog. It was a glimpse into the lively, independent little kid Mike had known before the fire.

Now was as good a time as any to break through his mental barriers about being in the park and seeing the bridge. Mike couldn't live in his hometown and ignore everything that made it special. It was just too bad those places held raw memories he'd rather avoid. *Get over it.* He scoffed to himself. That might as well be his mantra these days.

When Jason scampered off to get dressed, Mike let himself toy with the vision of a furry puppy chasing Jason through the house or around the beach in front of the house. Maybe a dog was just what they needed. Jason would have to talk to a puppy, wouldn't he? Maybe giggle over puppy antics? Sometimes Mike grew so sick of the sound of his own voice he turned on the TV or streamed a movie for Jason just to break the silence in the house. Only last night at dinner, it took all his self-control not to outright beg Jason to talk to him—*say something, anything. Speak!*

As appealing as a dog sounded for all kinds of reasons, Mike shelved the idea, at least for now. He had enough to do to settle into this complicated new life he'd created. Besides, he knew the drill. He'd once been a kid with a little cocker spaniel, and decades later he could still hear his mother asking, in her good-natured mom voice, "Why do I end up doing all the dog work around here?" He'd been a lot older than Jason before he'd remembered to fill the water bowl and take the dog out without his mom's exasperated nagging.

Mom. There she was again showing up in his mind chatter. Since he'd been back in the lake house, his mother seemed always present in the back of his mind. Or, the front of it. He'd poked around the cabinets and the hutch in the dining room and some boxes in the pantry, and found everything from holiday china settings to an old meat grinder and a seldom-used blender. Sometimes he lived his boyhood days all over again when he opened his eyes and looked out the window at the lake, situated so it caught the early morning light. Even as a boy, Mom's favorite time of the day had become his, too.

The drive to the park took them through town and past the two River Street office spaces Mike had arranged to look at next week. The Realtor he'd been working with was almost too honest when she admitted people weren't lining up to rent either space. Would he like to buy a building downtown? He could get one in a heartbeat. Dirt cheap.

Once they parked and left the car, Jason ran off to the higher of the two slides and climbed the ladder behind a couple of slightly older kids. Even Elaine Cermak had remarked that Jason's silence had mistakenly led her to assume Jason had withdrawn into his own world. Not so. Here in the park among children he didn't know, Jason had taken off to the slide without hesitation.

Even as he kept an eye on Jason whooshing down the slide and running back to the ladder to do it again, the red covered bridge beckoned. It was the one thing in town that hadn't changed at all, although he supposed the old garish hearts and flowers had probably been painted over with new names. He and Ruby had playfully argued about what spot to stake out as their own. Ruby chose bright purplish-red paint for the heart, but he'd insisted they carve "Mike + Ruby," not "M + R."

He and Ruby had more than flimsy dreams, he'd boasted to his mom. They had plans. Ruby called them *strategies*. He could still hear her voice as she spoke in a tone that called up images of people dressed in navy blue suits gathered around tables in corporate conference rooms. But Ruby had been serious. She'd presented him with a spreadsheet showing her strategy for the two of them to squeeze in extra classes each semester and do independent study in the summer so they could finish college in three years instead of four. He'd collected information on law schools for himself and MBA programs for Ruby, at the same universities, or at least at schools in the same city. They'd all but set a date for their wedding—at the bridge, of course. Now, two decades later, he reminded himself to exhale. Their names were on that wall a few feet away and knowing that tore his heart one more time.

Mike abruptly turned his back on the bridge. One day he'd overcome the dread and come here by himself to get it out of his system. Feel the hurt and finally get some closure on the dreams of his past. Twenty years was long enough. Meanwhile, he was still struggling to find his place in his hometown. Even walking down familiar River Street he felt out of place, like a tourist trying to figure out what the town was all about. The diner where all the teenagers had ordered burger plates and BLTs and baskets of fries was still there, but the dry cleaner was gone, along with many other businesses. But here in the park by the bridge, not much had changed.

He walked closer to the slide, waving to Jason, who sat at the top. Jason waved back, but then his focus seemed to shift and he hesitated for a couple of seconds at the top. When he let go of the handholds and slid to the bottom, he ran toward Mike, but then passed him. Mike spun around and saw a golden retriever straining on the end of a long leash. He smiled to himself. He got it. That dog was much more interesting than Dad.

His gaze followed Jason coming to an abrupt stop a few feet from the dog. He glanced at the woman holding the leash who was coming through the bridge and smiling at Jason. His stomach flipped as he froze in place.

Ruby. Ruby was on the other end of the leash. She leaned over to pat the dog's side. Red-haired, brown-eyed, smiling Ruby.

Mike's jaw slackened as the present moment gave way to flashes from the past. Seventeen-year-old Ruby running through the bridge and leaping into his arms, a college acceptance letter in her hand. Ruby in a purple dress lacing her fingers around his neck as they danced under the dim lights at their prom. A vision of them skipping stones at the riverbank flashed and morphed into the two of them in sweatshirts and jeans rowing under a full moon on a warm fall night.

He stared at Ruby, who stood twenty, maybe thirty feet away. Then she looked away from the dog and Jason, and saw him. Motionless, expressionless, she stared back across the patchy grass. Barely able to breathe, he forced himself to close the distance between them.

"Ruby… I'm, I don't seem to…"

"I know," she said in a faint voice. "What are you doing here?"

"I, uh, moved back." He pointed to the ground. "I live here now."

Ruby opened her mouth as if to speak, but no words came out. Instead, he heard a choking sob come from deep in her throat and her mouth disappeared behind her hand. As if by instinct he stretched his arm toward her, but wasn't close enough to touch her.

He glanced at Jason, who was petting the dog but also looking at Ruby with a curious expression.

Ruby turned halfway around to put her back to Jason. Mike could still see her free hand brushing each cheek. She kept shaking her head, as if in shock.

Mike spoke the first words that came to him. "Oh, Rubes, don't cry." He took a step closer.

She nodded and held up her hand, as if to both reassure him and keep him at a distance. "It's okay, Mike." She took a deep breath and squared her shoulders. "I'll be fine. Give me a minute. Don't worry. I won't upset Jason." She took a deep breath and released it, and then smoothed flyaway strands of hair blowing in front of her face.

She knew his son's name. Of course she did. She'd already talked to Jason, but had no idea who this little boy was.

Still not looking at him, she turned around and smiled down at Jason. "You and Miss Peach meet again, huh? I know she's glad to see you." Her voice was stronger now.

Mike snickered as an old, familiar feeling came over him. "Miss Peach? You named your dog *Miss Peach.*" *She'd always been so easy to tease.*

She quickly ran her fingertips across her cheeks, wiping away any trace of tears. A faint smile appeared. "Nope. Her original owner gets the blame for that." She kneeled down and rubbed the dog's jowls. "I call her Peach for short. Right, Jason?"

Widening his smile, Jason nodded. Mike's heart pounded in his chest as he watched Jason with the dog, who sat with her head cocked and tail moving, eating up the attention from a little boy who wanted nothing more than to shower her with affection. "Is your Peach a therapy dog?" Mike asked.

Ruby seemed confused at first, but then her expression softened.

"Well, not *professionally.* It's more like a hobby with her."

He smiled and nodded, thankful for her quickly lightening the mood. Ruby could always be counted on to try to fix things.

"Peach is great with kids. See how she is with your little boy?" She looked up at Mike with curious eyes.

He read in her face what she wanted to know. "Long story, Rubes, and for another day." Mike pointed behind him at the row of benches. "Let's sit. Catch up. I moved back here for Jason. But what brought you back?"

Ignoring his question, Ruby said, "So, Jason, would you like to walk Peach around the benches?"

Jason nodded eagerly.

"As long as it's okay with your dad…" She glanced at Mike.

"Sure." He had to force himself not to sound impatient, even demanding, but he so wanted to talk to Ruby. The reality of her standing this close left him stunned. Maybe because she was stunning. The really pretty eighteen-year-old girl frozen in his memory had grown into a breathtaking beauty. The easy, tender way she talked with his son showed Mike that the woman Ruby had become was still big-hearted and kind.

Ruby handed Jason the leash and he trotted off with Peach, who was soon circling the benches. "Look at that. I hadn't even known the dog was good with kids until just the other day."

"Ruby, please, I haven't seen you in twenty years. Let's talk about your dog another time." He heard the edge in his voice.

Fear? He wasn't sure what scared him, couldn't put it into words. Yet at the same time relief traveled through every cell, as if all along he'd been expecting this and the moment had finally come.

"You're the one who asked about the dog," Ruby teased.

He'd almost forgotten how easy it was for her to tease him, too. "I'm just glad to see you." He emptied his lungs and whispered, "To know you're okay."

Ruby's eyes filled again and she lowered her head.

"Oh, no, Ruby. I don't want to upset you. I'm sorry. I just can't believe you're here."

She held up her hand in a clear signal to stop. "I'm okay, Mike. Really. I don't want to worry your little boy. I don't even know what's brought on the crying."

She didn't? He knew exactly what *his* jumble of emotions was all about. He'd never loved anyone the way he'd loved her. Now he had to know what had brought her back to Bluestone River. "Uh, do you live here now?"

She frowned and flicked her hand. "No, no. I never imagined putting one foot in this town ever again." She spoke through a tight jaw. "I only came back for Emma."

"Ah, Emma. It's strange, but I just learned the other day that Neil died." How strange. He'd been the best man at Neil and Emma's wedding, but no one had let Mike know he'd died. But he hadn't reached out to any of his old friends for years, either.

Ruby nodded and filled him in about the couple. "They finally decided to split up after years of trying to figure out a way to make it work between them, but then Neil died." She then explained the surgery happening the next morning at the hospital in Clayton.

"I'm so sorry to hear that about Emma. I'll drive over there to see her and say hello." He hesitated, but finally said, "So, you two are still friends."

"Still best friends forever and all that." She looked behind her at the river and the bridge. "My one connection to this place."

"You were free to come here to be with Emma, then? I mean, you could leave your family or take the time off from...whatever." *Man, that was subtle.*

"Actually, it worked out great," Ruby

said in a buoyant upbeat tone he immediately pegged as so false it almost made him wince. "When Emma called, I'd just left my job in Florida and given up my apartment. The timing couldn't have been better."

She's never been skilled at pretending, Mike thought, watching her shift her weight and look anywhere but at him. Whoa, something was way off.

Changing the subject, she nodded toward Jason trotting alongside the dog. "Can you tell me why he doesn't talk?"

"Like I said, it's a long story. Complicated. But it boils down to Jason being in a fire with his mom. She died, and from what was pieced together, he likely saw it happen. We don't know for sure what he witnessed, but he hasn't spoken since." Mike told her about leaving the law firm in Cincinnati to come back to his family's old house on the lake. "It's a peaceful spot. Maybe it will help. It can't hurt."

"So, he's silent because of the trauma of what he witnessed. Maybe his injuries figure in, too." She spoke as if stating a fact, not asking a question.

"That's what they tell me. The therapists,

I mean." Relieved she hadn't dug deeper, he changed the subject. "He's in the special-education class at the school because of it. But once he's talking again, he'll go into a regular class. That's what Mrs. Cermak says."

Ruby tilted her head and smiled in obvious surprise. "Mrs. Cermak? No kidding. She's still teaching?"

Mike laughed. "I was surprised, too. At first she called me Mr. Abbot, but that was too weird."

"I'll bet it was." Ruby clasped and unclasped her hands. Twice. "I need to get back to Emma. She's impatient and restless today. If she had her way the surgery would be this afternoon."

Was that it? She'd take off and he wouldn't see her again? They had gone their separate ways so suddenly, no warning, no nothing. She fled in a state of shock and grief, according to Emma. Surely, she wanted to clear the air. Or talk about it...*or something*. But apparently not now. Mike called to Jason and waved him over.

"I have to get going now, Jason," Ruby said, taking the leash from Jason's hand.

"But maybe Peach and I will see you an-other time."

Jason gave the retriever a final pat.

"So, you'll tell Emma I said hello?" Mike asked. "I'll stop in to see her."

"Of course." She gave Jason a warm smile and then took off toward the bridge.

Just like that. Why was she in such a hurry to leave? She'd left him curious about so many things. "Ruby," he called.

She stopped and turned.

"Tell me, what was your job? I mean, what do you do?"

Planting one hand on her hip, she cocked her head and stared at some distant point across the park. She glanced back at him for several seconds, then said, "I guess you could say my work is in crisis and trauma."

Her words surprised him, leaving him without a ready response. It wasn't all about what happened to Jason, either. What hap-pened to him and Ruby had changed every-thing. Talk about crisis and trauma. As a teenager she'd focused like a laser beam on getting a degree in business, emphasis on advertising and marketing. Then a job, pref-erably in a top corporation. For him it had been about landing a position in a major law firm. And why wouldn't they have been ambitious? They were the lucky kids in school. The daughter of the principal, fifth in their class, practically engaged to the student-council president, who was also not a half-bad basketball player.

Crisis. Trauma. The already closed fist in his gut tightened its grip. Before he could respond, Ruby disappeared on the bridge, only to reappear on the other side of the river. She broke into a jog as she turned down the side road and was soon out of sight.

He looked down at Jason, who was standing by his side. Suddenly too tired to sort out anything more complicated than the grocery list, Mike had no answers to the questions zipping through his brain. "Let's go, kiddo. We've got to get more giant jars of peanut butter and grape jelly."

Mike took a last look at the bridge, where a lone biker bumped noisily over the wooden slats. Then he looked at the road where Ruby had disappeared. He wished she'd change her mind and come back. And do what? Fill in the whole twenty years? Hash over the past?

The last time he saw Ruby was in the emergency room of Bluestone River's one-floor community hospital, which didn't even exist anymore. No way could he handle ten minutes in the park as the last time he saw her for another two decades.

When they got to the supermarket, he hurried down the aisles tossing random items in his cart and keeping up his usual one-sided patter with Jason. Later, when they finally arrived back at the house, Jason took off to the water's edge. As if taking inventory, Mike scanned where he'd grown up without ever knowing how fleeting good times could be. The tire swing, the rowboat, the lake itself. They had Ruby's name etched on them just as sure as their names were carved in the bridge.

Yes, twenty years ago, she'd run away.

He hadn't gone after her then, but things had changed. This time they could figure out those answers together.

CHAPTER THREE

WITH EMMA AT the hospital, Ruby understood what it meant to rattle around in a big ol' house, an expression her Grandma Rachel used when she was widowed and still living in the home where she'd raised her large family.

Ruby knew how to live alone and had done so since the day she'd moved into a tiny studio apartment within walking distance of her first crisis-center job out of college. She'd never lived in a house with eight rooms spread out on one floor, plus a basement with a pool table and a giant-screen TV, though. Neil's choice, Ruby imagined, remembering him as an all-around sports guy.

This was her second morning alone in the house, and rain was beating down on the roof, bouncing on the deck and soaking the fading prairie grasses and remnants of wildflowers on Emma's field. Ruby stared at the dark sky and thought about how much her dad had enjoyed these intense storms. Such a contrast to the warm summer evening when she'd rushed out of the house as a teenager to meet Mike at the bridge.

Ruby had been the last member of her family to see her dad alive. Until the day he'd died, she hadn't thought much about death—and knew nothing of betrayal. In the years that followed, she'd relived those last minutes—sweet minutes—with him hundreds of times.

Her dad had been sitting at the kitchen table reading the newspaper when she'd hurried to the back door.

"You going to see Mike?" he'd asked, grinning. They both knew the answer.

She'd been so happy she'd rocked up on the balls of her feet and then back on her heels, as if revving up to launch herself into the air and fly to the bridge. "And Emma and Neil—there'll be lots of us, Dad."

"Don't be too late. Big day tomorrow."

Graduation. It was extra special for her because she would be the only one in her class to have her diploma handed to her by her own father, Timothy Driscoll, the popular principal of Bluestone River High School. "I won't forget, Dad," she joked knowingly. Planting a kiss on the top of his head, she added, "It's going to be the best day ever."

"Love you, Rubes." As always he added a reminder. "Be careful on your bike."

Ruby had answered with a quick nod and said, "Love you, too, Dad." Minutes later she was at the bridge. The way she pieced it together later, Ruby figured her dad had likely left the house about half an hour after her.

Peach's low whine grabbed her attention and Ruby suddenly remembered where she was. The dog was looking out to the yard with one paw on the glass, but Ruby had just let her out a few minutes earlier, fed her and filled her water bowl. "Your real walk will have to wait, my friend," Ruby said, rubbing the dog's neck.

Ruby waited a few more minutes for the rain to let up and then put on her purple hooded raincoat and left for the hospital. Knowing Emma, she was probably pestering the nurses about how soon she'd be mobile again.

She'd wanted to stay focused on Emma the night before the surgery, so Ruby hadn't mentioned running into Mike and his son. Emma was groggy after surgery on Monday, barely awake, and yesterday Ruby arrived as Em was being helped to get out of bed to stand upright for the first time. Ruby was just as happy to wait to mention it. Emma would read too much into what was nothing more than a chance meeting, anyway. Ruby almost laughed out loud thinking of Emma claiming it was a sign that she and Mike had shown up back in town at the same time. Ruby could hear her friend's sage words—"There are no coincidences."

Nonsense. Mike's presence only complicated Ruby's visit. As for her bout of tears upon seeing him standing a few feet away from her in the park, she wrote that off as nothing more than a physical response to the shock of it.

Having arrived at the hospital, Ruby pulled up the hood of her raincoat and jumped over deepening puddles of rainwater on her way to the revolving doors. She avoided the habitually slow elevators and took the stairs to the orthopedic and neurology floor. After greeting the now familiar nurse at the desk, she went to the room at the end of the hall and rapped twice before pushing the door open and stepping inside.

Her head jerked back. What? *Mike*. Sitting in a chair alongside Emma's bed. He shot out of the chair as if he'd been caught doing something he shouldn't.

"Ruby. Hello. Again." He flashed a lopsided smile, self-conscious and awkward.

She glanced at Emma, who held out her hand. Woodenly, Ruby went to Emma's side and took Em's offered hand and squeezed it. "Hey, you, looking good today."

"That's what I said," Mike offered.

"Pull up the other chair, Ruby. Two visitors. How lucky can I get?" Emma gushed.

Ruby rolled her eyes at Emma's over-the-top cheeriness. Her best friend knew exactly how uncomfortable she was. Mike, too. He shoved his hands in the front pockets of his jeans. The decades dropped away. As a young boy and even a teenager, Mike had always hid his hands in his front pockets when he a little nervous, unsure of himself.

Knowing he was self-conscious, just like her, challenged the wall she'd built between them. As if a switch flipped deep inside, Ruby decided to let down her guard and go with the moment. She dragged the chair from the corner over to the other side of Emma's bed. Mike still stood there, all six feet two of him, with eyes as bright blue as ever. Curious, intelligent eyes that could darken with frustration and anger, or be full of fun and soft with affection. Years ago, her mom had said Mike's eyes could twinkle for real.

Even after all this time, Ruby remembered the smallest things about him. He ruffled her somehow, made her self-conscious and jittery. She had best get used it. No doubt she'd have to see him now and again before she left town—new destination TBD. Besides, what was she going to do, demand that Mike leave Emma's room? Tell him not to bring his little boy to the park?

"So, Em, how're you doin'?" Ruby asked. "Do they have you training for a five K yet?"

Mike snorted. "She was just saying she intended to start running again. Soon."

Emma groaned. "Oh, please, you guys. Let a girl dream." She raised her hands helplessly. "As you can see, I'm not even sitting up straight yet."

"Ah, but your bed is raised a little higher than it was yesterday," Ruby said.

Emma lowered her chin to concede the point and the room went silent, until she finally said, "Uh, Mike was just telling me about looking for office space downtown."

"Oh, there's plenty of room on River Street," Mike said, inching toward the end of the bed. "The question is whether Bluestone River is busy enough to support another lawyer."

"You'll make it work," Emma said, then added, "Mike, please, sit back down. You look like you're trying to escape a prison cell."

Ruby swallowed back a laugh and pretended she hadn't heard Emma's remark. "You're setting up your own practice?" Ruby asked, watching Mike follow Emma's order and slip into the chair.

"I'm giving it a try," Mike said, lifting his hands in the air. "If it doesn't work out, then I'll look for a job with a firm over in Clayton." He paused. "I'll do whatever it takes so Jason and I can stay in the house at the lake."

He spoke like it was any old house, not a place that held almost a lifetime of memories.

"Mike said his son likes the ducks and geese," Em said.

"We, uh, row around on the lake most every day." His face reddening, he looked away.

Like we did. Right, Mike? "I'll bet he likes that." She smiled brightly and glanced at Emma, as if her friend could provide some kind of escape route out of the conversation, maybe the room.

"Ruby? Um, before you got here, I told Mike about—"

"About what." She winced at the sharp tone of her loud interruption. She glanced at Mike, but his gaze was fixed on Emma, his eyebrows raised in surprise.

"I told him why you're here," Em said softly, "other than for me, I mean."

Ruby's stomach rolled. "But it wasn't *your* story to tell."

"I know, I know," Emma said, raising her arm and letting it flop on the bed. "But I was telling Mike what a great career you've had so far. Your last job kind of came up on its own. I didn't plan it. Besides, there's nothing shameful about losing a job."

Easy for you to say. A sarcastic—and completely unfair—remark was up-front and ready, but Ruby squelched it. Emma was the only person Ruby knew who'd never had to work, and probably never would. Now and again, she envied her friend the freedom inherited money could buy. But that wasn't fair, either.

"It's my fault, Ruby." Mike got to his feet. "I pried it out of Emma. I wanted her to tell me what you do. What you said about your work the other day in the park kept running through my mind. Crisis and trauma."

She stared into his eyes and willed herself not to cry—again. "Because of Jason. I get it."

"Maybe we could talk sometime. I could tell you more about what happened to him." He wrapped his hand around the back of his neck as if working the kinks out of his muscles. "Get a new perspective. I sure need one."

She wouldn't refuse anyone a conversation about a child with a problem, but before she could say yes, two women swept into the room. Ruby got up and stepped back to clear space for them, and so did Mike, but the room wasn't big enough for four visitors. As soon as Emma had introduced Mike to her surgeon and the rehab specialist, Ruby went to the door. "I'll be back soon, Em," she said.

Mike stated he needed to leave, anyway.

Emma waved at Mike. "I'm so glad you stopped by, Mike."

"I'll see you again," he said. "I promise."

He followed Ruby into the hall. "I'll walk you to your car." He glanced down the hall. "Or are you staying?"

It would be so easy to be rid of Mike by ducking into the cafeteria and waiting there, but instead she said, "No, they'll keep Emma busy this morning. I'll go home and drive over this afternoon."

"Then could I ask a favor?"

She stared into the blue eyes of a man she hadn't seen in ages and wondered how it could be so easy to let the words *of course* roll off her tongue. Maybe it was his clear, confident voice, which hadn't changed at all.

"Would you come with me to look at a couple of office spaces?"

"In town, you mean?"

"Right. I've narrowed my choices down to two—for now. I need to make a decision—soon. Like today or tomorrow."

Keeping her voice light and hoping she didn't reveal the growing excitement inside her, she said, "Then I guess we better get going."

MIKE WATCHED RUBY study the long, narrow room, once a supply store that served most of the businesses within twenty or thirty miles of Bluestone River. According to the Realtor, almost all the fixtures and shelving had been sold off at auction more than a decade ago. Now only a couple of supporting columns broke up the empty space.

"What a barn." Ruby playfully tapped her fingertips on her mouth. "Oops, was I blunt enough?"

"No, no, you're right." He explained his idea of adding a couple of walls to create a private space and then fixing up the front as a reception area. The more he talked, the more impossible it seemed. "I'd have to invest a lot of time and money. It would be different if I had a couple of partners, or if I bought the building outright and rented out other offices." He pointed up to the ceiling. "Or, I could transform the second floor into Bluestone River's first trendy loft."

Ruby's eyes opened wide. "I'm surprised you'd even think about buying a building or taking on partners so soon. I guess you really are serious about staying here."

He looked at the dirty gray walls scarred by the shelving, which was long gone now. Half the floor was bare tile, the other half worn-out carpeting. With a sigh, he said, "I need this town now. Or, Jason does. I believe he can get better here." He gestured around the room. "But I don't want to buy this building. I'm considering renting it because it's roomy and empty. No heavy equipment to shift, like at the closed-up dry cleaner. The clothes press is still rusting in place."

"Let's move on to the next place." Ruby's optimistic tone told him all he needed to know about her opinion of this option.

Mike took another set of keys out of his pocket and held them up. "Our next stop is the building you'd remember as the insurance office. My dad used to go there to make his payments in person. It's smaller than this place, but it could work."

"I remember the insurance office," Ruby said. "The windows were perpetually dirty and the plants drooped."

Mike could only chuckle at the precise picture of the old place. "The Realtor tells me it's been empty for a while. It's only a few doors down."

"I'm game. Let's go see it."

She sounded pleasant, even eager, but she looked everywhere but at him. He didn't blame her. He also avoided looking at her directly in the eye—at least, not for very long. If he did, he might get lost in a game of pretending they were kids and that everything was still ahead of them. He'd take her into his arms and hold on tight.

Mike locked the former supply company's door behind him. They raised their hoods and hurried past the pharmacy, the beauty shop and a franchise exercise studio advertising a discount on new memberships. Two vacant storefronts later and they came to the small brick bungalow-style building with a wide picture window. There were a couple of others exactly like it on the street, built back in the 1950s, when the town was growing.

Ruby stopped in front of the window. "Some things don't change, do they? The window is as grimy as ever. But once it's cleaned it would let in lots of light on a sunny day."

He unlocked the door and held it open for Ruby to step inside. "And it has two offices inside and a supply room big enough for file cabinets and copiers. The rent is higher here, it's smaller, but the start-up costs would be less."

"Hey, this is nice." She glanced back at him. "Really. It looks exactly like a small law office—at least it wouldn't be hard to convert it into one." She pointed to the floor. "Hardwood floors, no ratty carpeting to pull up. A few *live* plants and comfortable chairs would dress it up."

Mike smirked. "I could put a few outdated magazines on a coffee table and the place would fit right into the rest of the street."

"Can't argue with that." Ruby grimaced. "Over the years, Emma's been frank about the struggles around here. You've seen it for yourself."

With the sound of the rain coming down hard on the flat roof of the one-story building, Mike led Ruby into the first of the two offices, empty but for an ordinary metal desk left behind. The ugly blue paint on the walls of the good-size room would have to go. First thing. "New paint and new furniture would make a substantial difference," he said, resting his hip on the corner of the desk. "So, what do you think?"

She looked down as if studying the wooden floor. "I think it's good. So much better than the other place. Certainly worth the extra rent money." She chuckled. "Easy for me to say. I don't know what…"

He waved off her comment. "Not a problem. I can pay a few dollars more. I'll be fine for a while. I've got some savings, and sold my condo. I can live on less around here, anyway, and make the money last longer." He stopped himself from elaborating more about his relative solvency. What did Ruby care? "But what about you? Emma said you've had some great jobs over the years, but you're at loose ends now."

"Loose ends?" She let out a cynical guffaw. "So that's what we're calling being unemployed these days."

"I didn't mean it as a joke. Really, I didn't."

Ruby perched on the other end of the desk and began her story.

Over the next few minutes, Mike took in an abbreviated version of Ruby's career. She hadn't been kidding about moving around from state to state. She developed preventative programs, mostly geared toward young people, that were intended to avoid traumatic events occurring in the first place, but when that failed, she helped people deal with the aftermath. Hotlines and women's shelters, plus pilot suicide-prevention networks, were all items in her work history. She surprised him when she mentioned the national fraternity that had consulted with her to develop new antihazing policies.

Her expression fixed in a thoughtful frown, Ruby said, "I started to understand post-traumatic stress disorder. I saw how PTSD can result from all kinds of situations." Once again, she studied the floor, where rainwater had dripped from her waterproof boots.

"Like Jason. The fire. His silence," Mike said softly. "The loss of his mother. It was devastating."

Ruby nodded. "He was physically injured, but he witnessed something much worse. From what you told me, he likely saw his mom die."

Mike closed his eyes against the imagined scene. He'd been told about the firefighters whisking away Jason and rushing him to the hospital in the small town in Pennsylvania. "Ever since, I've been worried about him being vulnerable to bullying. It's one of the reasons I moved back. I know there are mean kids everywhere, but…"

"You think you can protect him better here. Right?"

"That's the plan." And Mike wanted Jason to experience the kind of childhood he'd had growing up in the huge house and discovering every inch of the lake.

"For what it's worth," she said, "if we stop bullying at the first sign of it, kids are much less likely to bully other people when they're in high school and college and beyond. Bullying is abuse—stop it early, and you prevent abuse later." She shrugged. "That's not just my belief. Lots of research confirms it."

Mike was about to respond, but Ruby stood and took off to the back of the building. "Plenty of storage here. And a place for a coffeepot," she said. "What more do you need?"

Mike's mood was as good as it had been when he'd first driven into town with Jason. Being in the same room with Ruby changed how he felt inside. Self-conscious, nervous, yes, but maybe more optimistic, even confident that he could make his plan work. Sometimes impatience for his son to be well again ate away at him. As long as his son was living in silence, Mike felt like he was living on the edge of something unknown. It made no sense, but only a few minutes with Ruby softened that edge a little.

That's how he'd been as a teenager falling in love with Ruby. What could go wrong? They were invincible. Nothing would stop them from going after their dreams. He glanced around the office space and had to laugh to himself. Here he was, a single dad of a troubled child, putting up a shingle, Mike Abbot, Attorney at Law, in his more-

or-less crumbling hometown. Maybe not crumbling, just a place that had seen better days. He was either truly optimistic or completely naive. Time would tell.

"I need to go," Ruby said, breaking his train of thought.

Mike could almost hear his heart drop with a thud. He didn't want to end this time with her. But he realized Emma was her priority.

"I'll hang out here for a bit." He took a deep breath. "It's time to call the Realtor and tell her to draw up the lease. I can settle this today."

Ruby's face registered that as good news. That emboldened him to ask for more. "I know you're busy with Em, but one day soon can we have a talk about Jason? I want to pick your brain. Maybe you could come to the lake with that peachy dog of yours. Jason likes her a lot. You could watch Jason just being himself and tell me what you see."

He saw the hesitation in her face. Then she opened her mouth as if to speak, but changed her mind and looked away. Finally, she said, "Or, maybe you could come to Em's house when she's home. It's quite the place that she and Neil built. Not far from the park."

"Sure," he said quickly, "I can do that. I value your opinion." *It was going out to the lake that threw her off*, he thought. Too many memories. He never should have suggested it. Sadness and grief gathered steam inside him. Along with the powerful urge for answers.

"So, I guess I'll see you." She opened the door to leave.

"Ruby, wait."

She turned. Her light brown eyes were filled with fear, but he wouldn't back down.

"Why did you run away, Ruby? Without even calling to explain, to talk about what happened. To even say goodbye. *Why?*"

Hours ticked by, or at least it seemed that way, with Ruby standing there and staring at him with an expression of despair.

"Because you hated me so much."

The door slammed. She was gone.

Mike braced his hand on the wall to steady himself as he absorbed the blow. He shook his head, forcing himself to breathe again. *He'd never hated her. Never.*

HER HANDS TREMBLING, Ruby drove down

River Street toward Emma's house. She considered going another half mile to the bridge, but nixed that idea as fast as it came to her, and not just because of the rain. What if Mike showed up? The place held as many memories, happy and terrible, for him as it did for her.

The windshield wipers beat back and forth at the highest speed as she made her way slowly through town and turned into Emma's short tree-lined drive. The drops falling from the leaves onto the glass were like the tears she held back, not ready or willing to shed them. Flashbulb moments rushed back. Her mother's anguished wails in the hospital emergency room. The sounds of shock and grief—and anger—that took years to quiet.

But even as the memories slipped through her mind, she had no inclination to wail or cry herself. She knew better. The buckets of tears shed years ago had failed her. She could declare herself done with being crushed and controlled by the past. Almost uncontrollable crying when she saw Mike at the bridge didn't count. She'd written that off as an anomaly—a clinical word, but it fit. That was about shock and surprise.

Long ago, Ruby faced the simple fact that tears wouldn't heal the broken place inside her. Ever. The best she could do was avoid ripping open that place, and that's why she'd never set foot in Bluestone River until Emma needed her. Now, it was too late. The wound was open. She wouldn't let it poison her, though—not again.

Taking a deep breath to toughen her resolve, she ran through the rain, then let herself into the house and greeted Peach, who bounded toward her in her typically joyful way. Ruby bent over and hugged the dog and then let her out through the patio doors in the kitchen. Too restless to sit, Ruby folded her arms and leaned against the wall next to the doors so she could keep an eye on the dog.

Couldn't Mike have left well enough alone? Why had he asked the one question sure to bring on nothing but sorrow? For her. For him. He'd known the answer, anyway. How could he not?

That's how it had been during her three frantic college years, when she made herself too busy to reflect on anything more than classes and part-time jobs. That search to fill up her time—her life—kept up as she job-hopped from one state to another. Maybe looking for a place she could finally consider home.

After the last "love you" exchange with her dad she'd pedaled her bike through town to the bridge and into the park. Mike was already there, along with Emma and Neil. The three had claimed a picnic table under the trees. She'd waved at others from their senior class who were like islands of kids dotting the sea of green grass. A few sat in a row on top of the railing that extended beyond the bridge.

Such high spirits that night. Their sense of freedom filled the air around them as they held up soda cans and made toasts and cheered over graduation. The day they launched their *real* lives. Ruby was excited about another summer working alongside Mike at the Hidden Lake Resort, where they'd count the days before packing and driving away together to college.

They'd been so immersed in their own happiness they barely noticed the police car, sirens silent, but lights flashing, emerging through the bridge, typical of a routine drive-in/drive-out check done two or three times on summer evenings. But in this instance the cruiser stopped and two officers got out. Neil left the picnic table and jogged over to join the group gathering to find out what the police wanted.

Neil was gone barely a minute before he yelled, "Ruby, Mike. Get over here. *Now*."

She and Mike exchanged a glance as they got up from the bench. She recalled the tiny detail of Mike grabbing her hand as they ran to Neil. Someone, Ruby was never sure if it was her mom or her sister, or maybe Mike's dad, had told the police where to find them. By the time they sat in the backseat of the cruiser with their arms around each other, their friends and classmates were gathered on either side of the road to watch them leave. Ruby remembered Emma cupping her hands around her nose and mouth as she watched them leave.

The rest was a blur. The ten-minute trip to the ER. Rushing through the automatic doors. A man with a minister's collar standing with Mike's dad in the waiting room.

Spotting her mother and sister sitting in chairs in the far corner. Even if Ruby hadn't seen her mom, she'd have heard her wailing while Dee sat stoically with her arm around her.

Ruby glanced up at Mike. His face was fixed in disbelief. She broke away from him and hurried to her mom and Dee, dropping to her knees in front of their chairs. It didn't take long to piece it all together. Her dad, dead. Mike's mom, dead. Killed on the highway just out of town in a two-car collision.

Before she understood the whole of it, Ruby looked back at Mike, maybe twenty feet away in a huddle with his dad and the minister. Mike caught her eye, but his grimace didn't change. Then he turned his back on her.

Later, Ruby understood why his expression hardened and why he didn't want to face her. They'd each lost a parent that night, but that wasn't the whole of it. Mike's dad and the chaplain on duty had other facts she didn't. So did her mom and Dee.

"I don't *ever* want to see Mike again." Her mom had spit out the words. "Do you *hear* me, Ruby?"

"Mike? What?" She turned to Dee. "What's she talking about?"

"I can explain," a voice behind her said, as a warm hand circled her arm and helped her to her feet. "I'm Gray Austin, the chaplain on duty tonight."

Ruby stood. "Explain what? My *dad* was killed. And Mike's *mom*."

"Oh, no, you don't understand," Ruby's mom shouted.

Chaplain Austin immediately stepped around Ruby and sat in the empty chair next to her mother. Ruby again looked at Mike, who now stared at her across the expanse of the ER. His expression, grim before, was icy now. The bright blue eyes she loved so much were narrowed into slits. She read the loathing in his expression.

Suddenly, Mike's dad was pointing a finger at her. "Your father killed Ellen," he shouted. "Do you get that, Ruby? The high-and-mighty principal killed my wife."

Disbelieving, Ruby lifted her open hands, as if imploring Mike to say something, do something. But the cold, hateful look was fixed on his face.

"Ruby, listen to me, now." The chaplain

got to his feet and gently took her elbow. "Your father and Mrs. Abbot were in your dad's car. He was driving, you see."

"They were having an affair. *Cheating* on us." Her mother's words echoed through the room, empty but for their families and a couple of nurses.

Ruby spun around to face Mike. He was watching, but he shifted again. She started toward him, but Chaplain Austin held her back. "No, Ruby. Not now. You and Mike can talk later. Stay here with your mom and sister."

The loud male voice boomed in the room again. Mike's dad was pointing at her mom. "Ellen is dead because of Tim. You know that's true, Stephanie."

Her mother stood, ghostly pale but for her reddened eyes. In an unnaturally calm voice, she said, "Come on, girls. We're done here."

The chaplain put his arm around her mom's shoulder and guided her to the registration counter. Dee took Ruby's hand and led her in the same direction. Dressed in shorts and a tank top to spend the warm June night outside, Ruby suddenly shivered in the air-conditioned room. She rubbed her arms and drew in her hunched shoulders, but nothing stopped the shivering or the goose bumps on her mottled skin. Ruby closed her eyes and half listened to talk of death certificates and a back-and-forth with a nurse about an autopsy. Her mother said a loud *no* and that was that.

Ruby's mother waved her hand at Mike and his dad. "You stay away from us, Charlie. And that goes for you, too, Mike."

Ruby wanted to run to Mike. They needed to comfort each other, didn't they? But how could they? *His* mother with *her* dad? She stood by the door, shaky, and her knees were almost too weak to support her weight, let alone go to Mike. What would she say?

Her mom's shouts got Charlie's attention, but Mike didn't look up. He kept staring at the floor, shaking his head.

Charlie lowered his voice and said, "Tim Driscoll ruined everything."

In a flash Mike glanced her way, with that same way-beyond-grim expression. She'd never wipe away the message of loathing—hate—his expression sent. It was silent, but clear—*they* were over.

As if her mother dug deep and took control of herself, she lifted her chin and, with dry eyes, motioned for Dee and Ruby to follow her through the automatic doors that opened as if obeying her command.

Even then, Ruby understood exactly what those words meant. Confusion and grief and shock aside, she and Mike were done. Ruined. Her dad killed his mom. Or that's what Charlie Abbot said. Two other people died that same night in the other car. And her dad had been driving the car with Mike's mom in it. Even in all that pain, though, Ruby didn't believe, not for a second, that anyone died because her dad had been reckless. She held on to that over the few days after, as she changed every plan she'd so carefully designed and, instead, drove out of town forever.

Ruby slid open the patio door to let the dog back inside and dried her off with a towel. Tending to the dog helped Ruby's emotions settle once again. It was a relief, actually, finally confronting Mike about the last time they saw each other.

"Just a few more weeks and we'll be off to a new home," she whispered, as if Peach

would understand her words or the sadness
behind them.

But like Emma said, no matter where she
went the memories would come along like
wispy ghosts.

CHAPTER FOUR

"HEY, BUDDY, SCOOT OVER." Mike playfully huffed and puffed in his game of pretending Jason was so heavy he had to strain to slide him across the sheet. "You're getting so big I can barely move you."

That brought a smile to Jason's face as he wiggled his body to make room for Mike to sit next to him on the narrow bed. Mike's old bed. Jason handed him two books, one about a couple of giraffe families that had been so well loved, Mike had to drag out the stapler and tape to keep it in one piece. Jason himself had dropped the book into the box of things Mike had taken from his room at his mom's house. The other story was a brand-new book written by a local author about a boy on a farm. They'd only read it six or seven times already, Mike thought, amused. At least it was a book Jason had chosen himself in last week's trip to the local library.

He was letting more new things in with the old, Mike thought with satisfaction.

When he'd first gone to Pennsylvania to be with Jason at the hospital, he'd read the same stories again and again to the silent boy. Jason hadn't wanted to look at any books that weren't taken from the shelves in his room at home. Only since coming to Bluestone River had Jason discovered the wonder of the library. It was a sign he was moving forward and adjusting to his new life.

That afternoon, Gloria had spoken to Mike about Jason's progress in therapy. She believed Jason's love of stories was a coping tool that helped him make sense of what had happened to his mother. He was unconsciously sorting out his memories of the fire. His burns and the loss of his mom included. According to Gloria, the mysterious mechanisms of memory were forming a story, a version of events he'd remember and be able to tell. Then, when he was older, his mind could handle a more complex explanation of the fire and what happened to his mom, and to him.

No one had to explain that mechanism of

memory to Mike. For years he'd been telling himself a story about Ruby running away. *She* abandoned him. She was the one who destroyed any possibility the two of them could get past what had happened to their parents. Ruby proved it by rushing out of town, telling only Emma where she'd gone. Emma said it was a secret and kept her word to Ruby and refused to say. Barely a week later Neil told him a For Sale sign was stuck in the grass in front of Ruby's house. Before the end of the summer, Ruby's mom and Dee had left for Florida. Nothing was left of the Driscoll family, except Timothy Driscoll's headstone in the cemetery.

All that happened before Mike could accept his mother was gone, and it took much longer for him to face the reality that his mom had been unfaithful to his dad. He'd stayed stuck as an immature boy about that. He had to grow into a man before he could see his mother as a woman with her own private thoughts and feelings, as well as troubles and desires that had nothing to do with him. He hardly knew how to talk about Timothy Driscoll. He thought of Ruby's dad as a principal who expected a lot from the teenagers he was in charge of. He had a little swagger, too, like a man aware of the respect he commanded. Mike had secretly liked that about him. He didn't mind taking his share of jabs over dating the principal's daughter. A couple of decades later, Mike still could shut his eyes and swear he heard Neil's voice leading the razzing.

When Jason's breaths were soft and regular in the deep first stage of sleep, Mike closed the book and eased himself off the bed. With any luck, Jason would stay peaceful through the night. No way to predict how those hours would go, though. Mike had had to get used to that in the first few days after he'd brought Jason home from the hospital.

Mike closed the door behind him and started down the hall to the kitchen, passing the open door of his own room and the spare bedroom he planned to turn into his home office. He also passed the door to the enclosed stairway to his parents' bedroom and other smaller rooms upstairs. He'd avoided the second floor and his parents' room altogether after moving back in. As much as he welcomed the familiarity of the house, he wasn't ready to move into their large bedroom, even with the full bath his dad had added to please his mom.

Earlier, he'd called Emma and asked for Ruby's cell-phone number. Now he stood at the island in the kitchen with his phone in his hand. Waffling. Telling himself it was okay to call her, but then talking himself right back out of it. What would he say if she picked up his call?

With a frustrated groan, he let his head drop back. His mind made a detour as he stared at the patch of peeling white paint on the ceiling. Every day he saw something in the place that needed fixing. His parents had updated the house, but now it looked kind of dingy and old. The walls, the windows and the floors were calling for attention. But after Jason, his law practice was his priority. Figuring out the house could wait.

Still hanging on to the phone, Mike walked out to the porch. It was only 8:30 p.m., but it was dark at the lake and the sky was dotted with clouds moving fast in the breeze. But being away from the lights of the highway and town made it dark enough for a few stars to break through. He and Ruby used to sit side by side in the rowboat and look up at the stars. In the summer, Ruby usually found the points of the Big Dipper and at other times she searched for Sirius because it was the brightest star in the sky.

"Nope, you're the brightest star," he'd quipped, snorting at what he knew was a pretty lame joke.

Ruby had responded with a quick laugh, but then she'd kissed him and they'd let the boat drift around the far end of the lake while he kissed her back. Ruby's soft full lips, her warm skin, her easy, hearty laughter used to be on his mind all the time, starting in the morning when he got ready for school. Sometimes he drove a little too fast to get there just so he could see her before their first class. They studied together and hung out at the bridge and stuffed themselves with big platters of fries in the diner downtown. And rowed around the lake until it froze over in the winter. Starlight, moonlight, no light at all. It didn't matter.

So many memories had faded over the years, but his time with Ruby came back in colors as vivid as her red hair. Or the purple raincoat she'd worn just the other day.

He still remembered purple was her favorite color.

He picked up his phone.

MIKE THREW OFF the sheet and blanket and his bare feet hit the cold floor. Pulling a sweatshirt over his head, he hurried across the hall, the grogginess of being awakened from a deep sleep disappearing fast. Jason's piercing cries were louder still when Mike opened the door and then scooped his son's rigid body into his arms and pulled him to his chest. "Shh, shh… It's okay, it's okay. I'm here, Jason. You're safe, you're safe." He rested his cheek on the top of Jason's head, comforted by his soft curls.

"You're fine now," Mike whispered, rocking him slightly. "It was only a dream. Not real at all. You're home in your own bed, safe with me." Mike tugged up the blanket, tucked it around Jason's shoulders and enveloped him in his arms until he could feel the muscles in the boy's back and neck begin to let go. "See? What did I tell you? Everything is okay now."

Tension eased in Mike's body, too, and he leaned back to let the headboard support his weight. Like other nights, the cries quieted into weak whimpers until they trailed off altogether. Mike closed his eyes, thankful for even this small sign of improvement. Week by week, fewer of his son's nightmares jolted Mike in the middle of the night, and they didn't last as long, either.

He listened to Jason's breathing and when the inhales and exhales returned to a reassuring rhythm, Mike kept him covered while he rolled him fully onto the bed. He waited a couple of minutes before creeping down the hall into the kitchen and pouring himself a glass of water. Outside it was dark and silent. Inside, Jason was sleeping, but Mike was wide-awake at 2:30 a.m., a time guaranteed to build Mike's fears into monsters waiting to pounce. In the middle of the night all he could see was a future spent raising a child who wouldn't or couldn't speak. *Ever.* And a failed law practice. His savings would shrink month after month. If he wanted to stay in Bluestone River, then what?

Mike put his hands flat on top of the island counter and stretched back, feeling the tension build in his body. When the world was dark, Mike's natural optimism, so real and strong during the day, felt like a pretense. And he never felt more alone than in these moments.

RUBY KEPT HER distance as Jason stood with the toes of his sneakers at the edge of the lake. It was October now and what was left of the turning leaves on the trees reflected orange and gold on the flat surface of the water. "I can almost see the wheels turning in that little head," she remarked to Mike. "All he wants is for one of those tiny lake waves to come close so he can jump back from it and win the challenge. Boy triumphs over the wild sea."

"Looks like he's in for a long wait to feel heroic today." Mike chuckled as he spread his arms and looked at the brilliant fall sky. "Not many more warm afternoons like this." He paused. "I'm glad I convinced you to visit us here, on Jason's turf." He nodded in Jason's direction. "So, what do you think?"

Ruby continued staring at Jason while she formed her thoughts into a tactful answer to his question. "Let's start with the obvious. Jason looks so much like you it's almost comical. He's obviously bright and curious—and so engaged. But, I'm wondering how fearful he must be underneath that sweet, compliant mask he wears."

"*Mask?* I'm not sure I'd call it that." Mike shoved his hands in his front pockets. "Just because he's compliant, as you put it, doesn't mean he's…afraid."

"Hold on, Mike, I'm not saying he's really a bad kid underneath it all, but don't you think he's a little too, oh, I don't know, placid?"

Mike grunted in frustration. "That's what Gloria said."

Ruby had heard Mike talk about Jason's therapist, and given the natural way the boy played and acted—minus the mutism—it was clear somebody was doing something right. Zoe before she died, and Mike in the months since. Behaving like a model child, Jason had everything he needed more or less handed to him. Even Peach was standing quietly at his side. Given all the other circumstances, Ruby had to admit that being pleasant and compliant seemed like a smallish problem.

"He doesn't really need to talk, does he?"

Mike frowned. "*Need?* What do you mean?"

"Like I said before, Mike, I'm not an expert on his situation. This is just my observation. He has all his needs met. Just now at lunch you asked if he wanted mayonnaise or mustard on his turkey sandwich. Both jars were out, so all he had to do was point to what he wanted."

"But what else should I do?" he asked defensively.

Ruby let out a light laugh. "Well, I suppose you could start by not giving him a choice. Put mustard on the sandwich and let him object if he doesn't want it. Maybe he'd get a little frustrated that you didn't ask."

"Wow. Why didn't I think of that?" Mike snorted. "Seriously. I'm not being sarcastic, Rubes. Such a small but obvious thing to do."

Ruby ran the toe of her sneaker through the leaves and broken twigs gathered under the tree. "Didn't you say that at school, he does the work and Mrs. Cermak leaves him alone? He's learning to read and spell words."

"It's not a typical classroom," Mike said.

"But I'm guessing she doesn't ask him

questions that demand complex answers. She tells him what to do—"

"And he does it!" Mike took his hands out of his pockets and jabbed his finger into his chest. "I second-guess everything. I pick out his clothes, wait for him to point to books he wants read and tell him when it's time to eat, take a bath, go outside...wow."

"Well, I wouldn't feel bad about it." She spoke in a low voice. "You've been one-hundred-percent focused on making him feel secure and loved. You want him to know for sure you'll take care of his needs. Trouble is, he never balks. It could be quite a shock when he acts up."

Mike sighed. "Before Zoe died and I was visiting, he was always on his best behavior, like kids are with their grandparents. While it was good that he was polite, it was weird, too. It didn't feel genuine."

Mike rubbed at his cheeks in what to Ruby looked like frustration.

"I keep thinking back to the couple of days I got to spend with him last Christmas. I took him to some water park near their house. Very exciting...not," Mike said flatly.

She studied Mike's face, but he wasn't

looking at her. Instead, with a pinched expression he focused on Jason running back and forth along the shore with Peach.

She reached out to touch his arm, but quickly changed her mind. They'd maintained their distance and she intended to keep it that way. "So why do you look so pained?"

"Oh, don't get me wrong. It was fun." His snicker punctuated his sarcasm. "I'm being cynical. It had slides and waterfalls and rope swings. A kid's dream. I mean, what's not to like?"

He didn't need to fill out the picture. "Ah, I get it. Not your idea of Christmas."

"Thank you." In a voice edging toward anger, he added, "My friends at the firm didn't understand why I'd found the holiday so—so *empty*. It didn't feel like a real Christmas at all. And it was my first holiday with him and our first overnight trip."

"How did that happen?" Ruby asked. Mike had told her he and Jason were a story for another day. Well, maybe this was the day.

Mike stared off at the lake. "It's not that hard to explain, Rubes. I had a casual fling with another attorney at the firm. Zoe left and moved to Pennsylvania, and when a few women at the office came in all excited one day and told us Zoe had a baby, I did the math." He paused and closed his eyes.

Not knowing what to expect, Ruby shouldn't have been surprised by Mike's story, but she was. And she was impatient for him to fill in the blanks, which he quickly did. *A kind of emotional roller coaster,* Ruby thought, when he explained he'd been told Jason was another man's child. Naturally, he more or less forgot about Zoe and the baby.

Mike scoffed. "But she was wrong and the other guy eventually got a paternity test. Out of the blue, at least for me, she called to tell me the truth."

Not how Mike would have chosen to become a dad, Ruby thought, *no matter how much he'd changed in twenty years.* "So, you weren't in his life very long before his mom was killed."

"Less than a year. And I was an out-of-state dad, not even a weekend one. I saw him briefly at Thanksgiving and then again at Christmas. The water-park Christmas."

Ruby glanced around her, remembering the trees circling the lake covered with snow on Christmas Eve. Or the fairyland Mike's dad created by stringing white lights around the trees near the house and along the porch roof and the railings. Mike's mom elaborately decorated their tree, which filled at least a quarter of their living room. Ellen had added new ornaments every year, but she always hung the ones Mike had made as art projects in grade school.

In Ruby's mind, nearly every surface in Mike's house was covered with candles and her collections of ceramic angels and Swedish trolls. When they were kids Mike rolled his eyes at what he called "Christmas gone wild." No wonder the water park rang hollow.

"A water park would be a far cry from the festivities at your house." Almost as an afterthought she said, "Emma and I always said your mom was the coolest of all the moms we knew. She ran around all year in jeans and T-shirts or big comfy fisherman's knit sweaters. She was either in boots or sneakers and her long blond hair hung straight down her back. We loved her big hoop earrings."

For the first time in years, Ruby allowed herself to get a kick out of the memory of Ellen Abbot's holiday spirit. "Your mom was so different from mine. Mom always styled her hair carefully every day and wouldn't leave the house without meticulously putting on her makeup. All her clothes seemed perfectly matched. Red sweater sets with tailored slacks. Plaid blazers and navy skirts."

Mike looked into her eyes and smiled sadly. "That's true, but my mom had lots of running around to do with running a resort."

"Sure, but your mom had the most elaborate holiday rituals—the candles alone…" Laughing, Ruby raised her hands in the air for emphasis.

A scary mix of emotions swirled through her. They stumbled into shared memories and she was to blame for bringing up his mother. This had to stop, this slow walking up to the edge of the cliff that would tumble them deep into the past. In her defense she realized it was almost impossible to think about Christmas without Ellen's enthusiasm coming to mind. Ellen herself had talked about her holiday extravaganzas.

Changing the subject, Ruby forced a chuckle. "When I moved to south Florida I was sure I'd detest Christmases amongst the palm fronds. But I surprised myself. Balmy is good."

"Ha! Like I believe that."

"No, really." Then she blurted, "But I always missed Thanksgiving here in Bluestone River."

"Your favorite holiday, Rubes. I remember."

She drew back her head, surprised. "You do? Really?"

Mike reached for her hand and before she could pull it back, he caught it and squeezed her fingers. "I remember everything, Ruby."

Her heart pounding, she pulled away from him and moved closer to his son. "Let me show you something, Jason."

When the boy turned around she hurled a stick into the water and Peach raced into the lake and captured it in her mouth. Splashing water all around her, she bounded back to Ruby. She threw it again and again, and each time Peach took off like a shot.

"Better stand back," she called to Jason. "She'll soon be shaking her coat to get rid of all that water."

Jason responded by searching the ground around him until he picked up a good-size stick and ran closer to the water. When he threw the stick in the lake, the game immediately changed for Peach, who ignored Ruby and had eyes only for her new partner.

Aware Mike was at her side again, Ruby remained focused on Peach. "Peach spent most of her life with an elderly woman who lived alone, so I don't know how she became this good with kids."

"Golden retrievers have a reputation as good family dogs, don't they?" Mike asked.

"So I hear. I guess it's in her nature to be happy when she's around children." Steering the conversation back to Jason, she said, "Even playing these kinds of games with the dog, Jason doesn't have to talk. Peach knows what to do."

Mike smiled watching Jason playing. "He's getting wet, but so what? Jason knows where his dry clothes are. He won't need to ask."

"Don't get me wrong, Mike," she said

softly. "I'm not saying it's a bad thing that you anticipate what he needs." She gestured to the house and then the lake. "You've given him such a secure world now. And a beautiful one."

"He's the biggest challenge in my life, Ruby. It isn't all about me now, that's for sure."

Ruby nodded to acknowledge what he'd said, and for reasons she couldn't pinpoint, more memories came up. One Thanksgiving Day her parents had put their seal of approval on Mike when he stopped in late in the afternoon and watched football with her dad. She and her sister, Dee, kept her mom company in the kitchen and shared second helpings of blackberry pie while they listened to her dad and Mike banter about this or that quarterback. At one point, her mother whispered, "Your dad and I agree, Ruby— Mike is becoming a good man."

"Ruby? Where are you?"

Suddenly pulled out of the scene in her mind, she glanced at Mike the man, and from what she'd seen so far, he really was a good one. "Oh, I'm sorry. My mind drifted." *To you.*

"I saw that," he said with a grin. "But I wanted to know what *you* think it will take to get him to speak."

"Nothing like asking a tough question, Mike." It saddened her to think about how many months it had been since he'd heard his son's voice. What would finally compel the boy to break his silence? A shock of some kind? Ruby had heard of that happening. But sometimes it was a more subtle trigger. She didn't know what to say and her silence was a poor answer.

"Don't feel bad, Rubes. No one else knows, either." A deep frown showed his concern.

"I can only imagine how difficult this is."

Mike shifted his posture and turned toward her, his expression matter-of-fact now. "Enough about my problems. I'm really curious, you know, about you. Emma mentioned you've never been married, either."

She laughed nervously. "Emma really knows how to share the news. Not that it matters. No, I never got married. I had a couple of close calls, but I got used to my freedom." If she told the whole truth, she'd admit the calls weren't all that close. If anyone sidled up and wanted to stick around, she soon found herself applying for fascinating jobs a state or two away. Dee wrote her off as a runaway date, never letting it go far enough to become a runaway bride.

"I'm surprised, somehow. You're smart and funny—" he leaned in closer "—and easy on the eyes."

She winced. "I can't believe you said that. It's like something our grandparents would have said, you know, back in their day."

Laughing, Mike said, "I know, I know. So call the sheriff and have me arrested me for corny humor."

Ruby looked at his amused face—his blue eyes were doing that thing her mom called twinkling. Ignoring the warmth spreading through her body, she said, "I guess I've been like you. I've dated, had relationships, but never wanted to make that ultimate commitment." Ruby pointed with her chin toward Jason. "I just didn't have a child along the way."

She let out a quick laugh and met Mike's gaze. "My work has been like my child. It's odd to be without it, but it's also made me face what a big bite of my life it owned."

She lowered her head, suddenly studying her sneakers and regretting that she'd said more than she'd meant to.

When she raised her head again, she was greeted by Mike's quizzical expression. If he had questions for her, she sure had a bunch for him, too. But no more today.

She pulled her phone out of her pocket and checked the time. "I should get to the hospital. Did I tell you Emma is coming home soon? Like Monday, maybe."

"She texted me," Mike said. "She's excited about doing her rehab at home with you there to drive her to physical therapy and other appointments."

Emma hadn't mentioned she and Mike were texting now, but why not? Now that Mike was back in town their friendship would continue long after Ruby left.

"I get the feeling the work you've been doing all these years is more important than the kind of work that's eaten up my time," Mike said. "Contract and commercial real-estate law for the first few years, and then later, I branched out into public law."

"Citizen-advocacy issues?" Ruby asked.

"A couple of good cases about preserving

landmarks. That sort of thing." He shrugged. "I'm not sure what I'll handle here in town. Maybe real estate. Some family law, I suppose."

"I hope it goes well, Mike. I mean it." The intensity of her words embarrassed her and she distracted herself by calling out to Jason. "Why don't you say goodbye to Peach now, Jason? We've got to get going."

Jason responded by running toward her and Peach followed.

"Wait, Ruby, you're running off again. But you never told me about your last job, except that you were let go."

"Fired, Mike. It wasn't some congenial parting of the ways."

"But why?"

Ruby wasn't prepared to relive the story, not with Emma waiting and Peach and the little six-year-old running in a circle around Mike. She said the first thing that popped into her mind. "Arrogance."

"Huh? You mean your boss was arrogant."

She shook her head. "Nope. I was."

Mike's expression changed to frank curiosity, but leaving no time for any other response, she called Peach and said a quick goodbye to Jason. "I'll stop by again with Peach soon," she promised.

Already halfway to her car, she looked over her shoulder at Mike standing with his hands on his hips. She raised her hand, waving goodbye. "To quote you, Mike, it's a conversation for another day."

"Okay," he said, "but I'm going to hold you to that."

She'd already said too much. Especially since she wasn't ready to chew it over one more time and sort out how and why her big idea had gone so wrong.

CHAPTER FIVE

EMMA'S HOUSE WAS easy to find. Bluestone River didn't have many log homes, and those few were vacation cabins downriver and not typical dream houses. River Street took him toward the park, but he veered off on a street that ended at the road that led to Emma's place. Sure enough, there it was.

The imposing structure wasn't merely a big house, it was a small lodge. The place was so like Neil—tall with some heft, but not overpowering. He'd been the kind of guy who'd taken up a lot of space in any room he'd occupied just by the force of his personality. Mike could see why Neil and Emma chose the site on uncultivated prairie acres, some of them wooded. A nice piece of land. He smiled to himself. Not quite the prime real estate of his house on Hidden Lake. There was no more beautiful setting anywhere in Illinois.

As he reached the bottom of the stairs to the front door, Ruby came out. "Uh, hi. I didn't expect to see you here."

With her handbag slung over her shoulder it was obvious she was going somewhere. Showing up without calling first suddenly seemed like a very bad idea. "I see I caught you on your way out."

"I'm picking up Emma." She frowned. "I thought I mentioned she's coming home today."

Right. He'd forgotten that. That left him feeling foolish standing in her front yard for no particular reason other than wanting to talk to her. He failed miserably at playing it cool. No way could he pretend what happened to Ruby's job, for one thing, didn't interest him, especially because of the path she'd chosen. Ruby, the young girl on a quest for a prized MBA, had changed course somewhere.

"You did say that, Ruby. Sorry. It slipped my mind." He sighed. "I'll be on my way."

She came down the stairs and headed toward her car, not toward him. "Is everything okay with Jason?"

"Yes, he's fine," he said, opening his car

door. "He had a nightmare last night, but it didn't last long. He went right back to sleep."

"Good to hear. I've really got to hurry. I don't want to be late."

He nodded, but was slow to turn away.

"Mike...what's going on?" She raised her hands in a clear "what gives?" question.

He couldn't avoid answering. "Man, I should've known better than to just show up here. But... I mean, you ran off yesterday. *Again.* One more conversation we didn't finish." He took a deep breath and stepped closer to her. "Ruby, I want to know what's happened to you in all this time. I don't mean to intrude, but—"

"I'm here for Emma, Mike." She looked away and stared at the house, one hand resting on her hip. "Yes, it happens that I lost my job, so I was free to come to help her, but what difference does it make? You're planning your life with Jason. I actually think it's wonderful you're back here. What better place for your son to grow up? But that's you." She raised her shoulders in a half-hearted shrug. "As soon as Emma is better, I'm moving on to whatever is next for me."

Her words came at him like a boulder

threatening to knock him over. But why? She'd been clear from the day in the park her visit was about Emma, end of story. He'd never have bumped into her in the first place if Emma hadn't needed Ruby's help. He nodded his understanding, but balked at the truth of it. There were no coincidences. He was sure of it.

"I'm happy to talk with you about Jason, and sure, I can recount all the gory details about my last job, if you really want to hear them." Her voice grew louder with every word. "But why would you? What's been going on with me isn't any of your concern."

No? Then why did it feel so critical to hear the details. "For twenty years, I've had what felt like an open wound that's never closed up. How about you?"

She closed her eyes.

After dropping his guard this way, he had nothing to lose. "What about the talk we never got to have twenty years ago? Ruby, anytime we get even a little close to the personal stuff you rush off."

Ruby kicked around leaves and gravel with the toe of her shoe. He'd watched her do that before plenty of times. Was it a case of nerves or was she gathering her thoughts? He couldn't say. When they were kids, long before they were teenagers and falling love, they'd used their shoes to draw pictures or write their names in the gravel in the schoolyard and in the sand at the lake.

Finally, she raised her head. "Don't you dare put all the blame on me just because I left. Besides, why stir up all that pain again? There's nothing we can do to change what happened."

"Don't you think I know that?" he snapped.

Ruby's features softened, but she shifted her weight and looked at her car.

From the expression on her face, all he'd accomplished was making her feel torn between responding to him and taking off to get Emma. No fair. This was on him. He held up his hands and backed up. "I'm sorry. I don't know what I was thinking. I don't want you to keep Emma waiting." Wanting to lighten the mood or at least sound like a guy on a day like any other, he added, "Besides, I'm supposed to be rolling paint on those office walls right about now."

She laughed lightly. "I guess it's obvious I

can't think about much else except Emma at the moment. She's given me a title. I'm her 'life manager.'" Along with the air quotes around her title, a sly smile appeared. "I may even be forced to cook a few meals."

"Emma's my friend, too, remember. I can bring lunches over now and again. Or, pick up a carryout dinner. You can't say no to that."

How's that for inviting yourself? Nice.

"Nope. I won't say no to carryout food. I may send you on jelly-donut runs. I'm sure you've discovered Sweet Comforts. Emma can't go a day without scarfing down at least one of those. Then she complains about the sugar and carbs."

"It's a deal. I'm kind of partial to those sticky donuts myself." He opened the car door and waved. "Give Emma my best." With that, he got in and drove away, embarrassed for showing up in Emma's driveway like an eager teenager hoping for a few minutes with his girl. After he'd dropped off Jason at school, the car had seemed to steer itself toward the river and in search of Emma's house.

Ever since Ruby had mentioned her job

she'd been in his thoughts. Her amused grin hadn't changed at all, nor had her thoughtful, startling eyes. Always unusual and gorgeous, her light brown eyes made her mood easy to read. During their first conversation in the park he saw a trace of sadness in Ruby's eyes that hadn't been there when they were young.

As if on autopilot, Mike headed to the bridge, with her words echoing through him. *What's happened to me isn't any of your concern.*

That should be true, especially because he'd spent years burying questions about Ruby. So successfully, in fact, he'd never searched for her, not even online in recent years. Even before that, he'd let his friendship with Neil and Emma wither away, rather than being reminded of Ruby. When it came to Ruby, he'd worn blinders, particularly when his dad was still alive.

Mike had stayed behind to go to college close to home to pick up the slack and run the resort while his dad grieved. Eventually, he'd gone to law school, but also close to home, so he could lend a hand with the resort most weekends. Ruby's name was never spoken, and eventually, Mike perfected his detached act when it came to Ruby. Now, it had taken only one glimpse of her to expose what a fraud he was when it came to her.

He parked the car on the edge of the farm road, then walked to the bridge and leaned on the railing. The recent rains had raised the level of Bluestone River. The rush of water over the stones sparkled in the morning sun and gave off the flashes of the deep blue that had given the river—and the town—its name. Nothing changed with the river. It still rose and fell with the rain and dry spells, unaware the town desperately needed a shot of fresh energy.

He stared at a point on the sandy flats downriver, where it was deep enough to swim, but the currents made it dangerous all the time. Posted signs made it clear it was a no-swimming zone. But when he and Neil were about twelve, and their middle names were Swagger and Bravado, they decided those signs were just for show. Or didn't apply to daredevils like them.

"Grounded for a month," his mom later declared with a slap on the kitchen counter.

Caught red-handed. Or, more like caught

dripping wet with no way to fib their way out of it. Other adults had spotted them and alerted their parents. Neil resentfully complained about the tattling. Mike's mom, with a dry sense of humor, smiled smugly and said, "I hope you learned the real lesson. You won't get away with much in this little place. Even the river has eyes and ears."

His hometown was the kind of place where the adults kept an eye on all the kids. But standing at the bridge all these years later, he smiled at the memory of his mother grounding him and then tossing her hair back as she turned away. That familiar hair-toss gesture always meant she was punishing him because she was obliged to. She'd probably taken a few dips in the river herself at about the same age.

Mike tipped back his head to feel the sun on his face. He'd crossed into territory every bit as dangerous as the river currents. His mom. Since he'd been back in the house, one memory after another pushed their way to the surface. Along with trying to block out Ruby over the years, he'd run away from images of his mom as a woman with energy and humor and enormous patience.

He'd turned over stone after stone of his childhood, especially his high-school years, searching for signs his mom had been unhappy with his dad. Angry, hurt, or dissatisfied with her life. He almost wished he could find something—anything—to explain why she'd been willing to risk everything to sneak off with Timothy Driscoll in this little town where she knew so well secrets were hard to keep. He'd not had an "aha" moment over it, not in all these years.

He always came back to what Ruby said. His mom was one of the fun parents. Kids liked to hang out at his house and shoot hoops on the basket mounted on the garage, or sprawl out on the wraparound porch. They'd spread out towels and blankets under the tree by the swing. Of all the summer jobs in town, the most coveted was working at the Hidden Lake Resort and having Ellen Abbot for a boss.

"Speaking of bosses," Mike said aloud. "I'm the boss now." He had paint to buy, windows to wash, office furniture to scare up. Up until now, his days in Bluestone River had been taken up with settling in Jason and bringing the house back to life after it had been closed up for over ten years. But now he had a law practice to launch.

He hurried to his car, hoping that getting into action would quiet the anxiety sending out flutters in his gut as warning signals. Mike had no idea if another law practice could work in Bluestone River. But he had to try.

EMMA GRIMACED AS she gripped the walker and took the first step on a postbreakfast walk. This was the first of three five-minute walks inside the house. It was about sixty steps from the front entrance to the patio doors. The first walk had eaten up the whole five minutes. "Sounds like you told Mike to get lost."

"I did not," Ruby insisted, wincing in empathy as she watched Emma's careful movements. Ruby shadowed her, staying close enough to catch Emma if she lost her balance or needed a supportive hand. Last night, over cups of hot tomato soup, she'd first told Em about Mike's surprise visit that morning.

Emma rolled her eyes. "When you tell someone—in so many words—to mind his own business, that pretty much means you want him to go far away."

Ruby rested her hip on the arm of the couch. "That's not the same as getting lost. Besides, we haven't seen the last of him. He's going to bring us lunch now and again and do bakery runs. He wants to see you."

Emma reached out and captured Ruby's fingers in hers. "Then why do you have such a guilty look on your face? And sad. You look troubled every time Mike comes up in conversation."

Ignoring the question, Ruby pressed Emma's hand between both of hers. "You're cold. Why don't I make a fire this morning?"

With Peach standing close by, Ruby arranged the kindling and a couple of the smaller logs on the grate. She had filled the wood basket and made sure they had everything they needed for fires as the days grew chillier. "I'm rusty at this," Ruby said. "It's been a long time since I had a fireplace. Not since that cottage I rented in the mountains."

"I remember," Emma said. "The rooms were like postage stamps, but the view of the mountains was so great you didn't care."

She snickered. "Your job-hopping had big advantages for me. I had new places to visit every few years."

When flames from the paper and kindling shot up between the logs and the bark caught fire, Ruby sat back on her heels and gave Peach a pat. "There. Done."

"You've still got it, Rubes," Emma said, a giggle starting in her throat.

"What? What's so funny?"

Emma shrugged. "I don't know. You. It's not funny, but it's like a party being together here in my house after I made so many visits to see you. Even with my back aching, I'm loving this time with you."

"Me, too. We'll take trips again, Em." Ruby had great fun planning almost every long vacation around a special trip with Emma. A bike trip in the Netherlands was their first European adventure, but their walking tour of olive groves and wineries in Italy was their favorite.

As if reading her mind, Emma said, "Are you up for a trip sometime soon? How about London?"

"In a heartbeat. But I should wait until I'm, you know the phrase, *gainfully em-*

ployed." Not so for Emma, who had luckily inherited a not-so-small fortune before marrying Neil. She could pay for trips and support her favorite causes without a budget or having to save so many dollars a month to pay for a trip. Whereas Ruby's skimpy, not-for-profit salaries didn't buy trips without careful planning.

"Right," Emma said, "but another walking trip is my goal."

"I get it. And these short walks every day are a step toward that goal. Speaking of walking, when Brenda gets here to do the housekeeping I'll take Peach out for her long walk of the day."

"And yours," Emma said. "I like it that you and Peach are rambling around town. That's how you ran into Mike, right?"

Ruby didn't have to respond one way or another because Brenda arrived with a cheery hello and a bag of groceries in her arms. Ruby quickly leashed Peach and grabbed her jacket and let the dog lead her down the drive, but instead of turning toward the river, she tugged the leash the other way. "Something different today, Peach. We're headed into town."

She took a turn at the next corner and jogged a couple of short blocks to River Street. Mike had been weighing on her mind ever since his visit yesterday. She'd pretended to be nonplussed when she saw him, even detached, as if her stomach hadn't done flip-flops at the sight of him. Why was she intent on avoiding Mike's questions about what happened to the job she'd loved so much? Simple answer—*pride.* It was all about losing face. She'd failed in a big way.

On a whim, Ruby ducked into the gas station and scanned the candy aisle until she found what she was looking for and paid for it at the counter. Smiling to herself she headed for Mike's office. She wasn't sure he'd be there, but if not, she'd leave her little gift by the door and send him a "sorry I missed you" text. Offering an olive branch after being so curt was the least she could do.

Ruby knocked on Mike's window. His car was parked nearby and the office lights were on. When he came into her line of vision, his warm smile let her know he was happy to see her. When he opened the door, she handed him the bag from the store. "Enjoy," she said.

Mike opened the bag, peeked inside and laughed. "Red licorice. My favorite study food. You remembered, Rubes."

The sight of his face all lit up made her cheeks warm. She didn't need a mirror to tell her she was blushing. "You said something about painting this place, so I figured you'd be here."

"Come on back. I've got a card table and a couple chairs." He glanced at the dog. "No stepping in the paint, Miss Peach."

"Don't worry. I'll keep her close. She'll be all tuckered out from our walk, anyway." When they went past Mike's office, she saw the wall had gone from the ugly blue to a pale gray, almost white. In the back, half of one wall had one coat of paint and drop cloths covered the floor. "Good color, Mike. Better than a darker law-firm gray. It feels good in here."

"Thanks for saying that. It confirms that brightening the place was more important than communicating a solid, stuffy image." He took out the licorice and opened the package. Putting it on the table, he said,

"Have some. I remember how to share a bag of licorice with you." He then patted the back of a wooden folding chair. "Do you recognize the table and chairs? I found the set stashed away in the basement."

She remembered them. Mike's mom brought out the classic black-top card table and chairs when they were having dinners and parties for more than ten or twelve people. Ruby brushed her hand across the smooth top as a sudden bout of bittersweet nostalgia left her almost shaky. Over a table? "There was always room for one more at your house."

Even though she was restless, she took a seat. She was as ready as she'd ever be. "I actually came to apologize. I was kind of, well, *rude* yesterday. I don't believe you're idly nosing around in my business."

"I'm glad you understand that." Mike sat on the other chair across the table and looked at her through the same bright blue eyes that had drawn Ruby to him in the first place. "But I don't know what got into me, thinking I could show up like that and demands answers. That's not who I am—usually."

Maybe it was the honesty in those eyes, but being alone with Mike in that moment transformed into the right time to explain what had gone so awfully wrong.

"You asked about my job, but you already know I was fired." She smoothed her hands over her cheeks as she gathered her thoughts.

Mike opened his mouth as if to speak, but apparently thought better of it. Instead, he offered a slow nod.

"I think what hurts the most is that it was my dream job. I was so sure…of myself, of the strategy."

"Antibullying. Right?"

Ruby nodded and reached for a licorice string. She bit off the end of it and made quick work of the rest of it. Then she shaded in the background about years of working with crisis centers of various kinds. The details were different, but they all added up to the kind of trauma that was challenging to overcome. "The rewards were huge when we had successes. It was a relief to watch people get past the problems holding them back. Seeing that happen again and again is what kept me in the field." Hearing the pride in her voice, she quickly pointed out that she didn't do the work by herself. "I usually had a great team of dedicated people around me."

She shook her head. "It's hard to believe, Mike, but when I first got involved in this work as a volunteer in a crisis center in college, I didn't connect what I heard from other people to what happened to our families. To us."

The words caught in her throat. Mike stared at her, his jaw slack in the silence.

Finally, Mike smiled sadly. "I probably would have been the same way. I was so wrapped up in taking care of my dad because I thought—assumed—he was the one with the problem." In a voice barely above a whisper, he said, "Sounds like what you've been doing is truly hard work, Ruby."

Ruby bobbed her head while she thought about the roughest parts. "The more important the title I earned, the less I worked directly with the clients—the survivors—and the more I designed the programs and argued for funding. I saw trauma on a more massive scale when I organized emergency services after tornadoes and hurricanes."

She shook her head thinking about the solemn-faced kids hanging on to a parent with one hand and a stuffed animal with the other, not fully understanding their house had been flooded or was flattened. Gone forever.

"You climbed a ladder, Ruby, just not the corporate one, huh?"

Ruby smiled nostalgically. "Ah, yes, me and my MBA were going to set the business world on fire. I have a master's degree, but it's in public administration." She shrugged.

Restless, she bit off more licorice and stood to study the room. "Let me help. I'll finish telling you what happened." She picked up a new roller from a pile of supplies on the floor.

"You don't have to do that," Mike insisted.

"Of course I don't. But I want to." She gestured toward the unpainted wall. "Is there anything worse than a half-finished paint job?"

Mike laughed at her teasing voice and attached the fresh roller to a long handle while Ruby seized a gallon of paint and filled a tray. "Okay, Ruby, you start at the far end. We'll meet in the middle."

"Gotcha. I've painted many a funky apartment in my travels. Turns out I'm pretty good at making places more or less livable." She enjoyed the physical work of it, too. There was something satisfying about rolling paint on walls or polishing up woodwork or dressing up ancient kitchen cabinets. "Unlike the way I've made my living, painting a room or a bookcase provides a road to instant gratification."

Mike laughed. "I need to think that way when I start redoing my house. Opening it up and letting in some fresh air was the easy part."

"Should be fun, though, making that place your own." It was one of the best houses in town, filled with woodwork and cubbyholes, built-in hutches and alcoves.

"Keep going, Ruby," Mike said, his voice serious. "I didn't mean to interrupt."

"When I boil it all down, it's not all that complicated." She told him about a fraternity contacting her after a hazing incident. A nineteen-year-old had died of internal bleeding and the guys in the house tried to cover it up.

She told Mike about accepting a job with a school system in South Carolina that wanted a fresh approach to curbing bullying. "After what happened later in Florida, I wished I'd stayed in that town. It was on the coast. I had a little rental house on the marsh side of an island. It was so pretty and peaceful."

Mike filled his tray with more paint. "Sounds nice. So, you liked the place or the work? Or both?"

"Both." She stepped back to gauge how much Mike had done of the wall at his end. He was inching closer to her, not the other way around. "No fair. You're working faster. You've got longer arms."

"It's not a competition, Rubes," he teased.

"Oh, really? I don't know about that. I remember trying to win a few races to the raft out in the lake. Or get more skips in the stones we tossed in the river." She laughed, but stopped abruptly and put down the roller. "Remember the other day when I said I lost my job because of arrogance?"

Mike quit painting and braced his hand

on an unpainted spot on the wall. "You bet I do. Why do you think I'm so curious? You? Arrogant? I never saw that side of you."

"Well, let's just say the work I did in South Carolina went well. It wasn't just fewer bullies gaining traction and terrorizing kids. The whole point was to talk about communication as a baseline, and nurturing empathy and valuing other people." During the dark days after Florida, Ruby clung to that earlier success as she tried to coax herself to get out of bed and face a new day.

She'd accepted an offer as head of special programming for a midsize school system in Florida because it had a wider reach. "I was seduced by promises of expanding our mandate into cyber-bullying and suicide prevention."

"Wow, Rubes, apparently, you're still fearless. You jumped into the middle of the most controversial—and potentially tragic—problems kids face."

Picking up the roller again, she covered a swath of wall, satisfied that she'd quickly improved the look of it. She kept going, explaining that her program was designed to roll out over three years. But it ran into trouble with an impatient school board demanding instant results. Punishment schemes were more to their liking than the character-development approach. "Once I got there and jumped in, they more or less ridiculed the plan for the first year—the part of the program that depended on communication training. My system to promote empathy was way too soft for this board."

"Oh, yeah?" Mike asked sarcastically. "I've met a few people like that in my line of work."

"I bet you have. It went wrong all around, but my first mistake was staying after I realized the job wasn't the same one I had interviewed for. My second mistake was agreeing to launch their watered-down anti-bullying program, instead of the next phase of my plan."

She dropped the roller into the pan and opened a bottle of water Mike had put on the table. "I had no time to train or even prep everyone and get them to buy in. The board started bragging about the program and put me on radio and TV to declare it a success."

Beads of sweat formed on her forehead, from exertion, for sure, but also from feeling so bad about the jumble of memories that were part of this awful time in her life. She'd warned the board but fell for empty promises to do their part. "I helped oversell the program with a media blitz. After the incident happened I saw a replay of myself promising that bullying would soon be history at the county's public schools."

Mike looked at her thoughtfully, hand still braced on the wall. "Had you done a lot of media before? I can see you being good at it."

A little pride crept in, flustering her in front of Mike. "I had a little experience with it—interviews were part of the jobs I had. I had to get good at PR. But I'd never had interviews then used against me by my employer to prove what was bad judgment."

She told Mike about a boy named Benton, a freshman who had been a target for the mean kids for years. "He's smart, a little nerdy, pushed around most of his life."

"He was alone? Isolated?"

Ruby could almost hear Mike's worries about Jason inside that question. "He hung out with a couple of bullied girls." Ruby shook her head and took big gulps of water out of the bottle. "Counselors had worked with Benton and the two girls, trying to help them not take the bait but still hold their ground."

What happened next felt like a nightmare that would never end. "Benton's old nemesis, Nash, an older kid, pounced the first day of school. Grabbed his backpack and flung it into the fountain pool in front of the school. Then he shoved Benton into the water. Nash the bully had all his mean-kid friends there egging him on."

Benton had texted his older brother to bring him dry clothes, Ruby explained, and somehow that was the final straw for Benton's family. It was going to be another year of this sort of aggression. "The principal was supposed to call Nash's family. He was supposed to call me. But no one followed through—as I feared would happen when we'd finished the first phase of training."

This was the part of the story where Ruby's sense of helplessness was raw, like it had all happened yesterday.

"Why do I get the feeling you blame yourself for all this?" Mike asked.

"I am partly to blame. I should have spoken out more, been stronger and stuck to my plan." Not waiting for Mike to ask, she picked up a brush and started to cover missed spots along the baseboards.

"I can do that later, Ruby." Mike came closer, gently took the brush from her hand and rested it on the edge of the paint can. "Tell me."

She turned her face to look at him full-on. "Benton's older brother and cousin went after Nash with baseball bats. They caught him from behind and poked at him and threatened him. They pushed him all the way to the fountain, shouting and taunting."

Ruby hadn't been there and Nash's buddies had folded fast and scattered. "In the end, Nash took his best swing and Benton's cousin shoved the bat in his gut and sent him flying into the fountain, but he missed the water and hit the concrete rim first."

Mike's mouth dropped open. "Did he kill Nash?"

Ruby closed her eyes. "Almost. It was a miracle he survived." Ruby recalled the moment of relief when she'd been assured Nash was expected to recover. "Nash had a concussion and was in a coma for two days.

He doesn't remember getting hit, falling, or even waking up."

Ruby stared into the corner, where Peach, her nap apparently over, had stood and stretched her front legs the way only dogs can do. Peach had been her best friend from the day of the attack on.

When she looked back at Mike, his face was screwed up in disbelief. "And you lost your job because of what happened? Why were you at fault?"

Ruby scoffed. "Well, that brings us back to where we started. My arrogance." Ruby leaned down and rubbed Peach's neck and jowls. The dog loved it, but it also comforted Ruby in an odd way.

She told Mike about the crush of press that showed up at the school and how at first she tried to keep a lid on it. But one of the most vocal school-board members, who had been pushing for tougher penalties, sucked up the oxygen before Ruby or the principal could respond. "He claimed my program, which had no chance the way they rolled it out, had led to the violence. He called for stepped-up school suspensions and all sorts of other new punishments."

She let out a long groan as she shook her head. "Oh, Mike, I knew when I counter-punched it would be much wiser to wait. But I shushed the voice in my head and issued my statement blaming the school board. I was harsh."

Mike stared at her as if trying to solve a puzzle. "Why was that arrogant? Isn't it the truth?"

"It was, but I went off on a tangent about communication training for young people in this cyber age." Sweeping her hand dismissively, Ruby added, "And I made sure the public knew I'd warned the administration, the board—everyone—that the counseling programs were inadequate. In other words, Mike, I made it all about me."

Ruby flopped in the chair, tired as all the subsequent events flashed before her. Her interviews. The phone call to Benton's family. The one to Nash's mom. "I may have blamed everyone else, but in my heart I knew I'd failed Benton. And Nash. I wanted to intervene with Nash the year before, and offer Benton more help, too. I was told the counselors would handle it."

Mike took a step toward her. Ruby was

sure he would have swept her into his arms if she reached out to him. That's why she kept her hands in her lap.

"Must have come to a head fast."

"I recognized I was in trouble when a couple of teachers I knew in South Carolina emailed to ask what was going on. *With me.* One of the counselors called, naturally furious after hearing one of my public statements, the one I made in front of my apartment building with the press camping out there." She shook her head. "That one still embarrasses me. I had no right to blame the counselors. Their department's funds had been slashed, which left them underpaid and understaffed. I've apologized, but I don't blame them for not responding."

With a thoughtful expression, Mike spoke in a matter-of-fact tone. "You saw your mistakes, but couldn't stop yourself from making them."

Ruby shifted in the chair. "Exactly. My buddies from South Carolina tried to gently, even kindly, suggest I'd burned out."

Ruby shook her head. If she could have forced Mike to look away from her she'd have done it, but he kept watching her through sympathetic eyes. "I caved to the superintendent. I let something half-finished pass itself off as complete. Worse, I made claims I couldn't back up." She gave him a pointed look.

Mike folded his arms across his chest. "Sounds like you were up against an unmovable mountain. We had that kind of situation at the firm now and then. We lost cases because a partner wouldn't budge on doomed trial strategy."

"But I went public, Mike. That's where my own arrogance really stood out. Way too much anger and resentment had built up. Classic burnout symptoms."

The decision to resign had been almost instant. "The head of the school board drafted a letter firing me and went public with it. Then he called me, but I'd already submitted my resignation."

"Did your letter have a time stamp?"

Ruby chuckled. "Oh, Mike, what a lawyerlike question. I'd sent it by email and via registered letter, so they were forced to retract what they'd originally said and opted for general talk about how I'd lost my ability to effectively carry out my role in the system and that my leaving had been our mutual decision. The principal's a popular guy, and has been there forever, so the only available head to roll was mine." Her phrasing made her laugh, and the corners of Mike's mouth curled up, too.

Mike leaned closer. "Don't slug me, Ruby, but it sounds like facing up to your mistake and making a clean break was for the best."

"Ha. No need to duck, Mike. I'm not in the mood to hit anyone. No, I admit I am burned out. The old Ruby would never have let herself be pressured to do a boatload of PR about a weak program. I had no ducks to even put in a row." She'd realized just how badly she needed a change when nothing in her apartment meant much anymore. Even the ocean, a half hour ride away, failed to give her comfort. "I made my amends to Benton's and Nash's families and my colleagues, who understood the political dynamics rippling below the surface. In the midst of this, Emma called, and Peach and I drove north."

"What's next, then?" Mike asked.

She shrugged. "I don't know. But it won't be with schools."

"I can sure see why."

Ruby got up and pointed to the wall. "Hey, I made a little progress, but I need to get back to Emma. It's almost lunchtime. Brenda has probably already left by now."

"Thanks…and I don't mean just for the help in making this place a real law office. I'm glad you told me what happened." His voice low, he said, "And now, here you are."

She ignored the intimate tone and turned to Peach. "Okay, girl, you've been a lazy bones long enough. Let's get moving."

"Hey, Rubes, I need to grab lunch. Let me pick up soup and sandwiches and bring them to Emma's." He cocked his head. "I said I'd contribute."

No, no, this is dangerous. It was way too easy to hang out with Mike. But she couldn't make herself refuse. Instead, she said, "Sounds good. Emma likes turkey."

"And you like roast beef on dark rye, just mustard, no cheese."

Ruby tapped her temple, appreciating how he'd spoken without hesitation. "What a memory."

He liked crusty rolls and thick slices of ham and Swiss cheese. She was good at remembering, too.

CHAPTER SIX

"I'LL PUT ANOTHER log on the fire," Mike said, getting to his feet. "Nice, Emma, having lunch by the fireplace." Almost too nice. Emma was stretched out across the couch. Ruby was making a pot of coffee, and once he'd had a cup, he had to get back to what waited. Painting, paperwork and calling on his River Street neighbors.

"Peach is pawing at the patio door," Ruby called from the kitchen. "I'm going to take her for a quick run around the field. I'll be right back."

Mike and Emma were quiet for a minute after the sound of the door sliding closed. Finally, he said, "This is going to sound really lame and way too late, Em, but I'm sorry I didn't stay in touch with you and Neil."

"No, no. You don't need to say a word," Emma whispered. "No regrets about Neil. He spent his time with the guys at the auto shop. He made them his crowd after he took the place over from his dad." She grimaced, as if in pain. "He could have reached out to you. I could have, for that matter. I owe you an apology, too. But, honestly, Mike, things with Neil and me were never great. I'm not sure you'd have wanted to be around us."

"Like my life keeping my dad glued together was so great?"

Emma struggled to move into a sitting position. "Turns out, Neil and I had little in common. We were like good friends in a really bad marriage. The older we got, the more we diverged, rather than melding together."

Mike couldn't pretend to understand. His friends had always seemed perfect for each other.

"Listen, Mike, I need to say something before Ruby gets back. There are things you should know."

"I know what happened in Florida, the awful way her job ended. If that's what you mean."

Emma shook her head. "I'm not talking about that. Ruby will snap back from that. I told you at the hospital about the important work she's done all these years. No wonder she burned out. I'm not worried. She'll get her confidence back. This is about Ruby herself."

His heart beat faster. "I'm listening."

"I'm not sure she ever got over losing her dad the way she did. Not to mention losing you." Emma huffed the air out of her lungs as if she'd been holding on to these comments for a while.

"She said she came close to marrying," Mike said, feeling a dull ache in his chest.

"Could have been Clay, a heart surgeon in Pennsylvania, or there was Harrison, a history professor in North Carolina."

Oh, sure, there'd be Clays and Harrisons. What guy in his right mind wouldn't fall for Ruby? But he wasn't in the mood to hear about men in Ruby's life. He held up his hand to stop her. "Emma, really, you don't have to tell me—"

"*Yes*, I do." She jabbed the air. If he'd been any closer her finger would have poked his chest. "Ever since she came inside this house, she's goes on about how she's leaving. She's afraid to let her guard down even an inch and refuses to give herself a chance to consider making a life here."

The ache inside got scraped raw at the thought of her leaving. He hadn't let himself go there yet.

"Last night she was looking online and came across an opening for a trauma consultant at a hospital in *Montana*, for Pete's sake. Montana's lovely, but that's thousands of miles away from the people who care about her."

"I don't want her to go—that's the truth. But she still breaks into a run anytime our conversation threatens to lead to *our* past." He flipped one of the logs and it sent sparks flying. "She ran away all those years ago believing I hated her for what happened to my mom."

Emma nodded. "And that you'd never look at her the same way again."

It was true. At first. "My dad was so bitter, Em. Over that summer, I had no one to confide in. Neil was the only one I told about my dad not getting out of bed for weeks. I did everything at the resort, and got the high-school kids working double shifts. I pretended the resort was going fine."

"And while that was happening, Ruby sent cheery emails from a resort in Wisconsin," Emma said. "But I could read between the lines. Then she got a last-minute acceptance to a university in Iowa. Still, she never once mentioned her dad. Or you."

"I spent most of my days poisoning myself with hating Timothy Driscoll and wondering about my mom. Ruby's right. I did hate her dad," Mike confessed. "When I think how I resented my dad for being too weak to get a hold of himself, I still feel shame. I'd gone to such an ugly place inside my head."

Restless, Mike left the fireplace and grabbed the back of the reading chair, thrumming his fingers on the fabric. "It took me a long time to eventually accept things and understand them for what they were. It was just so hard to get my head around it all. *Our* parents didn't have affairs."

"Think about what *you* want, Mike. You and Ruby need to clear the air. Fine. But please, be careful. She's not so tough, you know. When the boy in Florida was in a coma, she was in tears. I talked to her two or three times a day until that boy opened his eyes and spoke his first words. She didn't sleep, she didn't eat. She blamed herself, not a little bit, but one-hundred-percent."

"She said as much earlier while we painted my office."

Emma gave him a look filled with suspicion. He hadn't seen it coming. "How cozy. The two of you fixing up your new law office."

"Whoa. You think I'll hurt Ruby? Is that it? I'd never let that happen. You must believe that."

Emma nodded.

"And as for what I want? You mean like going back twenty years and starting all over again?" He stuck his hands in his front pockets. "You know, I'm pretty vulnerable myself."

"Maybe so, but you've made up your mind. Your life is here. You have a little boy." She paused and offered a weak smile. "Ruby is taken with him and wants to help. After spending a couple of hours at your house, she filled me in on every little thing about Jason, including how happy he seems."

He closed his eyes as he relived that afternoon one more time. Every minute of it. It had given him such a lift.

Mike sat down in the chair opposite Emma. "I was young and I made a bad decision. I let my dad dictate the rules and he demanded that I not see Ruby again. I heard Ruby's mom that night at the hospital. She didn't want me around, either." He propped his elbows on his knees and held his head in his hands. "I put my feelings for Ruby in a box and tried to keep the lid on tight."

Emma rested her cheek on her palm. "But, twenty years later, here you are in my living room still heartbroken and angry."

"Yep, that's me." He let out a loud snicker. His hadn't lost his sense of irony. "So, Em, it wasn't that long ago I negotiated a significant settlement for a property dispute—millions at stake. It was an important case for the firm and the rumor mill buzzed about the brass making me a full partner."

"Really?"

He looked down at himself and pointed to the stains on his worn-out T-shirt. "Can't you tell what a hotshot I am? Instead of moving into my new corner office in a deluxe skyscraper at the firm, I'm about to hang my shingle on a street where half the storefronts are empty." He tapped his temple. "Smart, huh?"

Emma laughed. "Piece of cake, Mike. Besides, in the movies, everyone loves a small-town lawyer."

Glad the tension between them was melting away, he tapped his temple again. "I'll remember that."

Emma glanced behind her to the kitchen door. "Here's the thing," she whispered, speaking faster now. "You and I are friends, but you and Ruby can't be casual painting pals. Her heart isn't made that way. Not when it comes to you."

Like my heart is? Emma was so right. And there was more than just their hearts at risk. With so much on the line, could he honestly say he wanted to pick up where they had left off before their parents died? Then again, why did it seem not only possible, but also easy? A part of him would marry Ruby right now and carry all her stuff—and her—into the lake house and settle right in.

"She and I have left a lot unsaid." Unable to sit, he went to the fireplace and leaned against the stone facade. "But Ruby brought up my mom for the first time. She mentioned how she and all her girlfriends liked her so much."

Emma looked amused. "More than other moms, she was her own person. She had a swagger about her."

Mike laughed. "Like Ruby. A one-of-a-kind girl, my mom once said." What *did* he want from this one-of-a-kind grown-up woman, as complex and gorgeous as she was?

The sound of the patio door opening interrupted his thoughts.

"Think about what I've said, Mike. *Please.*"

He nodded to acknowledge her and looked up in time to smile at Ruby coming into the living room.

"Hey, you two," she said, rubbing her palms together. "Getting cold out there."

"But the blaze will keep you warm." He grabbed his jacket off the chair. "I've got to be on my way. School's out soon."

Hurrying to the door, he said, "I'll be by again. Soon." He pointed to Emma. "Lunch today, dinner next time. You haven't seen the last of me." He grinned at Ruby and quickly let himself out.

All the while, everything that Emma had said echoed through him... *What do you want from Ruby?*

His head kept trying to shush his stubborn, nagging heart.

TWO DAYS LATER, Mike pushed the refinished table between the two chairs and stepped back to have a look. Not bad. All he needed was a stack of magazines. A business journal, a sports monthly and a health magazine. Something for everyone.

Thanks to Ruby he even had a plant. She'd left it in front of the office door early that morning, along with a note:

Enjoy this jade plant—a symbol of luck and prosperity. Some think of the leaves as coins—so, may this office bring you great good fortune and happiness. Best, Ruby.

Now the green plant sat on the low window shelf, alive and well. A far cry from the yellowing plants in the dirty window of the old insurance company. He'd also hung two black-and-white photos of River Street, vintage 1930 or so, in the reception area. He'd saved two colorful photos of Hidden Lake in the fall for his office.

He turned to the sound of a knock on his glass front door. A tall woman with long, wavy gray hair was smiling at him. She lifted her hand to greet him. When Mike opened the door to let her in, she didn't hesitate to barrel inside and scan the room.

"Welcome to River Street," she said. "I saw the crew painting your name on the door and putting up your banner, so I already know you're an attorney. Rumor has it you came from a fancy firm somewhere in Ohio."

Laughing, Mike held out his hand and introduced himself. "So, news still travels fast here. Yes, I came from Cincinnati, but my roots are in Bluestone River. I moved back here to raise my little boy. He's six now."

"Aw, that's nice. This is a good place for little kids. By the way, I believe we share a rental agent. Last time I saw her she was doing a little happy dance over filling another space." She gave his hand a quick shake. "I'm from Florida myself. But here I am in Blue…oops, I should tell you my name before I give you my whole life story. I'm Margaret Hall. Everyone calls me Maggie." She reached into her jacket pocket and pulled out a business card. "I'm an experienced web designer—ten years."

"Have a seat," Mike said, pointing to the two chairs. "Be the first to sit in my brand-new reception room." He tapped the business card on his palm.

Not waiting to be asked, Maggie described her web-design business with clientele in eight states. "Doesn't matter where they live."

"You stopped by at the right time. I need a website, and soon." He'd noticed a sign on the door of her office, housed in a bungalow-style building, same as his.

She beamed. "I was hoping to work with more local businesses now that I have a real office. My first one." Maggie tilted her head toward him. "And I earned it. My oldest is off to college and the other one is in her senior year. My husband is the chaplain at the hospital in Clayton, but no more morning goodbyes in the kitchen when he leaves for work. These days we're doing our kisses in the driveway next to our cars—in full view of the neighbors."

Mike laughed out loud. What a character. He wanted a website on the offbeat side. Upbeat, too, with a neighborly image. He was a Bluestone River guy through and through.

"Anyway, as it happens, I need an attorney to help me incorporate my business," Maggie said, getting to her feet. "And if I take on a part-time designer, a goal of mine, I want to be sure I follow all the rules—the laws dealing with employees. I imagine you know what I mean."

He offered a nod in her direction. "Absolutely. Happy to help. Just let me know when you'd like to sit down and talk about it." He gestured around the room. "The paint dried yesterday, and I've been officially open for business the minute you walked in the door. I've got lots of holes in my schedule."

She shook his hand. "I'm glad I stopped by. Seeing you move in makes me even more determined to be part of the River Street revival."

"Hey, I like your attitude," Mike said, his spirits climbing. "I'm hoping I came home at the right time." *Home.* It sounded better to his ears every time he said it. "I grew up here, so I've got a stake in the place."

He and Maggie agreed to meet in his office in two days. Incorporation, employment law. This was the kind of work he could practically do in his sleep.

With her hand on the doorknob, Maggie said, "Oops, I almost forgot to mention the town-council meeting tonight. Are you coming?"

"I plan to be there. I want to introduce myself, or in the case of the mayor, reconnect. I went to high school with Kristine Laughlin. So, I'll see at least one friendly face—two, counting yours."

"Good, I'm looking forward to it." She frowned in thought. "If you ever need a babysitter...well, you have my number. My high school senior is a good candidate for you."

"I'll keep that in mind." And he would. Maybe not right away. But after Jason... The blank was easy to fill in. *After Jason starts talking.* It always came back to that. And was followed by the next intrusive thought: What if he doesn't? What if years passed by and Jason stayed silent? In special-education classes he didn't need?

Stop. Fear trapped him in its vise grips whenever he allowed his thoughts to drift to a hazy future. Today. Stay focused on today. Wave goodbye to Maggie as she passes the window.

Back in his office, he entered the woman's information into his files. His fingers flew across the keyboard. His first meeting with a client pleased him more than he could describe. He grabbed his phone off the desk. He had to tell Ruby. She'd get a kick out of knowing he'd launched his practice with someone down the block. "Hey, Rubes," he mumbled to himself, "in my freshly painted office with its jade plant and sparkling clean windows."

He stared at the phone in his hand and took a deep breath. *I can't call her every time I have some news.* But it was his first impulse. Then Emma's concern about him and Ruby becoming close again flashed in his mind like a neon sign. Reluctantly, he put down the phone.

The framed poster of the covered bridge sat propped in one of the two client chairs across from him. It would fill some empty space in the reception area and remind his clients of one of the town's best—and revered—features. He'd chosen the one showing the bridge in the summer, when the maples and elms and a smattering of birch tree surrounding the approach to the bridge were thick with leaves. The bright blue lettering at the bottom read Step Back in Time—Visit the Historic Bluestone River Covered Bridge.

Just looking at a picture of the bridge led him back in time. For him, the first part of the caption could have just as easily been Stay Stuck in Time. He stood and carried the poster out of his office.

Then the phone rang.

CHAPTER SEVEN

"COME ON, PEACH, a good pal of yours is at the door." Ruby chuckled as she opened Emma's front door to greet Mike and Jason. "Hey, Jason, Peach has been waiting for you. The three of us are so glad you could visit."

Jason's serious face brightened at the sight of the dog and he hurried inside. The attention temporarily diverted Peach's busy nose from the mixed aromas coming from the shopping bag filled with burgers and fries in Mike's hand.

Mike followed Jason inside. "I really appreciate this, Rubes. Like I said on the phone, I'd have canceled plans to go to the council meeting if I hadn't told my new client I'd see her there."

She could barely keep her eyes off him standing there in jeans that fit like they were custom-made for him, like his navy blazer. With his curly hair brushing the collar of his light blue shirt, he carried off the professional-casual look to perfection.

"No problem. Emma is happy to meet your son. And you know I'm always glad to see him." She grinned at the boy, who was absorbed in the dog.

"We've got plenty to keep him busy," Emma called from the couch. "Jason is going to think I'm some kind of slouch, though. Sitting around, being waited on."

"That's okay, I didn't come empty-handed." Mike held up the bag. "Dinner is served."

Taking the bag of food from his hands, Ruby saw him glancing at the fireplace. "Uh, we let it burn out. I wasn't sure if it was okay…" She gave him a knowing look, assuming she didn't have to finish the sentence.

They'd had a fire going all afternoon, as they did almost every day now. Then Mike called and said Heather's baby was feverish and she had to cancel afternoon day care. Ruby was almost too eager to jump in and offer to watch Jason even before Mike asked. But it's something she'd have done for any friend, she told herself.

"Good thinking. I haven't used mine at the house yet. It can wait."

Ruby pointed to Jason's backpack. "What did you bring?"

"His super tractor, and a book about a farm." He pulled out a jigsaw puzzle. "We're big on *The Wizard of Oz* these days," Mike said. "He's especially taken with Toto." "This is plenty to keep him occupied, even if he gets antsy before I get back." He reached into his blazer pocket and pulled out a box of crayons. "I brought these just in case. He draws a lot. I figured you have paper, but not necessarily crayons."

"As a matter of fact, I brought some art supplies with me from Florida—colored pencils and some pastels." Why had she even mentioned that? She hadn't even told Emma she'd squirreled away those things in the back of the desk drawer in her room.

When Mike looked past her, she followed his gaze to see Jason perched on a chair, keeping himself busy rubbing Peach's jowls.

"All's well for the moment. Come with me," Ruby said, gesturing for him to follow. "We'll get dinner on the table in the kitchen."

Ruby set out place mats and forks while Mike unwrapped the burgers and put them on plates Ruby stacked for him. She didn't need a mirror to know she was smiling. For what? What was the big deal about putting a fast-food spread on Emma's table? Maybe because they'd fallen into an easy rhythm as they moved around Emma's tidy kitchen, like they'd been teaming up on dinner for years.

"All set," Mike said, glancing at his watch. "I don't want to eat and run, but I have to. I won't be gone long, though."

"He'll be fine."

Mike frowned. "I'm not sure. Just don't be surprised if he seems a little upset that I'm leaving him here. He's used to being with Heather after school a few days a week. But I've never left him at night after dinner." His forehead wrinkling even more, he added, "Uh, you see, we have a routine."

"Whatever happens, we'll handle it." Lowering her voice to a whisper, she added, "You're a great dad, but you can't prevent him from getting out of sorts or even angry sometimes." Seeing his troubled expression, she acknowledged, "I get it, easy for me to say."

"I know you can handle whatever happens. Besides, I'm what…? Ten minutes away. If anything comes up, send me a text." He turned away and called over the divider shelf. "Dinner's ready, you two."

Ruby put Peach's food in her bowl and by the time they'd gathered at the table, the dog had flopped in front of the patio door. "We'll take Peach out after dinner," she said to Jason. "She always needs one chance to run around before it gets too dark."

Jason scrunched up his face and stared out to the backyard. She could almost see the thoughts popping into his head as he put two and two together. He wasn't so sure he liked the idea of his dad leaving him. Dog or no dog.

As they sat around the table, Jason was distracted by his fast-food dinner. Emma filled in Mike on how the town council and the mayor had taken advantage of complacency—some called it apathy—to keep the town running in a predictable way. "What it really comes down to is being stuck in a rut."

"Well, I'll find out, won't I?" He pushed away from the table and stood. "Okay, Jason, time for me to run. I'll be back to pick you up before you know it."

Jason's eyes opened wide as he slid off the chair and followed his dad to the front door. Ruby went behind him but kept her distance.

"Hey, Jason?" Ruby said. She looked into Mike's amused eyes. "Your dad has to go to some boring meeting, but you get to be here and play with us."

"So, have fun, buddy. Be good."

Jason shook his head, and tugged on Mike's jacket, but Mike eased away. "We went over this before. You'll be here with Peach, Ruby and Emma."

Again, Jason shook his head and grabbed at Mike's blazer, but like he and Ruby had talked about on the phone, Mike gently removed Jason's fingers and pulled away from the squirming boy. Ruby put her hands on Jason's shoulders, but he shrugged her off. Mike held up two fingers. "I'll see you in about two hours."

Ruby stepped forward and closed the door behind Mike as soon as he was on the porch. "Come on, Jason, let's wave goodbye, and then we can take Peach outside." She again rested her hands on the boy's shoulder, but still, he was having none of it. He rushed to the front window and pushed aside the curtains.

Ruby stayed behind him, watching the boy splay his fingers on the window. In the light, Ruby saw the dull streaks of scarring on his lower arms and a couple of spots on the top of his hands. Only after Mike made the tight turn, so he could drive out nose-first, did Jason wave.

When the car disappeared from view, Jason's shoulders sagged and he got down on his knees and braced his elbows on the windowsill. Through the reflection on the glass, Ruby saw him wiping away tears. In that moment, the forlorn little boy looked younger than his six years—more like a pre-schooler not used to babysitters. *So this was what Jason's rebellion looked like*, Ruby thought.

A good sign? Maybe not. A loud and rousing meltdown could be a breakthrough sometimes. She'd seen that with adults and kids coping with the aftermath of trau-matic events. Keeping it all knotted up inside could have consequences. Hit with a wave of sadness that left her nearly queasy, she backed away and went into the kitchen, where Emma still sat at the table sipping coffee. Ruby shrugged helplessly, but Emma silently responded with a "what did we expect?" look.

Ruby motioned for Peach to come to her. When the dog followed her to the edge of the living room, she pointed to Jason. "Go to Jason," she whispered, patting the dog's side.

Peach ambled toward Jason, stopping to look back at Ruby. She motioned for her to keep going, which the dog dutifully did, finally plunking down next to him at the window. When Jason didn't respond, she pushed her body against him until he relented and moved his arm so Peach could slide closer to him.

Ruby killed a few minutes wiping down the kitchen counters, but still, no Jason.

Finally, Emma asked, "Shouldn't we start cracking the walnuts for the cookies?" Her raised voice filled the air.

Ruby feigned surprise. "Right. I *forgot* we were going to bake those cookies tonight."

"You promised me, remember?"

She gave Emma a thumbs-up, wishing she'd had the idea first. No child, even one momentarily unhappy, could resist the offer of homemade cookies. But so far, Jason seemed more interested in kneeling by the window, keeping an eye out for his dad.

From what she'd seen of Jason, he wasn't especially distractible. When he'd thrown sticks to Peach, he was focused like a laser beam. No flitting around from one thing to another for him. It took persistence to produce those detailed drawings Mike had taped to the refrigerator. *Like dad, like son.* Ruby's stomach did a little tap dance, as her mind took a huge leap into the future and saw Jason as a teenager with his curly hair and a sturdy, lean body. He was already a little tall for his age. It was so much more than looks, though. Curious. Self-contained. Careful without being overly cautious. So much of Mike to see in his son.

Ruby smiled to herself. As devoted as Peach was, she was no Jason. She'd be bored soon and needing to stretch her dog legs.

"I better take *Peach* out before we start cracking those nuts for the oatmeal cookies." Emphasis on *Peach*—Jason couldn't miss it.

"Okay. I could start showing Jason how to crack the walnut shells."

"Or, he could come outside with me. Let's go, Peach," Ruby said, walking halfway to the window. Jason hadn't moved. Seeing him from the back, he looked lonesome in his vigilance. How much this boy had lost was never far from Ruby's mind. "You can come, too, Jason. Or, you can do a special cookie project with Emma."

Hearing herself, Ellen Abbot came to mind again. Mike's mom used words like *project* to describe stripping the linens off the beds in the guest cabins. So much more important than a chore. Mike's mom was the reason Ruby had called the plan to finish college in three years a *strategy*. It had an impressive ring to it.

Ruby went out via the patio door. It was a warmish night and through the trees she saw the new moon rising while it was still light. Noisy geese were flying overhead. Most would move on, but a few stayed behind, although she didn't know why. She broke into a light jog toward the trees and then took a hard right through the field, making a game of it for Peach, who stayed close. Ruby ran the dog back and forth a few times before detouring along the side of the house to get a view of the front windows. If Jason had moved, all the better, but if he was there, she'd wave and then disappear in the back again.

The wind had blown dry leaves into rows of hills in the side yard and they crunched underfoot as she walked to the front. When she got to the porch, Jason's solemn little face was still in the window. She forced herself to smile and wave and then disappeared. Now what? She hadn't thought that far ahead. When she reached the back, she went up the stairs and let Peach take off for the trees while she watched her from the railing.

Finally, she called Peach back and when she went to open the patio door, Jason was dragging a chair closer to Emma.

"We're just getting started," Emma said, spreading newspaper over the tabletop.

"So I see."

Emma picked up the nutcracker. "Here's

the idea, Jason. Ruby is going to show you how to use this little tool."

"Right," Ruby said, laughing. "We have to work really hard to get our cupful of nuts."

Ruby glanced at Jason, wondering what had changed his mind. She'd probably never know, which left her with a jumble of contradictory feelings and thoughts. Playing with fire came to mind. Mike's need for a babysitter happened just as an afternoon malaise had settled over Ruby, mirroring Emma's intensifying frustration at being mostly cooped up. She'd graduated from the walker to a cane and her three in-house walks were now ten minutes each. The physical therapist that came to the house had declared her progress impressive. But it was still too slow to satisfy Emma.

She and Emma had been on the verge of getting on each other's nerves. That didn't happen often, but it signaled the need to retreat to her room to read or check her email. Or, she could argue with herself about the job search she'd barely even started.

Ruby pulled the stepstool to the table and sat next to Jason, who kneeled in his chair and rested his arms on the table so he could lean in and watch her. She handled the first walnut and squeezed the nutcracker until the shell broke and the walnut fell out in pieces. "See? Easy as can be." She held up one of chunks and handed Jason another. "We get to eat the first ones. It's the rule. Your dad made it up when he was about twelve."

That caught Jason's attention. He stared at her expectantly.

Jason looked happy again when he watched Ruby toss the nut in her mouth and then copied her perfectly.

"Your dad was always fun that way," Ruby said, inching closer toward Jason. "He liked his routines and rules. You know he likes to turn things into games. Like eating all the crusts on a peanut butter sandwich before you bite into the middle."

She'd once again landed among danger- ous memories. She'd seen Mike's playful side coming out with Jason. With so little history with Mike, though, all his son knew of his dad had been recently learned and limited to the present day. No aunts or un- cles or grandparents were around to tell old stories about Mike's childhood quirks. Were there even photos of Ellen and Charlie in the house? What about signs of Zoe?

Ruby pushed aside those questions as they fell into a comfortable silence. Ruby put her hands over Jason's and helped him squeeze the nutcracker. They tossed the loose nuts into the bowl.

"You try now," Ruby said, pulling her hands back.

Jason's face broke into a smile when he'd cracked the first one on his own. Then he looked serious and determined as he did the next one, and the next. He put them in the measuring cup and then tapped it to call attention to it. He smiled as the level rose closer to the top.

"You're doing a great job," Ruby said, taking another nut. "We're almost done."

Ruby caught Emma's eye, certain she was reading her friend's mind correctly. The six-year-old working so hard could have been Mike concentrating on sanding the hull of one of the boats at the lake. Or shooting baskets, one after the other, until a full one hundred had swished through the net. Ruby couldn't keep from staring at Jason, her heart aching, but not so much for this boy. Jason would be okay. With Mike as his dad, Ruby was sure of it. She was worried for herself.

Ruby started to assemble bowls and ingredients, putting the eggs and butter in front of Emma.

"Time to break these eggs." Emma cracked the shells on the side of the bowl and started to beat them. "You two better get the other ingredients ready. No time to waste."

"Okay, Jason, you heard Emma. It's up to us to measure the sugar and oats…and a bunch of other things. How about that?" Ruby asked. With his eyes open wide, Jason nodded.

She gathered the flour and sugar and correct measuring cups and brought them to the table along with two bowls.

Offering a measuring cup to Jason, she said, "Time for you to measure the oats?"

He didn't hesitate to take the cup from her hand. She brought the box of oats closer and Jason dipped it in and came up with a full cup. She held out the bowl. "Great. Dump it in here."

He smiled shyly at her when he'd emptied

the cup and looked up at her. She handed him another measuring cup and opened the canister of flour. "Now we need two scoops in the same bowl as the oats."

Ruby measured the spices and gave him the teaspoons so he could drop the cinnamon and nutmeg into the bowl.

"We're close to the grand finale." Ruby brandished the spoon in the air. That brought a delighted smile to Jason's face. Maybe he even came close to laughing out loud. Almost.

Once Ruby had combined the dry ingredients with the butter, sugar, and eggs, she mixed it all up until it was just about ready. "Now you can finish it for us. Stir really hard."

She turned on the oven and got out Emma's cookie sheets.

"The nuts come last," she said, "and then we get to plop the batter on these sheets. That's always fun."

Ruby watched Jason put all his energy into stirring the cookie batter. She shook the nuts in the mixture a little at a time and he made them disappear with his spoon. Looking at him having fun as he worked so hard, warmth spread across her chest. She could no longer say her feelings for Jason were linked to him being Mike's son. Jason kept touching her heart all on his own.

Ruby positioned the cookie sheets and bowl and showed Jason how to load a spoon and drop it on the cookie sheet. She lowered her head to get closer to him. "We're allowed to use our fingers to get all the batter off the spoon," she whispered, as if sharing a secret.

His expression surprised, Jason opened his mouth…a word, maybe an exclamation almost came out. Ruby was certain of it. Even her heart beat a little faster. But then he looked away and concentrated on filling his spoon.

So close, Ruby thought. *So close.*

"Uh oh," Ruby said when they'd filled two cookie sheets. "I almost forgot."

Jason's gaze followed her when she went into the kitchen and opened the cabinet. She glanced at Emma, who looked just as curious as Jason.

"We almost forgot the raisins. How are we going to put faces on the cookies without raisins?"

Emma laughed, but Jason kept his eyes on her hand as she shook some raisins in a bowl. "Want to watch me do one, Jason?"

He opened his mouth again, but then closed it. Ruby let that moment slide right by and showed him how to make two eyes and a nose on the cookies. "And these cookies will all be smiling, just like you."

Jason took his job seriously and by the time they were done, his cookies had giant smiles.

"All set then," she said, laughing. "I'll pop them in the oven." Before she left the table, she leaned over and told him, "You did a great job."

She gave him a little wink.

"It's odd how familiar everyone looks," Mike said. He stood with Maggie, his neighbor and new client, behind a row of folding chairs facing the dais, where the town council was gathering. "Some I can easily identify, including Kristine Laughlin."

"Now there's a woman with a very tough job."

"She was a year behind us in school and the incoming senior class president while I was the outgoing one. I remember coaching her a little before I graduated. The same way my predecessor helped me. It was kind of a tradition in those days." Mike left out the part about Kristine being indifferent to most of what he had to say. Talk about yesterday's news. None of that mattered now.

"Now she's the mayor," Maggie said with a laugh. "See what can happen to people who stick around this town."

Mike chuckled. "Right. Maybe she's got some new ideas."

"We can only hope." Maggie paused and tried unsuccessfully to gather her hair at the back of her neck. "By the way, who is *us*?"

Puzzled by the question, he must have looked blank.

"You said she was a year behind *us*," Maggie explained, "so I wondered who you meant."

Slip of the tongue. He'd meant Ruby. Maybe Neil and Emma, but Ruby had been on his mind. "I was unconsciously including the kids I hung around with back then. It's a small high school, so we all knew each other."

"It's still a tight-knit sort of place," Maggie said. Then she pointed to the rows of empty chairs. "See? A total of two dozen chairs set up for regular folks—people like you and me. And that's optimistic."

In the past, Mike would have been surprised, but no more. Elaine Cermak had opened up to him a little more and described the downward turn Bluestone River had taken after its biggest employer, a food-processing company, shut its doors. Swallowed up by a bigger firm, she'd said. Out of the corner of his eye, he saw Kristine move up to the podium. She chatted informally with the town-council members, an even split of three men and three women, who followed her and took their seats at the long table.

"Plenty of room in the front row," Maggie said, leading the way.

Including the stragglers, Mike counted eight people—citizens—in addition to the seven officials. "So, this is a typical crowd?" Mike was jolted back to days when the room was filled with at least thirty or forty people at these meetings, sometimes many more. His mom and dad almost always showed up. They had a big stake in what went on in town. The shabby room with its institutional green walls looked worn out, a lot like his office before he'd spruced it up.

"Sometimes as many as fifteen of us attend," Maggie said. "Usually we have an issue we're pressing, like getting rid of the parking meters on River Street. It took us a year to get that done." She pointed with her chin to a couple farther down the row. "That's Star Lenski and her husband, Mason. They own the bakery, but she runs it. Mason works in a lab over in Clayton."

Lenski. Not a name he recognized from years ago. But he filed it away, if for no other reason than Emma loved that bakery.

Mike saw glimpses of the teenage Kristine when she smiled at the handful of people in the room and then opened the meeting. "I'm glad to see you all here tonight. We won't keep you long. So let's get started."

Hmm…a smile, a greeting, a reassuring remark to the audience and then a quick call to action. Right out of Principal Driscoll's playbook. He offered all the class leaders little tricks to run meetings. Mike had opened a few meetings at the firm using the formula he learned from Ruby's dad.

Old business was dispensed with quickly, followed by a brief rundown on sidewalk repairs. As for substance, the only important issue involved approving the building permit allowing Sweet Comforts Bakery to add a café to their building. *Yes, please,* Mike thought. He wished they'd located on River Street, but even one expanding business was a good start.

Maggie nudged him and whispered, "Watch that older councilman on the end, Jim Kellerman. He'll vote no because he's afraid the café will take customers away from the fast food restaurants and coffee business at the plaza out near the highway exit. That's a popular part of town with older people now. Well, younger people, too."

"A little competition would be a great problem to have," Mike whispered back. "Not to mention another factory or other company to take the place of the food processing plant. As far as shops and restaurants and businesses are concerned, it shouldn't be a matter of either-or. Let's have as many cafés and coffee shops as possible." *And the sanctuary and the bridge and the trails,* Mike thought. *Why couldn't they have it all?*

"And more tourists," Maggie chimed in. "It's such a pretty town. I'm glad they're adding the café."

Mike found Jim confusing. Something had changed. "Aren't the Kellermans still an important local family? They used to be." Mike left out other details, like how Jim had snubbed his mom and dad. Jim and his family acted like the Abbot's no-frills resort wasn't quite up to the high standards of their Bluestone River. Jim threw his weight around and publically threatened a lawsuit to block his dad from deeding over his valuable acres to a conservancy. Fortunately, he had no legal grounds, so his words had fallen on deaf ears.

"It's time we put this to a vote." Kristine spoke into a microphone she didn't need and the sound echoed unpleasantly. "Do you have anything you want to add, Star? Mason?"

Tall and slender with short, almost white-blonde hair, Star stood and raised her hand to greet the council. *Good, she's maybe midtwenties*, Mike thought. Young energy to invest in Bluestone River. Star rubbed her palms together in a show of excitement. "I just want to add that we can't wait to get started. Before the first snow, we hope. A café off the highway will help bring more business to town in the winter."

Mike could see from the nods and friendly expressions on the council members' faces that this permit was a done deal. Sure enough, when the hands went up, only Jim Kellerman voted no. The reaction was light applause rippling through the room.

When Kristine asked if there was anything else, Maggie raised her hand and stood. She held up a flyer and announced she was looking for a part-time graphics designer. "I'm going to post this notice on the community board. Spread the word. I'd like to hire locally."

Kristine planted her hand on her hip and gave Mike a sidelong glance. "Is that Mike Abbot I see next to you?"

Her sultry, flirtatious tone threw him, but he managed to get to his feet to acknowledge her. "Nice to see you, Kristine—Mayor Laughlin, I should say. I just opened my law office on River Street, where Benson Insurance used to be. I'm here to catch up with what's going on in town and introduce myself."

"When did *you* come back?" Jim called out gruffly.

"A few weeks ago," Mike said. "My son is in first grade at the Roosevelt school."

"Quite a surprise to see you, Mike." Kristine lowered her gaze to the file folder in front of her.

"I'll say," Jim added in a loud voice. He leaned back in his chair and folded his arms.

A couple of council members shifted in their seats in response to Jim's icy tone.

"It's great to be back home. I grew up here and a part of me never left." *Take that, Kellerman.* Amused by his own words, he wondered what made both Kristine and Jim so uncomfortable. Maybe his dad had been right about people in town having long memories.

The meeting adjourned and he and Maggie filed out of the room in silence. Mike sensed Maggie's curiosity about the undercurrent in his exchange with Kristine and Jim. He glanced at his watch. "Looks like

I can go pick up my son earlier than I expected."

Maggie touched his arm. "Do you mind my—"

He raised his hand to interrupt. "When we meet in my office, I'll give you the thirty-second version. It's personal."

Maggie nodded. "Gotcha." She said good-night and took off for her car.

Mike did the same, suddenly more drained than he'd been in a long time. And sad. Sad about the state of the town, Jason's continuing silence, and having to dip into savings to get his office ready. With no guarantee it would pay off.

Seeing Jim hadn't helped. He'd always been a "get off my lawn" grumpy man, old when he was young. Jim had been his parents' only real adversary in town. That was his mom's word for the guy, as opposed to calling him an enemy, which his dad liked better. A contractor, he'd wanted to build vacation homes on the Abbot land. He'd hounded Mike's parents to sell for years before his mother died and his father up and left. Jim complained the stupid bird sanctuary wouldn't produce a dime of return on the investment. At the time, Mike and his dad amused themselves by making up lame imitations of Jim's protests about the lazy, "good for nuthin'" birds not earning their keep.

What a hoot. Climbing in the car, he laughed out loud and reminded himself to tell Ruby about Jim and his attitude. Less entertaining was the odd welcome from Kristine and Jim's public gruffness. Maggie hadn't missed it, so he couldn't write it off to his imagination. It brought back the way his mother's death had been like a crash itself. Without a chance to take a breath so many lives had instantly spun out of control, just as Timothy Driscoll's car had done on the highway.

As he drove through town, images flashing through his mind put Mike inside the police car with Ruby, the last time he held her in his arms. Then it was to stop her shivering from the cold. He and Ruby had exchanged few words, at least that he could recall. But his memory of clinging to each other in the backseat of the cruiser was sharp and clear. Ruby's head was on his chest. As if it happened yesterday, he remembered the minty scent of her hair. His favorite smell back then. He'd rubbed his hand up and down her arm to warm her up.

Mike pulled the car over before he turned onto the shortcut road to Emma's house. He had to stop these memories from taunting him, especially the moment he'd learned that Ruby's father was driving the car with his mother in it. It took a second or two, maybe even three, to let his thoughts take that next leap.

By the time he accepted the truth, the whole town knew.

CHAPTER EIGHT

CONTAINER OF LEFTOVER cookies in hand, Ruby approached Mike's office as a very tall, slender woman came out with Mike. Standing on the sidewalk, they shook hands and the woman walked down the street, her long gray-white hair tousled in the wind.

Before he could go back inside, Ruby called his name.

Mike's tight smile looked forced. "I didn't expect to see you this morning."

"Uh, is this a bad time?"

His expression neutral, he said, "Not exactly. Come in. I'll explain."

"I won't keep you," Ruby said. "I thought Jason might like the extras. He seemed to really enjoy baking them, not to mention eating them last night."

"Nice of you to think of him, right." Mike's smile changed—sort of.

He was distracted. "Was that your new client?" Ruby asked to change the subject.

"Maggie Hall. The web designer in one of the other offices just like mine." He pointed down the street. "We had our first meeting." He grinned—for real—and flexed his biceps. "I'm back. A pro again."

He eyed the container in her hands. "Do you think Jason would miss one or two of those?"

She held out the plastic box. "Go ahead, have some. I packed plenty. Like I said last night, it's the same recipe I used years ago."

"C'mon in, have a cookie," he said, opening the door to let her in. "Probably best to eat in my office and not sitting at the window."

She followed him and sat in the chair across from the desk. "True, we wouldn't want the stodgy new attorney to be seen sitting around munching cookies."

"I don't do stodgy too well, or so I've been told."

"No, I don't suppose you do," she said with a laugh.

Instead of sitting in his chair behind the

desk, he chose the other client chair and put the container on the desk between them.

"Nice touch." She pointed to the vintage photos of the resort back in the 1940s. "I like the shots of old River Street, too." She slipped off her jacket and curled one leg under her, feeling at home. "You've done such a great job with this place."

"With your help," he said, opening the container and holding it out to her. He glanced at his open computer, obviously preoccupied.

She edged forward in the chair. "You've traveled miles away. I should go so you can get back to work."

That got his attention. "*No*, no. I mean it, Rubes. Stay." He laced his fingers behind his head and stared at the ceiling.

"If I stay, then you need to tell me what's going on with you."

His expression, even his body language, told her he was discouraged. "I hate admitting this, but you were probably right about Bluestone River's long memory."

She liked being right, but not this time. "What happened?"

"There's no smoking gun, so I can't prove

anything," he said, "but when Kristine Laughlin spotted me she acted surprised."

Well, that seemed logical. He'd been gone for years. What was Mike's point? "Tell me more."

He glanced up to meet her eye. "She said it so publicly, Rubes, and in a certain tone. And then Jim Kellerman chimed in with his icy remark."

She remembered the name, Kellerman, an old Bluestone River family. Like the Laughlins and the Abbots. Not like her family. Her parents adopted the town as their own when her dad started teaching high-school history with ambition to become a principal. Every now and then her family was reminded they were "from away." Her mother had felt that acutely in the groups of women charged with planning the town's Christmas celebrations or organizing the Halloween parties for the kids. She had a certain status as Timothy Driscoll's wife, but lost a few points by being from Indiana.

"You seem upset by this, but the Kellermans were known snobs. My mother was on the receiving end of their snooty ways a few times. But Kristine? Do you believe she cares much one way or the other about what happened with our parents?"

Mike shot her a look full of meaning—but she couldn't interpret it. "What am I missing, Mike?"

Mike propped his elbow on the arm of the chair and rested his chin on his closed fist. "What about my mom and your dad?"

Her heart beat a little faster. Buying time, she raised her shoulders in an innocent shrug as if pretending she didn't know what he meant.

"Seriously, Ruby? Like you haven't thought about it?" He rubbed the back of his neck in a way familiar to Ruby. It wasn't relaxing his muscles so much as showing frustration. "Other than an offhand remark about my mom's Christmas extravaganzas or your dad the football fanatic, our parents' secrets are off-limits between us."

"And Kristine and Jim's reactions to you at the meeting last night stirred this up?"

It was his turn to appear perplexed. "I don't know. It was like being put on the spot. They absolutely remember what happened."

"Only the smallest, pettiest people care," she said, waving him off. And sounding a lot like Emma. "You're here to make a life. So what? Kristine will have to adjust. Jim will keep on being Jim. You didn't do anything wrong. Neither did I."

Her spirits were sinking like the stones they'd thrown in the river as kids. They could talk, laugh, have fun with Jason and Emma, but they'd always be the kids of parents who'd died because of an affair.

"I still find it almost impossible to think about my mom with your dad...the secrets they kept. For a year or more."

No kidding. Ruby got to her feet. "I better get back to Emma."

"Sure, leave, go ahead." Mike gave her a sharp look as he flapped his hand toward the door, as if shooing her out. "What will you do when you don't have Emma as your excuse to run from every uncomfortable conversation?"

Whoa. She was in no mood for his attitude. She matched it as she hurried out of the office and toward the front door. "As a matter of fact, Emma is having a really bad day. If you must know. She sat at the table too long last night because she was having so much fun with Jason. She still gets tired, and some days everything aches."

Mike followed her, his apology coming fast. "I'm sorry. I really am."

"Okay, I'll forgive you this time," Ruby said, forcing a breezy lilt, despite the pressure building behind her eyes. If she stayed another minute tears would start rolling down her cheeks. Over what?

Suddenly, Mike's arms were around her, gently pulling her close. "Oh, Ruby."

Her muscles gave way as she let her head drop against his chest. In an instant Mike's lips had found her mouth and everything about him rushed back. The voice in her head screamed a warning not to let down her guard. *Ever.* She broke free of his arms and stepped back. "I can't… I can't."

Without looking into Mike's eyes, she turned away and fled out of the office and down the street. She heard him call her name. When she reached her car, she glanced behind her and saw him approaching.

"No, Mike, not now." She left him standing on the sidewalk. He lifted his arm in a goodbye wave.

Every time she ran away, she fought the urge to go running back. *Every time.*

All the way back to Emma's house Ruby repeated her plans in her head. *Get Peach, go for a run. Fix dinner for Emma. Call Mom.* She'd been putting off that call. But it was time. Her mother was encouraging her to come back to Florida for the winter to get a good long break and take time to figure out her next step.

It was time to take her up on the offer. She had to.

When Ruby let herself into the dark house, she inhaled the lingering scent of burning wood from their almost daily fires. Peach was curled up on the rug in front of the fireplace. Holding out her hand to stop Peach from rousing herself and following, Ruby tiptoed down the hall and peered through the half-open door to see Emma on her side, sleeping. Seeing the slow, easy rise and fall of her friend's back, Ruby realized Em wouldn't need her much longer. This was one bad day, not a setback. Ruby felt better knowing Emma was optimistic about a complete recovery most of the time. But now and again in the four weeks or so since the surgery, doubt would creep in. Emma admitted she feared that even the surgery wouldn't give her back her full life. To Emma, that meant walking without a cane, hiking, dancing and doing everything she did before the fall that started her troubles. Ruby wanted that for her friend, too, but even Emma said she was given no guarantees.

She went back down the hall and let Peach out into the backyard, and stood on the deck watching the sky change from blue to slate as thickening clouds slid across the sky from the west. Another day was passing quickly. On the drive home, she saw a mom and a couple of toddlers arranging pumpkins on their front stairs. The house down the street from Emma was already decorated with scarecrows and giant spiders and ghosts hidden in the empty tree branches. As much as Bluestone River had changed, marking the changing seasons and their holidays stayed the same.

As she watched the sky, the memory of Mike's mouth on hers and the warmth of his arms holding her close pushed away everything else she tried to think about. Those few seconds lifted her back to an old, once-familiar feeling of being exactly where she belonged. For a second or two the years dropped away. Even the texture of Mike's blue sweater on her cheek was as familiar as the color of his eyes.

"Stop, stop." Ruby said the words out loud to drill the reality that all the memories, sweet or painful, were behind her. Done with. Halloween was around the corner, and next up Thanksgiving. Em likely would be cleared to drive by early December. By New Year's Eve, Emma the list maker would be jotting new goals in her journal. Maybe Ruby would do that, too. But not in Emma's homey room with its desk and comfy reading chair. Instead, she'd think about her future on the deck of her mom's condo in Florida.

Leaving Emma to her nap, Ruby let Peach back inside and went into her room and dashed off a quick text to Dee to let her know she was fine. Dee emailed and called and texted often, always in a serious older-sister tone. Ruby did her best to reassure her, but Dee worried if she hadn't heard from Ruby every couple of days.

Finally, her calls and texts done for the day, and email checked, she left her room and went outside to gather logs from the stacked wood next to the deck. She carried them into the house and put them in the log basket. She kept her hands busy brushing ashes out of the fireplace and starting their afternoon fire. Growing up, her mom and dad used the fireplace almost every night in the fall and winter, unlike Emma's family, who reserved the living room in their three-floor home for special occasions, the fireplace tools pristine in their wrought-iron holders.

"Hey, Rubes, you're back." Emma stood in the doorway, leaning on her three-pronged cane.

Emma's voice startled her. "And you're awake. I looked in on you a few minutes ago." She pointed to the fire. "I thought I'd get an early start."

"Fine by me." Emma looked comfortable in sweatpants and a red flannel shirt. "I'm much better now. Not nearly as achy all over."

"I was thinking about your fireplace back

when we were kids," Ruby said. "Did you ever use it?"

Emma laughed. "Heaven forbid. You had to be company from out of town. Funny thing. We didn't have many visitors."

Ruby struck a match to light the scrunched-up newspaper. "That's all changed now. You've got me."

"I like thinking of you as a roommate." Emma held up her hand. "You don't need to contradict me. I know this is temporary."

"Turns out I was right and you were wrong," Ruby said with good-natured smugness. "According to Mike it seems people around here haven't forgotten all about the messy lives of the Abbots and the Driscolls."

Emma slowly made her way to the couch and used the armrest for extra support as she sat down. "What do you mean?"

She repeated what Mike said about the council meeting and Kristine. "One of the Kellermans was there and a little gruff. I forget his name."

"That would be Jim," Emma said with a low groan. "He hasn't met a new idea he likes in a decade. Or probably a person, either. He objected to the bird sanctuary and gave me a hard time about it." Emma smirked. "That's not quite true. Jim gave Neil a hard time for not *controlling* me better."

"Sounds like a real charmer," Ruby said, frowning. "I think Mike was bothered most because they were surprised to see him."

"So?" Emma signaled she wanted more info.

"Mike sees it the way I do. We had nothing to do with what our parents did." Mike had seemed a little defiant, too.

Ruby watched the kindling ignite and catch the birch bark. "This was the first time Mike and I inched a little closer to talking about his mom and my dad. The affair." She had to pull the word out of her own mouth.

Emma responded with a cautious tone. "Was that weird?"

"Excruciating. But not for long. I ran out of Mike's office as fast as I could." Yes, she admitted running away from another conversation. She kept quiet about the rest of their meeting. Like Mike's warm lips on hers. She startled herself when she pushed a log so hard with the poker, it almost fell off the grate. She glanced at Emma, waiting for the remark that was sure to come.

Emma rested her head back on the couch cushion. She pulled a tube of lotion out of her pocket and squeezed some into her palms, then began massaging it into her hands and arms. "Rubes, I love you, but you have no idea how much I envy you sometimes."

Ruby almost dropped the poker. "Huh? You envy me?"

Emma nodded to the fire. "It's a blaze, Ruby. Roaring. Leave it alone and come sit down. Thanks to my lavender lotion, we'll have the softest arms and hands in Bluestone River."

Ruby saw a tempting ploy. She knew Emma well enough to be certain a heart-to-heart was coming and that it wasn't going to be about the smell of the hand cream. She sank into the chair cushions across from Emma.

"And my envy isn't limited to your glowing health, which can be kind of annoying, by the way." She tossed the tube to Ruby, who snatched it out of the air before it hit the floor.

"Oh, Em, I'm sorry."

"Don't you dare apologize. Just hear me out. I watch you skip down my deck stairs and take off across the field with Peach. Effortlessly. I used to be loose and agile, too."

"That part, I get," Ruby said, pushing up her sleeves and squeezing a dab of lotion on her arm. A little envy was a part of their friendship. Not good, not bad. But not something they could deny, either. It was no secret she'd long envied Emma's freedom to do exactly as she pleased without the need to glance at the price tag. She'd never had to work nine-to-five and was free to use her money to support all kinds of projects. Few people in town knew she covered Millie Kress's salary at the bird sanctuary. "You've had a setback, Em. A big one. But you're getting strong again."

Emma smoothed the lotion over each finger. "Just once in my life, Rubes, I'd like to have a man look at me the way Mike looks at you."

Boom. The reality of Emma's words was a blow to the center of her heart. The teenage Emma and Neil were no Ruby and Mike. It would be silly to argue otherwise.

"Your silence speaks for itself," Emma said with a heavy sigh. "You know exactly what I mean. Neil and I were a mismatch. We should have realized our colossal mistake the first year." She paused. "The truth is we did, but pride took over and we couldn't admit it. Stupidly stubborn, that's what we were."

"Look, I've never argued with you about Neil."

"You couldn't argue. Not when you lived it all with me. Year by painful year."

Emma and Neil had spent years in counseling, looking for a way to make it work. Since they'd gone to separate colleges, their high-school infatuation was never tested. They didn't get to know each other any better, so their summer wedding after they graduated took place as if a long-awaited fairy tale was about to start.

"The same thing could have happened to Mike and me," Ruby said with a shrug. "Odds are we'd have ended up the same way as you and Neil."

Emma shook her head, showing a surge of energy. "Right. Like I'll let that statement stand. You and Mike were the real deal. We all knew it. Even our…" Emma clamped her mouth shut.

"You were about to say our parents knew it, weren't you? Don't you think that's one of the worst parts?" She clasped her hands, the intensity in her voice increasing. "Mike's mom and dad loved me. My parents thought he was the best. Right up until the night Mike and his dad became my mom's bitter enemies."

"You should let it go." The words sliced the air. "That was shock talking. *Trauma.* Of course your mom hated Mike. She hated his dad, too." With narrowed eyes she stared at the fire. When she spoke again, her tone had softened. "As for Charlie Abbot, he was ruined…he was never the same person again. Mike was forced to scrap almost every plan he had so he could keep his dad functioning."

"Yeah, well, I had to change a few things, too, didn't I?" Ruby was instantly ashamed of the self-pitying tone seeping into her voice. It had been so long since she and Emma battled out their different stories of the past. Emma's impatience up against Ruby's defensiveness.

"Oh, I know all that," Emma said. "I was there with you. But I'm not backing down. You and Mike had something good. I can't believe you're letting this chance—a real chance—to reconnect slip away and be gone forever."

For once, Ruby couldn't think of anything to say. She felt like nudging her peacefully sleeping dog and escaping the house. Running away, Emma would call it. Mike, too. She stared at the fireplace, unwilling to face Emma.

"You know I'm right. Mike is giving you every sign he wants to be close to you."

"But, what if...?" She shrugged.

"It doesn't work out?" Emma said. "Then at least you'll know. Right now, you're not even giving it a chance."

Once again, Ruby had no quick comeback at the ready.

She stood and moved behind Em, and squeezed her shoulders. "Okay. I admit you could be right...at least about some things. But I can't talk about it anymore now, okay?" She gave Emma a final pat. "I'll get us coffee and donuts."

She left Emma to enjoy the fire and Peach

to doze. The rain started as Ruby put the jelly donuts on a plate and made them each a mug of coffee. When she was done, she watched the rain fall and allowed herself to answer Emma's what-if? Instead of picturing the worst, Ruby let her mind spin the images of what could be if her feelings and Mike's weren't just wisps of long-ago young love.

What if slow dancing with Mike at their prom turned into a fast dance in the kitchen with Jason giggling at their antics? What if they grilled burgers in the yard and watched the moon rise over the lake? What if they showed Jason their names carved into the bridge? What if they got caught in a rain shower? That had happened more times than she could count when they were kids. They'd huddle under a shared umbrella, giddy as they flipped it into a moment of playful romance and shared a few kisses. They could do that again.

What if…the magic was still there? Grown-up magic this time.

CHAPTER NINE

MIKE CLOSED HIS laptop and slipped on his gray blazer. Reaching for his red-and-white striped tie, he had second thoughts and draped it over the chair. He wasn't heading to court. He wasn't taking a deposition. He was hoping to meet the hairdresser next door.

After locking up his office, he took a minute to glance up and down the street. Not many people in sight on this string of late fall days, when the temperature hit seventy-plus. Soon enough, a couple of storms with high winds would strip the last of the leaves off the trees and cold air would settle in and stay a while.

He took the few steps to the shop next to his office. When he opened the door a bell jingled and the dark-haired woman he'd seen a few times appeared at the back of the shop. "Hey, it's the lawyer next door."

He held out his hand. "Yes, Mike Abbot."

"Georgia Greer," she said, grinning and shaking his hand. "I saw your sign. It says *Michael* Abbot, but you go by Mike?"

No one had ever asked him that, but he didn't have to think about the answer. "I've been Mike all my life. I might not even respond to Michael."

"So, Mike, you looking for a haircut? A trim for those curls?"

Some people had an infectious laugh, but Georgia had an infectious smile.

Suddenly self-conscious, Mike ran his hand through his hair. "Uh, maybe some other time. Today I have another purpose for dropping in on you. I wanted to introduce myself and offer my legal services should you ever need them. I'm visiting all the folks who are new to town. Well, new to me."

"I figured as much." Georgia drew back her head and looked at him like she was studying his face. "I hear you come from Cincinnati. You live out by the bird lake. And you have a little boy."

He might have known. Maybe Maggie mentioned him. Or Kristine. "Yes on all counts, except I was born and raised here in town. I moved away for a few years, now I'm back for good."

"As a matter of fact, Mr. Mike Abbot, I might have a job or two for you."

Still grinning right along with her, he said, "Okay. What do you need? I'm listening."

"A will—two of them. One for my husband and for me?"

"I can definitely handle wills and estates. Trusts, too." He welcomed the happy stirring in his gut. Just the hope of another client gave him a life. "Do you have wills now?"

She buried her face in her hands and shook her head. "I'm turning red. I'm so embarrassed."

Another neighbor, another character. He liked her teasing demeanor. "You aren't the only two people in the world to let that slide." He hoped his tone was reassuring enough. He pointed to the row of stylists' chairs. "You especially need one if you're in business."

In an instant, the mood changed. Georgia's jaw tightened and her mouth turned down. "At the moment, I am. But who knows for how long?"

In the next few minutes, Mike listened to

Georgia's five years on River Street waiting for the grand revival that never materialized. Her mouth twisted to the side in what Mike interpreted as a show of disgust. According to Georgia, the owners offered her a three-year lease to give her some security to get the business off the ground. "I renewed it once, but I'm going to think real hard before I renew again next year. We have trouble getting folks who live half a mile away to do business on River Street—and it's not about the parking."

"What do *you* think would bring more people to Bluestone River?" Mike wanted to gather opinions instead of grousing by himself.

Georgia gestured to the chair. "Since you've asked the question and gotten me started, you might as well have a seat."

"Happy to. I've got some time before I pick up my son from school. Since I grew up here, I'm probably extra curious about what it's going to take to bring Bluestone River to life again."

Georgia scoffed. "A little PR might help. We could stop acting like that bird sanctuary out there on the lake is a secret site."

As if she'd just thought of it, she said, "But you must know all about that. Your family owned a resort."

"For a couple of generations we ran the place. I was already gone when my dad deeded the land and rights to the lake to the conservancy," he explained. "But I hear it's not lived up to what people expected."

"It's barely mentioned in the brochures about the town," Georgia said. "One, maybe two photos on the website. And a shot of the covered bridge."

"The bridge used to bring people to town. It's old and just weathered enough to be called quaint. We hung out there a lot—as kids, I mean."

"We did, too. Such a pretty town," Georgia said with a quick shrug. "It's got the river and the bridge, trails, state parks nearby." She waved toward the window. "Tree-lined streets. Seems odd not to market the natural beauty of the place."

"I have the same thought every day," Mike said. Even Ruby wondered why no one had put more effort into promoting Bluestone River as a good place to bike after a trip to the Oak Forest park, or talk up the bridge as a photo-op destination.

"I used to go to town-council meetings, but they don't do much. Seems it's mostly status quo. I suppose I shouldn't criticize too much," Georgia said. "The town council does sponsor things for people who live here. They still have the family Halloween party at the town hall."

"Ah, yes, Halloween." It loomed for him. He'd seen the flyer about the town-hall party. He'd been putting off the costume issue. What would work for a kid who couldn't respond to a friendly compliment or a question about his costume?

"You be sure to take your son to that party. I used to go when my kids were little. It's a good time."

"I will," Mike said. "Who knows? Maybe I'll run into more pals from my high-school days."

Bringing the conversation to a close, Mike encouraged Georgia to meet again briefly to talk over the wills the next morning, before her shop opened. He left feeling a little lighter. Two business neighbors. Two clients. Not bad.

RUBY PICKED UP her pace on the trail adjacent to the river. With Peach home with Emma, Ruby could run easier. Clear her head on this golden day and get a new perspective. Each step brought her closer to the road ahead—not a major highway, but it divided the town more or less in half. It curved up ahead, and if her memory was accurate, the road dead-ended at a now defunct gas station. The trail extending this far along the riverbank was new, so she wasn't sure where her route was taking her.

The trail took her under two causeways, crossing side streets, and followed the natural twist of the river until it led away from the water and ended at the edge of some woods with a couple of benches and a parking area big enough for three or four cars. Not breaking her pace, she looked in the other direction and saw the stripped-down gas station and its boarded-up building on the gravelly strip of bare ground. Beyond the gas station, another narrow farm road began. She crossed the gravel and jogged past acres of recently harvested fields of corn.

Off in the distance, the road ended at a

T intersection. She kept going to see where
another road crossed, but nothing appeared
except for a sparsely wooded area that gradually thickened into a forest as she ran. The
familiar sound of geese brought her to a fast
stop. She shielded her eyes from the late-
afternoon sun to see the geese on the move
and telling the world about it. She counted
five *V* formations looking like long trails
being pulled across the sky.

Could it be that the back corner of the
sanctuary was on the road to the right? She
ran ahead and made the turn, but stopped.
She could wander in the woods and see if
she ended up at Mike's house, but she didn't
want to show up unannounced—and unin-
vited. She pulled out her phone and made
the call. He picked up on the third ring.

"Hey, Rubes."

"I don't want to bother you, but I'm out
jogging, and followed the river trail and now
I'm not sure where I am. Is there a road behind the sanctuary?"

"A couple of short farm roads can get you
to the back of the property, but there's no
road through the woods to the buildings."

"Well, I think I'm only a short walk

away," she said, more eager to see Mike than she should be. "Is it okay if I stop in for a glass of water? I went farther than I planned. And I know my way back home if I leave through the front entrance and go to River Street."

"No problem. Jason and I can scare up a glass of water—maybe even some juice."

"Okay, I'll head your way, or what seems like your way. Funny, I don't recall ever being back here."

"Be careful—no one maintains the trails that far back in the woods," Mike said. "You'll have to pick your way through the fallen branches and undergrowth." He let out a quick laugh. "Or, Jason and I can drive back there and pick you up."

"And ruin my spirit of adventure? No way." They ended the call on that note. Amused, she jogged along the road until she found an opening into the forest. In the distance, she thought she heard the sound of the water in the creek that ran across the back corner of the resort. She and Mike hadn't explored back there so much, mainly because all the action at the resort had been closer to the front entrance and on the lake.

She navigated around water-filled holes in some places and stepped over downed trees. The ground was dry in spots, but mostly soft and damp under her feet. The soles of her shoes were soon covered in mud. The honking geese overhead reassured her she was at least trudging along in the right place.

A few minutes later a building came into view—the back of a cabin, one of the guest cabins that had been closed up for years. It was a dusty blue with white trim, pretty at one time, but dirty and faded now. She'd end up coming into the lake around the middle of the shore.

Using the cabin as her guide, she looked for more exactly like it. They were built in clusters. Another one appeared between the branches the equivalent of about half a block away. Two more boarded-up buildings came into view. Finally, she saw the sparkles of the lake tinted almost pink under the sun. Emerging from the woods, she saw Mike and Jason by the tire swing in the yard. She waved both arms at them and shouted, "I found you!"

They waved back and Jason broke into a run down the beach toward her. He was looking past her, though. Uh-oh, he was looking for Peach.

When she reached him she put her hand on his shoulder. "I ran too far today to bring Peach with me. She's a good runner, but even for her strong legs, six or seven miles would make her too tuckered out." She panted to imitate a tired dog.

"And too ambitious a distance for me these days," Mike said, approaching. "No wonder you're in such great shape."

She scoffed and made a silly face for Jason as she raised her arms to the side. "And yuck, I'm really sweaty at the moment. I ran and ran and ran."

Jason stared at her and managed a little smile. It must seem odd, though, to see her without Peach. And disappointing.

"Come on up to the house. I'll get you a drink. Jason and I will drive you over to Emma's."

Ruby looked back at the woods. She'd started at the park and now, six or so miles and a couple of twists and turns later, she was at the sanctuary. Odd, without the newly added sections of river trail, she'd never known about a back way to get to the sanctuary.

Jason ran to the tire swing. "Ruby and I are going inside. We'll watch you from the windows."

"That swing is his favorite new hobby," Mike said, moving to the refrigerator. "I took down the one that had been there since I was a kid. The rope was weak, but the branch itself is as strong as it was over thirty years ago."

Ruby looked out of the kitchen window at the old maples and oaks, only traces of orange and red left now, and they batted in the breeze as if clamoring for attention. Brown oak leaves hung in clumps. "Seems to me what that yard needs is a dog to go with that boy."

"Don't you dare say that within earshot of Jason," Mike warned.

"Not ready to add a four-legged creature to the family?"

He shook his head. "Things are still too unsettled. I don't want one more item on my to-do list."

"Hmm...know what you mean. Rescuing Peach gave Em lots of ammunition to tease me about her, especially since I refused to have so much as a house plant for years. I rented apartments or cottages. Never had to replace an appliance or fix a roof."

"Rootless Ruby, huh?" Mike's quip didn't match his serious expression. He held out a carton of apple juice and a jug of orange.

"Exactly. For a long time my work was the only responsibility I cared to take on." She pointed to orange juice and Mike retrieved two glasses. "I'll be daring this time."

"Oh, speaking of responsibility, I have one with a short time line. Halloween. I need costume ideas suitable for a boy who doesn't speak."

Of course. It had to be recognizable. "You don't want people asking what he's dressed up as—it has to be clear."

"Right. But I've mentioned being a ghost or a pirate, and he shook his head. He didn't like any of the superheroes that popped to mind, either."

Ruby tapped her finger on her lips to mime being deep in thought. But sure enough, an idea came to her immediately. She almost blurted it, but decided to mull it over before suggesting it, just to make sure it would work. "I'll give it some thought. But tell me about your practice. How's it going?"

"So glad you asked," he said, grinning. "Yesterday I had one client, today I have two."

"Hey, your small-town-lawyer act is going to work after all."

They took their juice out to the porch and watched as Jason went back and forth on the swing. But he jumped off when the quacking from the ducks paddling to the shore caught his attention.

"Ducks and geese are his best friends," Mike said. "We don't feed them, though. Millie asked me not to."

"Looks—and sounds—like the geese are on their way south. Or are they settling in at the sanctuary?" Ruby asked, mesmerized by the sight of more *V* formations overhead. "Time seems to stop when I look up to watch them."

"I know," Mike whispered. "Autumn is something special around here. I'm not sure what it is. But there's nowhere I'd rather be when it's fall than in Bluestone River."

Ruby gulped back her juice, trying to

shake off the now familiar bittersweet feelings being with Mike evoked. Almost without fail they raced to the surface, throwing off her peace of mind, yet she came back for more. Sadness and pleasure, and the urge to leave even when she longed to stay.

"I take it there's been no change with Jason," Ruby said, deliberately switching the subject.

"Not really. Odd, though. Mrs. Cermak seems unconcerned. She's impressed with his artistic ability."

"A budding artist. I can see that with the exhibit on your fridge," Ruby said. "They give the place its homey touch."

Mike drummed his fingers on the porch railing, not taking his eyes off Jason. "I sometimes forget that my mom liked to draw. I never realized how much of her needlework is hanging on the walls—mostly upstairs. I'm no expert, but I think it's needlepoint."

The upstairs Mike avoided, Ruby thought. "According to Emma, what this town needs is a good craft shop."

"Both Georgia and Maggie want a Greek or Italian restaurant on River Street. The diner's good, but it'd be nice to have options."

"And leave the high-school kids to hang out and share giant French-fry platters." Ruby drained her cup. "Well, I should get back."

Mike didn't argue, but called over Jason and told him they were taking Ruby home. "Why don't you call Emma and see if she wants us to bring some dinner."

"Even better, stay and have stew with us. Brenda made us a huge pot. Let me give Emma a heads-up." Ruby grinned as she took out her phone. Her body tingled in the strangest way, as a surge of happiness shot through her.

Mike's face lit up. "Thanks. It's good for Jason—and for me—to be with other people."

She flashed a pointed look at Mike. "Emma's a big fan of yours. And she's not going anywhere. Long after I'm gone, you'll have Emma as your pal—and champion." Why had she said that? She wanted to inhale the words back out of the air the minute they left her mouth. The subtle droop in Mike's features said it all. She'd ruined the warm moment.

Warm moment? Warm moments between her and Mike led nowhere. Or to things they shouldn't.

In awkward silence, she and Mike walked to the car. Jason climbed into his seat and buckled himself in.

"Good job, Jason," Mike said, patting Jason's knee.

Watching Mike and his son brought back the warmth.

MIKE HAD MIXED feelings when he saw Ruby's name on his screen. He was in the middle of Maggie's incorporation document, so he let the call go to voice mail. Even though he got over his frustration, he was getting tired of hearing Ruby talk about leaving every time he saw her. All right, he got it. He needed a minute to get himself ready to sound like his normal self on the phone.

At dinner at Emma's last night, Ruby'd mused about the route of the bike trail, which was new to him, too. Unlike her, he wasn't much of a runner. Never had been. He liked basketball at the gym with the guys from the firm and anyone else who wanted in. Before Jason, he rode on bike trails in Cincinnati two or three times a week. Now he had a stationary bike in the house gathering dust. What a bore. He should get Jason a real bike. Maybe for Christmas, or he could wait…

Slow down…ease up. These days, his mind jumped all over the place, but that wasn't his style. He liked his orderly lists. First client work, then pick up Jason and finally off to Clayton for groceries and a Halloween costume.

It was gnawing anxiety that was robbing him of a peaceful day. Over last night's dinner he and Emma kept adding to the list of Bluestone River's shortcomings, and by the time he'd left Emma's, he was dragging what was left of his optimism behind him. Maybe returning to Bluestone River was like betting on the wrong horse. Even being with Ruby couldn't lift him. Saying goodnight at the door left him empty. It was time for him to face facts. Ruby had her mind on some other place—as yet unnamed.

With his work for Maggie out of the way, Mike spent the rest of the morning polishing up the two oak file cabinets he'd brought from home and setting up a paper filing system. He'd found the cabinets in the basement, the same place he'd found the framed photos he'd hung on the office walls.

His phone signaled a text. It was from Ruby and read: Idea 4 costume & where 2 get it. Great. Now he felt like a jerk for not picking up her earlier call. Instead of responding with another text, he phoned her.

Ruby answered cheerfully. "Hey, you caught us as we're leaving. Em feels good enough to go wandering a little."

"That sounds positive. Sorry I couldn't pick up your call."

"No problem. I figured you were busy. But I'm excited about my idea. What if Jason went as a doctor? He could wear a white coat and drape a stethoscope around his neck."

"And maybe one of those lights they stick in your ears," Mike added, grabbing hold of the notion.

"Right. People will see the white coat and his costume will be obvious. They'll be more likely to make comments rather than ask him questions. If someone talks to

him, he can put the stethoscope in his ears
and pretend to check their heart—something
like that."

"Hmm…where will I find a white coat
in his size?"

"No worries. Emma and I have that covered," Ruby said enthusiastically. "We found
a place in Clayton. We were poking around
online. It's kind of an old-fashioned costume
shop with authentic period clothes for community theater and the colleges in the area.
They've got new and used stuff for adults
and kids."

Whew. His day just improved…a lot. "Really? That sounds great. Thanks."

"We called and they still have a couple of
white coats in stock for Halloween. And a
toy stethoscope to go with it."

Relief flowed through him. Over a costume? He almost laughed out loud. He
needed a life.

"Emma and I could pick it up for you
if you don't have time," Ruby offered, her
voice tentative.

"No, no. I have to go over to Clayton myself for groceries. I'll take Jason. Why don't

you come along? We could go today after school."

Silence.

He winced as if waiting to be hurt. Why had he pushed it? It seemed he was always giving her a chance to run away—or in this case, say no.

"Uh, that would be fun, but Emma and I have the afternoon planned, maybe out to the bakery, the park. Emma is walking with her cane now."

He couldn't be certain she was lying, but it sounded like she was making it up as she went along. "That's fine," he said in his best phony casual tone. "It was short notice, anyway. Tell Emma I'm glad she's feeling good enough to get out."

"I will," Ruby said, then added, "I almost forgot, but Em wants to come to the Halloween party at the town hall. So, we'll get to see Jason in his costume in any case. I'll take some pictures."

"Good, good." He had to get off the phone, or he'd repeat himself or ask questions that had one-word answers.

"I better go…and thanks for asking me to come along, Mike."

Later, when he was running his errands, Mike kept replaying in his mind his conversation with Ruby, feeling like a detective looking for clues as to how she felt. She and Emma had plans. On TV, the detectives would say "A likely story." On the other hand, she and Emma were coming to the party.

Not that any of it mattered.

When they got to the shop, Jason wasn't shy about wandering around, looking wide-eyed at period costumes, from fussy Victorian men's suits to a row of wide ties from the 1960s. A few always popular animal costumes came in various sizes.

He steered Jason toward the salesman, who directed him to the small rack of medical costumes in the shop. He spotted two white medical coats on the used rack, clean and crisp. The caduceus with its two coiled snakes stitched on the pocket. So authentic.

Jason was passive when Mike helped him on with the jacket. "You look so professional, just like a real doctor—Doctor Jason Abbot." He deepened his voice to sound authoritative and a lot older. "What seems to be the problem here? Let's listen to your heart."

Jason smiled at the put-on voice and looked on as Mike took the stethoscope out of the coat pocket and tore off the plastic wrapping. The pocket also held a prescription pad and pencil. Perfect. Mike put the ends of the stethoscope in Jason's and put the end on his own chest.

Mike laughed when Jason's eyes popped open at the sound of Mike's heart. It might be a toy, but it worked at least a little. "Let's listen to your heart now." Jason's smile got even wider. "Okay, buddy, the costume is yours, and you can even write prescriptions on the little pad, just like a real doctor. We'll put your name on the pad."

The woman at the register looked barely out of her teens and was dressed in the way that reminded him of an exaggerated version of his mom's favorite outfit—when she wasn't in jeans and sweaters. Jessie, according to her name tag, wore a long velvet skirt, a peasant blouse, beads and more beads, and earrings that grazed her shoulders. Unlike his mom, who hadn't dyed her hair, Jessie had sprayed some kind of tint to transform her spiked blond hair into a trio of sparkling orange and green, and a couple of streaks of bright blue.

Jason couldn't keep his eyes off her.

"You have the coolest costume ever," Jessie said. "When Halloween is all over, you can play doctor anytime you want. If your daddy gets a cold, you help make him better."

"You have a pretty cool costume yourself," Mike said, taking the bag from the woman and handing it to Jason. "Here. You can carry it."

Jason didn't speak, but he clutched the bag to his chest. Then before they went out the door, Jason waved at Jessie, who waved back and called out, "You have fun—hope you get a lot of candy. Don't save any of it."

Mike laughed as he opened the door and he and Jason went down the street. Still holding the bag tightly in his arm, Jason broke into a skip and bounced along to the car.

Every now and then, in moments like this, Mike ached for Zoe. He'd hardly known her, but he'd seen in Jason the kind of mother she'd been. These small things like trips to the park and Halloween were supposed to be fun times to share with her son. And strangely, now it stung all over again remembering how he and Ruby had planned to have a couple of kids. It hadn't all been about their ambitions and goals. Did Ruby ever see Jason and think of a child they could have had?

Last night, after their dinner of stew and homemade bread, Ruby had followed him and Jason out to say good-night. Jason gave Peach a quick hug around her neck and spontaneously put his arms around Ruby's waist and hugged her, too. She'd leaned over and squeezed him tight as she whispered sweet dreams.

Mike thought about the way Jason's hugging Ruby had surprised him. And softened Ruby's expression. In spite of enjoying seeing his son show that kind of affection, little fingers of fear had crept inside and latched onto his gut. As much as Mike hated to admit it, maybe it was best that Ruby get on with her life somewhere else before Jason began to think of her as "always-around Ruby." Then he himself could finally get the pain over with and let her go,

once and for all. He'd never forget about her.
He'd love her forever. But maybe, at last,
his heart would stop picking up speed even
thinking about how she'd looked coming out
of the woods yesterday into the afternoon
light. She'd raised both arms high in the air
and waved. Eventually, he'd stop thinking
about the tender look on her face when she
watched Jason run down the slope of the
yard to greet the ducks.

Good thing Jason hadn't had the stethoscope on Mike's chest then.

CHAPTER TEN

"WOW, YOU LOOK GREAT," Emma said, grinning. "Head to toe. Your shoes turned out fantastic."

"I know," Ruby said smugly. She stuck out her foot to admire her sparkly red shoes. "It's amazing what a little glue and glitter can do for a pair of old clogs." Emma had contributed the white ankle socks, and Ruby rummaged through some boxes in the basement until she came up with the light blue pinafore Emma had kept from a Halloween costume years ago. When she put the pinafore over a white blouse and her denim skirt she pulled off a fairly good version of Dorothy. "I think Jason will know who I'm supposed to be. I'm only wearing a costume because of him."

"Oh, yeah," Emma said, "he'll know Dorothy when he sees her."

The idea of a "Wizard of Oz" theme

had come to her the night they'd made the cookies with Jason. The puzzle they'd put together featured Dorothy and Toto prominently, with the other story characters in the background. She'd told Jason about Dorothy and Toto just wanting to go home. Maybe it was the little dog, along with Dorothy's red shoes, that captured his attention, but once they'd fit the last piece, Jason stared at it for a long time, munching his cookie.

Ruby picked up her tote bag and pulled out the black stuffed dog, the only store-bought part of her costume. "I'll give Toto to Jason when the party's over."

"Your braids are the perfect final touch," Emma said.

Ruby pulled at the end of one of her braids she'd embellished with a white bow. Then she touched her warm cheeks and looked down at her costume and shoes. "I don't know why I'm blushing." She shrugged. "Maybe it's because I haven't dressed up for Halloween in years."

"It could be that simple, Rubes," Emma said, grinning.

"The weather is helping," Ruby added. Halloween had dawned cool and crisp with a cloudless bright blue sky. Rain was in the forecast, but not until late that night and long after the party downtown was over for another year.

"You look good yourself," Ruby said. Emma was tall enough to pull off an elegant look in her coat-length red sweater with black leggings and boots.

"Next year maybe I'll come up with a costume. I'm going for comfort this year. As it is, I feel like I'm making my debut," she said, one hip thrust out and a hand behind her head in a model pose. She picked up her carved wooden cane and raised it as if showing it off. "If I have to use one of these for a while longer, I'm done with the plain ones. I'm into fashion canes now."

Emma had bought it on one of their trips to Clayton to see the doctor. With Emma feeling strong, they'd detoured into a gallery and found the cane made by a local woodcarver. The stick had intricate carvings of birds and a handle shaped like a duck's head. "It's beautiful," Ruby said. "And the day you bought it was one of your best so far."

"Did you reach your mother?" Emma

asked, easing herself into a chair at the kitchen table.

"No, but I left a message." She paused. "I told her I was thinking about coming down after Thanksgiving…really early December."

"And not for a visit, huh?" As if stating a fact, she added, "You're planning to stay there."

"It's open-ended." Ruby shook her head. "I don't know. All I know is I'm not ready to do serious job-hunting yet. My confidence is… It's…depleted. Still." Her once legendary spirit of taking on a challenge was still replaced with a fearful shakiness deep in her core.

"I've felt better about things, sort of, as the weeks have gone by. This has been a time-out. Now you're getting better every day, Em. You'll be driving soon and back to your regular life."

"That doesn't mean I won't miss you. It doesn't mean I want you to leave." Suddenly, Emma grinned. "You've hardly gotten on my nerves at all."

"Yeah, maybe so, but you're driving me bonkers." Ruby let out a hoot. She could make that joke because they both knew it wasn't true.

"We were the same on our trips." A pensive expression took over her pretty features now. "In any case, don't pack up and head out because of some false notion you're wearing out your welcome. Besides, you've spoiled me. You might not cook the food, but you do a mean cleanup act."

"I know. I'm the best dishwasher loader you ever saw." Ruby closed her eyes and recalled the week they'd spent in a beach house in Maine. They'd debated making themselves lobster but quickly abandoned the idea and followed the traffic to town and let themselves be waited on. Emma never traveled with Neil because vacations meant fishing or hunting, preferably in locations no farther than an hour or two away.

Relieved she could be direct with Emma and open about her intentions, she relaxed against the kitchen counter and let her hands hang loose at her sides. "I need to leave, get out of town. The other night when Jason left with Mike he gave me the sweetest hug as he was saying goodbye."

"I saw it. I was in the window."

"He loves my Peach. Now he's getting attached to me." She shook her head. "Mike sees it, too. I can tell."

"I'll bet he's torn, Rubes. How Mike feels about you is written all over him."

"How he *thinks* he feels," Ruby corrected. "Ever since I walked through your door and settled in that lovely room, I've been sifting through these last few years, you know, writing my thoughts. Clarifying where my job went wrong. Admitting I burned out and figuring out what to do next. I never expected to be sifting through my feelings about Mike, too. Do I even know the guy anymore?"

Emma impatiently gave her a "don't give me that nonsense" look. "That's the kind of question you only feel obligated to ask. As if you don't already know the answers."

"I don't know all the answers, Em. Really."

"What's so different about today's Mike versus the eighteen-year-old one? Except that he's even cuter now than he was back in high school."

"So I've noticed," Ruby said wryly. "But he's a dad now. That responsibility sits square on his shoulders and guides everything he does. There's no telling how long Jason will be silent. We don't know what kind of lasting problems Jason could have."

"Like that would scare you away. Rumor has it you know a little something about trauma." After a long pause, Emma blurted, "For all that happened to you and Mike and your parents, he's a real grown-up man. Surprise, Rubes, you're all grown up, too."

Ruby laughed in spite of the gloomy mood settling over her. "Maybe so, but he's not a golden boy with endless potential trying to make partner at a big firm. He's got a couple of clients for small jobs. And he knows he could fail. For all his talk about this being home, how long is he going to stick around here and try to make a go of it?"

Emma scoffed. "Ha! Another adventure for Ruby. You're not tied to this place, either."

"You have an answer for everything," Ruby said, rolling her eyes.

"I suppose I do." Emma grimaced, as tears pooled in her eyes. She quickly brushed them away before they ran down her cheeks. "I'm sad because Neil got cheated out of a second chance. Being mismatched with me didn't mean he was a bad guy."

Ruby squirmed in the chair. "I'm sorry, Emma. You've been through so much."

"I should back off." Emma pressed her temples and gave her head a little shake. "I don't know what gets into me sometimes. You're right. I have no way to know what you and Mike could be in the future. Maybe I'm the one stuck in your old dream."

Not really.

"If we don't leave for the Halloween party I'm going to lose the urge to go." Emma braced her hand on the table and got to her feet. "Besides, I'm tired of trips to the doctor. And physical therapy shouldn't be the highpoint of my week. I want to see the little kids in their costumes. Especially Jason."

"I'm kind of curious about Dr. Jason myself. It's kind of fun that we're all dressed up and we actually have somewhere to go."

Fifteen minutes later, they joined a stream of other people arriving. The committee had decorated the town hall's community room with orange and black streamers and cutouts of skeletons and witches covering the walls. Pyramids of pumpkins filled the corners. These town-sponsored parties were apparently new—well, a dozen years new—and were a way to make the holiday safe for the kids. Ruby remembered a couple of parties at Mike's house with lights illuminating ghostly sheets arranged in the trees. They were little kids then and, typical of Mike's mom, everyone in their class had been invited.

The glass atrium-style walkway that linked the town-hall building to the library was filled with adults who'd deposited their kids for the first activities. Ruby spotted Mike talking to parents and other volunteers, directing them to different corners of the community room. He was wearing ordinary clothes. Ruby took a quick look around. Only a few of the adults wore costumes, and those were the adults leading Halloween bingo in the corner or one of the other games set up on the far side of the room.

"Mike isn't in a costume, Emma," Ruby said, staring at her pinafore. "I thought you said the adults show up in costumes."

"Well, some do. I didn't say Mike would. I see a few adults in getups." Emma pointed to a woman in an orange body suit and green hat. "She's a pumpkin."

The woman was supervising a game of "Pin the Face on the Pumpkin." Ruby sighed. "I'm reminding myself I did this for Jason."

"And you had fun putting it together. Trust me, he's going to get a big kick out of it." Looking at Ruby's shoes, she added, "And so will Mike."

"Oh, look at those ghosts," Ruby said, as she followed Emma to an empty spot near rows of chairs off to the side. She pointed to a group of kids around Jason's age. A few were dressed as zombies, but the others were a mix of witches and superheroes. The kids were tucking cut-out ghosts about a foot high into the cardboard branches of a tree covering one section of the wall. Some of the paper ghosts peeked out of the branches with their mouths forming a perfect oval of surprise. Others had big impish smiles, but a few had frowns between their eyes, but not too many and not too fierce. It all added up to a fun display.

"They're like ghost emojis," Emma remarked. "So many kids. Wow. It's bigger every year. That's good news."

Ruby pointed out Mike, who spoke into the microphone to get everyone's attention.

"Time for the costume parade to be underway." He began directing parents to line up their kids in the library entrance before their trip through the atrium.

"Good." Emma chuckled. "The parade is the main event, and then once it's over they're free to play more games. We can't forget the table of treats! Caramel corn scarecrows, taffy apples and marshmallow spiders. And they have healthier stuff, too, of course."

Ruby nodded, getting a kick out of the squeals and giggles of exuberant kids. She watched the sea of faces, some familiar, some not. It was as if she remembered adults she'd seen around town in her childhood but whose names she never knew. Other faces were the grown-up versions of people she'd known when they were all kids.

"The passing of the generations," Ruby said, glancing at the parents and grandparents gathering. Somehow, the adults managed to get zebras and robots, vampires and zombies gathered all in one place.

"Let's find a couple of seats in those rows of chairs," Emma said. "We can see them all coming down the atrium from the library and they'll parade around the room. Everybody can get their pictures. We'll get a clear shot of Jason when he goes by."

"It was sweet of Mike to volunteer to help herd the cats," Ruby said.

Mike still hadn't noticed them, preoccupied as he was with getting the kids in line. She scanned the hallway for Jason, but didn't spot him. Fear started nipping at her. This was a lot of commotion for a boy who didn't speak. Her mind jumped ahead to what could happen, what she'd seen happen, when overwhelmed children and adults were in crowded spaces. They panicked. Some ran, some hid. Did Mike know that? On the other hand, Mike probably volunteered to help out in part to stay close to Jason. "I used to think he'd be a volunteer basketball coach one day," Ruby said to distract herself.

"It may happen yet," Emma said.

"Funny, despite being levelheaded kids,

Mike and I thought we could control everything, right down to the year we'd come back to town and raise a family." *Where was Jason?*

Emma shook her head. "Better than having no vision at all."

Ruby was saved from having to respond because two women came over to Emma. One gushed over Emma, telling her how great it was to see her at the party. Emma introduced them as mother and daughter members of a book club they'd been part of years before. They chatted about Em's physical therapy and she showed her optimism in reporting her progress. Ruby listened with half an ear, but stepped out of their circle to try to catch a glimpse of Jason in the atrium or at the library entrance. She kept an eye out for Mike, who was no longer in her line of vision.

She brought her attention back to the conversation long enough to agree that yes, Emma was almost her old self again.

"I'm not going to be satisfied until the cane is gone. But I know it will take time." Emma grinned at the women. "Ruby has to put up with all my complaining."

In the next few minutes, Ruby skirted questions about her work, how long she'd be in town and what was next for her. Amused with her skimpy answers, Ruby patted herself on the back for some half-decent social banter that revealed very little information. Not that it mattered. To these women, Ruby was just a best friend who'd put her job-hunting on hold.

EMMA KEPT CHATTING with the two women, but Ruby heard another voice coming from behind. "Hey, if it isn't Ruby Driscoll."

The unfamiliar voice interrupted her rising concern about Jason. When she turned to the sound of her name, she recognized the face.

"Oh, Kristine. Nice to see you." She gestured around the room. "You throw a great party."

"And you put together a terrific costume." Kristine gave her a prolonged pointed look. "Love the shoes."

"I had fun with the glitter," Ruby admitted.

"You and Mike are full of surprises, aren't you?"

She had no answer for that, but her gut

responded by tightening up. "I'm here visiting Emma. She just had surgery, but you probably knew that."

"I looked up from the podium at the town-council meeting a couple of weeks ago and there was Mike. Now, I run into you. After so many years."

And your point is? "Mike moved back—to stay, or so I understand." Ruby hoped she sounded noncommittal. She gave Kristine a once-over. "And what about you? Looks like you've done well here in town."

"Well, I started my accounting business—" she turned halfway around and back again "—and then local politics called my name. But what about you? You're not back for good?"

Ruby dismissed that idea with a quick flick of her hand. "Oh, no, no. Not at all. I'll be heading to Florida soon." *Home to Mom*, she thought, *but not for long.* Just after midnight last night, she'd responded to an online job listing for an outreach-program specialist in Seattle and for one in the Virgin Islands. Neither were positions with school districts and both were in places she'd never been.

Kristine lowered her voice and said, "No mystery why you wouldn't come back permanently. I understand. Same with Mike. But here he is. Go figure."

Don't take the bait. The snide message beneath the benign words was exactly why she'd sworn she'd never return to Bluestone River. *Never.*

"Oh, look, the kids are coming." Ruby checked to see that the head of the stuffed dog was sticking out of her tote so Jason wouldn't miss it when he passed by.

Then Mike came into view, patting Jason's shoulder as he went on his way to join the other kids. Ruby exhaled, aware that she'd been holding her breath until she saw Jason.

Mike glanced in their direction and even from a distance she caught his face light up. His smile broadened as soon as he recognized her costume. But then his expression changed when his gaze took in Kristine standing next to her. Ruby couldn't miss the apprehension flickering across his face. Recovering fast, he gave them a friendly wave.

Ruby didn't miss the way Kristine's face winced in response to seeing Mike.

"I better go," Kristine said, pointing to the crowd. "I have to give a little speech later." She reached behind Ruby and tapped Emma on the knee. "Thanks again."

Emma smiled and waved her off. "It's nothing. Happy to do it."

"She has a way of saying so much without actually being specific," Ruby whispered as she took her seat next to Emma.

Classic carnival music blared over the speakers and brought the adult conversations and laughter to an abrupt halt.

"Here they come," Ruby said, positioning her phone to take shots of a group of four superheroes leading the rest of the kids down the atrium and through the wide entrance to the room. A skeleton and a witch were next, followed by two toddler-size robots holding hands.

The adults broke into applause for each child coming through and kept it going as a volunteer led the kids around the periphery of the room.

Jason was the only doctor in the house. When he came into view he was hand in hand with a little girl who was smaller and seemed younger—and obviously a little scared. She was dressed as a witch, with a tall pointy hat and a long black cloak.

"Maybe she's one of Jason's classmates," Emma whispered. "She looks so tiny next to him."

Ruby was aiming her phone at the two when Jason's face suddenly changed. His mouth opened in surprise and quickly changed to the widest smile Ruby had seen on his wonderful little face. Jason waved with his free hand and Ruby responded by holding up her phone. She took a couple of quick photos of him and the witch, and then she turned her body to the side to make sure he saw Toto peeking from her bag. He nodded as if sending a signal he understood.

The kids kept coming, but Ruby followed Jason's path around the room. He was into it now, and so was his friend. They waved and smiled to the crowd like a couple of performers.

It took twenty minutes or so for all the kids to come through and take their turn to be in the spotlight as they circled the room. When Mike and a couple of other dads brought up the rear of the line, the older kids scattered in groups and the younger ones hurried to their parents. Jason disappeared into the crowd.

Kristine went to the podium, tested the mic and made her welcome speech before banging her gavel to declare that treats were on the tables. Ruby guessed that about one hundred kids began helping themselves to cookies and punch.

"I'm going to go get a shot of Mike and Jason together. I'll be back." With that, Ruby weaved her way through the crowd and found Mike with the little girl and her parents. Ruby approached slowly so she could watch Jason with half a cookie in his mouth, while his witch friend held the stethoscope against Jason's chest. Jason was smiling, apparently not minding at all.

It won't be long now. He'll soon be telling stories to his dad and asking a million questions. It was just a feeling, a hunch, but honeylike warmth poured through her body. She usually trusted her hunches.

"Hey, Dr. Jason," she said holding her phone, "I want a big smile so I can get your picture."

Jason grinned and pointed to her shoes.

"You like my fancy red shoes?"

Jason nodded and pointed to the dog in her bag.

"That's Toto," the little girl said.

"Right you are," Ruby said, taking the girl's picture. "You're a super witch. I love your pointy hat."

"I was just going to look for you." Mike said, his voice low. He looked her up and down. "I figured you'd be easy to spot. If I couldn't spot the red pigtails, then I'd keep my eyes open for the shoes."

His flirtatious tone brought on a giggle. Wanting to squelch that in a hurry, she turned to the little girl's parents. "I'm on a mission," Ruby told them, holding up her phone. "An amateur photo shoot."

Uncharacteristically awkward, Mike introduced Marie and Everett, and their little girl, Kelly. He explained the couple had graduated from high school a few years after their class. "As it happens, Marie's mom worked at the resort way back when."

Marie beamed. "One of dozens of people around here to have that experience. Working at the Hidden Lake Resort was one of the best jobs I ever had."

"I think all of us teenagers felt that way,"

Ruby said. "Looks like Jason and Kelly hit it off." The two sat cross-legged on the floor against the nearby wall still playing with the stethoscope and munching cookies. Even in their silence they looked content.

"Kelly is on the shy side," Everett said.

Then Jason is the perfect pal, Ruby thought. "Do you think Kelly would mind if I take another picture of the two of them?"

Both parents said their quick okay, so Ruby jumped in and acted like a professional photographer as she shot pictures of them together, alone and clustered with proud parents. She coaxed smiles and silly faces, close-ups and longer shots. Then she tucked Marie's business card in her handbag and promised to send the photos the next day.

Everett and Marie led Kelly away to the candy table and the kids waved goodbye to each other. Ruby glanced at Mike, who sighed happily. "I was worried about how he'd do in a big party setting, but sweet Kelly saved the day."

"Kelly's parents would say Jason did the same for her." She paused to gather her thoughts. "I was watching for Jason earlier but couldn't find him in the crowd. To be honest, I was concerned." She put her hand on her chest. "In all the commotion, I wondered if he'd get scared."

"Funny you should say that, Ruby. I kept my eye on him almost every minute. That's the main reason I volunteered to be one of the watchdog parents."

"I might have known," she said, gesturing over at Emma. "Before things wind down, will you bring Jason over to say hello to Em? She's doing really well, but she needed to grab a chair and get off her feet."

"I want to say hello anyway. But why don't you come with me now and we'll take Jason to the candy table first. And they still have a few caramel apples left."

"Sounds good." She spotted Jason, who was with a couple of kids playing a balloon version of volleyball. "He's occupied for the moment."

"So he is. I probably shouldn't do this," Mike said slyly, "but I can't resist." He took hold of her pigtail and gave it a gentle tug. "I'm in third grade again and you were the new girl with the long braids."

"So I was." What was she supposed to

say? She kept her eyes on Jason to avoid Mike's. "But you never pulled my braids. That would have been breaking Mrs. Cermak's rules."

Mike laughed. "Right you are. Anyway, I'm glad you came. And Emma. I wanted you to see what a big success your costume idea turned out to be." He patted the stuffed dog's head sticking out of her bag. And you? You're a perfect Dorothy."

Ruby held up her phone. "Dr. Jason is captured in here. He looks adorable. By the way, don't leave without taking Toto with you. I only bought it so I could give it to him."

Mike's frown lasted only a second or two. But Ruby understood. She debated if it was a good idea to give Jason that kind of gift. In the end, though, she decided it was a small thing and would be worth it to see the smile on the boy's face.

"And here he comes," Ruby said.

She reached out and squeezed Jason's shoulder. "You look like a real doctor."

She and Mike laughed as Jason nodded solemnly, apparently taking his costume seriously.

Mike ran his hand over Jason's curly hair. "Take us to the candy, Jason. We'll make sure you get one of everything."

She and Mike let Jason lead the way to the table, where he was given an orange bag decorated with black cats and bats. Then an older couple dressed as a king and queen filled it with miniature chocolate bars and bags of Halloween candy, along with a sheet of Halloween stickers and a puzzle book.

"Okay, Jason, let's go to the apple booth and get you one with lots of caramel and nuts." Mike steered him toward the table, but a man tapped Mike on the arm and asked if he could speak to him for a minute.

Mike glanced at Ruby, his expression asking a silent question.

"Go ahead, Mike. I'll take him to get one of the apples."

"Hey, Jason, we're in luck," Ruby said when they'd taken the few steps to the booth. "No waiting."

This volunteer was dressed as an old-fashioned farmer with bib overalls and a big straw hat. In a jovial voice he asked, "What can I get for Dorothy and the doctor?"

Jason pointed to Toto.

"Okay, and for the dog."

"One with caramel and nuts?" Ruby asked Jason.

When he smiled and nodded, the guy said, "One apple with everything comin' right up."

Ruby picked up Jason, who was surprisingly heavy in her arms. She held him around his middle so he could see the apple on a stick swirling into the creamy rich caramel. Then the man dipped the apple into the nuts and with a flick of his wrist gave it a spin and it came up covered.

"That looks almost too beautiful to eat," Ruby joked, when she took the apple from the man's hand. "Why don't I carry it for you?"

Jason nodded and they stepped away from the booth. "I suppose we could look for your dad or for Emma. What do you think?"

Jason shook his head. No? Hmm…puzzling. The pull on her pinafore got her attention. She crouched down next to Jason. "What is it?"

Jason took his prescription pad and pencil from his pocket and wrote something on it. Then he turned it so Ruby could see the letters: HUG.

Ruby had a bit of a struggle to keep her eyes from filling with tears. She managed to say, "That's easy enough." She opened her arms and he did the same, and when her arms circled him he rested his cheek against her shoulder.

"What a nice surprise," she whispered. She gave him an extra little squeeze. She relaxed her arms and drew back a little and looked into his smiling face. She then took Toto out her bag and tucked it under his arm. "He belongs to you now."

She straightened up and took Jason's hand. She headed toward Emma and saw Mike on the way. Kristine approached from the other direction.

"We got the best apple they had," Ruby said, keeping her voice even. But she wasn't on an even keel inside. She wanted the special moment back. She glanced down at Jason. "It was a wonderful party."

Kristine patted her arm. "I'm very sorry I won't be seeing you again, Ruby. But good luck wherever you go."

"Not so fast." Emma rose and laced her

arm through Ruby's. "I'm keeping her around until Thanksgiving—*at least.*"

Ruby's and Mike's eyes met for a split second. Then Ruby forced herself to look at Kristine, who wore an insincere smile as she glanced from Ruby to Mike and back again. They stood in silence. The energy around Ruby quivered as if something meaningful had happened, but no one could name it.

CHAPTER ELEVEN

WITH HIS FEET propped up on his desk, Mike flipped through the latest issue of the business weekly he'd recently subscribed to. It was unusual for him to have a quiet moment to himself. Jason was never far from his thoughts. Thankfully, the nightmares hadn't surfaced lately, but the resistance was showing itself daily. He shook his head to refuse scrambled eggs one day, green beans the next. Mike would put out a blue T-shirt, and Jason would put it back and take out the red one. Like Ruby said, a little rebellion was a good sign. Right. But that didn't mean it was easy to deal with.

The phone rang and Mike eagerly answered it.

"Are you in your office or at home?" Ruby said, dispensing with a greeting. Loud background noise told him she was outside.

"In the office." He put his feet on the floor and sat up straight. "Why? Where are you?"

"I'm at the bridge. I just finished a long run back to that road behind your place. I have an idea about something. If you're free, can I bring lunch to your office? I'd like to get your opinion."

Did he want vanilla ice cream on hot apple pie? Sunshine on a rainy day? Of course, he wanted her to bring lunch. "Uh, sure that sounds fine." Did he sound cool and casual enough? "I was just about to start some notes for a client. Ha! Listen to me. It's for one of my two clients."

She chuckled. "Two and counting, Mike. You want the usual roast beef?"

"That's it." They ended the call and curiosity consumed him. That river trail had sure grabbed Ruby's attention. He dropped the magazine on the stack and brought up Georgia's file. He added a few notes.

He could spend all day telling himself Ruby was just an old girlfriend, a first love, nothing more. But a devilish little voice deep inside belly-laughed and mocked him for the lies.

He pushed aside his laptop. When he

swiveled the chair, he faced the building next door and a slice of the gray sky. Against his better judgment, Mike closed his eyes and recalled the images of Ruby gently cupping Emma's elbow to provide support as she gingerly walked with her cane. How Ruby had been close to tears as she shouldered the blame for her antibullying program going wrong. Or, laughing and shouting encouraging words to Jason as he threw sticks to Peach and had kept the dog's tail happily in motion.

The bell on the door jingled and Ruby called his name. The chair squeaked as he straightened up fast—but not fast enough.

"Did I wake you, counselor?" An impish smile took over Ruby's face.

"Are you kidding? Couldn't you tell I was pondering Lady Justice herself?"

She tsked. "I think you're better off pleading guilty."

"And throwing myself on the mercy of the court? Go for a plea bargain?" Only Ruby—and now Jason—could bring out his playful side.

She sniffed the air. "I smell hazelnut coffee."

"I was pretty sure it's your favorite." He led the way to the back, where he poured coffee into the giant mugs he'd bought specifically to use in his office with clients.

They set out the sandwiches on napkins. "I keep meaning to bring plates," he said. "There must be five complete sets of dishes at the house. I had forgotten my mom had Thanksgiving dishes—she called it the harvest set. They have leaves and cornucopias and pumpkins. She used those in October and November. Then in December she brought out the holiday china."

"I remember those plates because they were hand-painted with snow-covered evergreens and stars and lights that almost twinkled." Ruby lifted her mug high in the air. "I like the glazes on these. Prairie colors, the browns and greens and a touch of blue—it reminds me of the sky in winter. Your mom would have liked them."

Her voice had gradually become hoarse with emotion. Nostalgia. He knew it well. But he also knew to keep his distance and not scare her away with kisses and talk of her moving to town. He almost laughed out loud. Scared away because it all felt too good.

"That's what drew me to them." A long-forgotten memory surfaced. Ruby in the small makeshift art studio at the high school showing him a bowl. "You made pottery bowls, Rubes. I remember." He'd been all thumbs, or that's how he thought of himself. He and Neil acted like Rubes and Em taking extra art classes was a girly thing. Talk about being dumb guys.

Ruby nodded. "I was thinking about that the other day. In the last few years, whenever I'd wanted to expand my life—you know, do something besides work…and work out—I'd think about taking a pottery class. But somehow, I never got around to it."

He studied her face, deep in reflection as she spoke. A mesmerizing face, with distinctive light brown eyes revealing the depth of the woman she'd become. Her rich red hair looked dark against the white headband that held it in place. "You're already a really good photographer."

Ruby grinned. "I like it, just like I had fun working with clay as a teenager. And Emma was always such a good sketch artist." She took a bite of her sandwich and chewed. "Speaking of sketching, Emma loaned me one of her notepads. So, have your lunch and you can see for yourself." She patted her backpack sitting next to her.

"This is getting interesting. What are you going to draw?"

"Eat first. You'll see."

It didn't take long to recap the Halloween party while they finished their sandwiches and coffee.

After he scrunched up the bag and napkins and threw them in the trash, she pulled a good-size tablet out of her pack.

"You really are going to draw," he said.

She sent him a self-deprecating glance. "An embarrassing and no doubt way off-scale map of the river trails and the roads I took on the day I ended up at your house."

"You've got my attention," Mike said.

Ruby opened the sketchbook and took out a box of colored pencils. "I told you I brought art supplies with me." She laughed. "I have a feeling Jason could do a better job with what I'm about to do."

"Ah, c'mon, Rubes, show me what you got."

Ruby chuckled at his teasing and in the bottom corner, she drew the bridge in red and, flashing a smile, exchanged her red pencil for a blue one and made a squiggly line up the page to indicate the river. Then she held up the green and brown pencils. "Okay, using these for land, here are the river trails." She looked up. "What I'm doing here is part of a bigger vision, for lack of a modest word. The other day, I noticed there's no sign anywhere that points visitors to those trails. There should be one of those posts with arrows pointing to the park and bridge and trails."

Good point, Mike thought, watching her fill in the trail and underpasses. "When we were kids, that area along the river wasn't cleared," he said. "The actual paved trail wasn't put in until about a year before my dad signed over our land."

"Which helps explain why no one figured out that the road behind the old gas station could be connected to the sanctuary. It's an extra mile, or a mile and a half, and could have been part of the trail system." Ruby circled the end of the trail at the parking lot, and then drew a line to create a back road to the dead-end *T*. "If you make a right turn you're at the rear boundary of the sanctuary. Why not extend a trail through the woods? It would come up here." She drew a rectangle and labeled it the office.

Mike pointed higher. "And the front entrance—that's way over here and the winding road into the parking here." He picked up the blue pencil. "And this would be the lake that's more or less off the paper."

"I'm no civil engineer," Ruby said, "but how much could it cost to create a gravel trail, if not a paved one?"

"A new extension would provide walkers and cyclists a route from one nature site to another. The covered bridge to the bird sanctuary. There's even a marshy area that could be covered with a boardwalk."

Ruby used a brown pencil to draw a line down the road to the left of the dead end. "When Emma and I were out the other day, we looked for the turnoff to the back road from the other direction. Near as we could tell, it's off Miller Road, where there are two very large farms. Emma said there used to be six or seven farms in that area."

"Likely part of Bluestone River's sad tale of decline," Mike said, tapping what Ruby had drawn. "My dad predicted bigger farms would gobble up the smaller ones. He was right. They're more like factories now."

"Not much we can do about that," Ruby said, "but allowing a trail from that road to the main building in the sanctuary would give the owners something to brag about. Taking their civic duty seriously and all that."

"The extended trail system would definitely draw more tourists—and local use," Mike said.

Ruby paused and then traced her finger down the page to the bridge. "Imagine a sign pointing the way to the Hidden Lake Bird Sanctuary here at the bridge." She held up her hands to form a rectangle. "I can *see* the photos in a brochure for the town."

"Millie doesn't care for many injured birds. The place isn't really fulfilling its mission as a sanctuary. But that could change."

"It was odd the other day to see cabins all boarded up."

"Neglected, probably not opened in years. My dad sold off the equipment and the freezers in the ice-cream shop to a guy over in Clayton." He rolled his eyes. "Naturally, Bluestone River's loss was Clayton's gain. The building is still there. Only two or three of the cabins have been torn down. Probably because the wood was rotting."

"So, what do you think about proposing the trail expansion?" Ruby asked. "Emma still has some pull in this town." She pointed to him. "So do you?"

"That's iffy," Mike said, wistfully. "Emma maybe. But no one is inclined to listen to me."

"*Yet.* Give it time, Mike. The Abbots were a big part of things around here."

Mike had his doubts, but it didn't matter. "How about this? I'll find out who owns the land where the farm road is. It's a start. Maybe they'd do a long-term lease or even sell it for public use. Could be a couple of ag-equipment companies that could use the PR." With the brown pencil he made a shoulder area on the side of both roads and curved a line through the grass and gravel for a path. "Unless whoever owns the land is willing to cover the cost, the project needs funding. I'm sure the tax base is lower now."

"You could argue the sanctuary is missing out, too. It's barely mentioned on the website."

"But it's so nice and quiet. Exactly how I like it. The birds probably would vote to keep it that way, too." Pretending to scold her, he said, "And now you, and probably Emma, want to *encourage* people to come here."

Ruby laughed. "Hey, it's your civic duty. Supports the environment, too. A good credential for you."

"Hey, isn't Emma on the board of the conservancy?"

"She used to be," Ruby said, "but that was before she fell and was so badly hurt. She had to give up most of her volunteer work. But she kept funding the two part-time salaries for Millie and a seasonal groundskeeper. Even after she and Neil decided to split up, she promised him she'd keep up the funding."

The image of his old friend Neil talking with Emma about divorce agreements tore at his insides. Even worse, it forced him to face the way he'd let his friendship with Neil slip away. Why couldn't he and Neil have been more like Emma and Ruby? Best friends forever. Neil had pulled away first, though, as Mike remembered. But he hadn't challenged him. Just like he'd never gone after Ruby. Now he realized Neil probably didn't want to confide his marriage troubles, they'd all been close.

Ruby leaned forward. "It hurts to imagine them having that kind of conversation, doesn't it?"

"Were you reading my mind?"

She shook her head. "Remember, I saw Emma a few times a year. With me, she had a chance to drop her defenses a little and admit how hard it was between them."

What if he and Ruby had ended up that unhappy? He couldn't stand even thinking about it.

"He and Emma were sad more than angry," Ruby said. "They parted when they were still friends who hoped they'd each get a second chance at finding the right person."

They sat in silence. The hum of the camper-size fridge was the only noise he heard.

When he started to jump back to the conversation, so did Ruby, so they were both talking at the same time. That lightened things up and Mike gestured to Ruby to go first.

She tilted her head and smiled smugly. "I'd like to brag a little."

"Well, then, be my guest," he said with a laugh.

"You don't know this, but I happen to be a champion grant writer. If I hadn't been, a couple of the crisis centers I worked for would have folded. I can put numbers together, statistics, budgets and cost-benefit analysis."

Mike found this side of Ruby easy to imagine. "I bet you're good. I would have liked to have done more pro bono work in Cincinnati."

"So, then you know what I'm talking about. We could do a proposal for the town council. Emma can talk to the conservancy and to Millie and get some figures."

"And I'll dig round and find out who owns the land," Mike repeated. "You sold me." He flashed back to Ruby, an aspiring marketing entrepreneur. "I'll drive over there soon and see the roads for myself."

"I just want you to see what looks like a real possibility," Ruby said softly. "Wouldn't it be something if this comes together? I'd be leaving a little something of myself behind this time."

"Other than a hole in my heart?" The words had just slipped out. Horrified, he shot out of the chair. So did she. "Ruby, I'm sorry. I can't believe I said that."

"Yeah, well, *my* heart wasn't in one piece, either." She started to leave. "I'll let myself out." At the door, she turned, but stared at her shoes. "It's always there, Mike. No matter what we do, no matter how much I care about you and Jason, or you care about me. It never goes away."

"But Ruby—"

"There's nothing you can do right now, Mike, that's going to make this better. Strange, isn't it? We've paid for what our parents did a lifetime ago. We've been paying for twenty years." She scoffed. "And what's worse, they weren't even our mistakes in the first place."

Ruby hurried away. He didn't go after her. Ruby was right. It was always there. He'd just proved it.

MIKE LOOKED THROUGH the one-way glass at Gloria sitting with Jason on the carpet. So far, Jason had followed Gloria's directions and, using blocks and plastic figures as well as items like cars and trees, he'd built a house and in it put two figures. Then he knocked the blocks over. The figure of a woman was half in and half out of the house and the boy was on the green grass. There was never anything subtle about Jason's art. Rather than upsetting Mike, he was relieved Jason's memories and fears were obvious.

"Activities, Mike," Gloria had said. "The path to what's inside Jason."

Over the weeks, following Gloria's lead, they'd captured their fears and sent them off in balloons. Jason and Gloria had treated wounds on stuffed animals. He'd drawn images from nightmares and used colors to show his changing emotions. Mike and the ducks were showing up more often and a lone woman in distress less frequently.

The pictures Jason created at the felt board usually included a lake and a boat, and now bare trees. Tumbling the blocks was something newer.

Gloria's assistant entered the room and the therapist said something to Jason and patted his shoulder. She left and, a few seconds later, came inside the observation room and greeted Mike.

"I don't know how close he is to talking," Mike said, "but he looks happy."

"Well, today was a repeat of something we've been doing for a couple of weeks. He's closing in on the fire."

Closing in? An ominous thought. "What do you mean?"

"I'm asking him questions, and because he likes to build and draw, and is good at it, he's creating real representations of the traumatic event. Little by little. We don't go too far at any one session."

He glanced at Jason putting together a puzzle. "What about his representation of Zoe?"

"Showing the woman not quite out of the house was as close as he's come to indicating her death. He included himself. But he hasn't filled in features on his own face." She smiled slyly. "Not the way he puts a big smile on the man with curly hair."

"I'll take it," he said, grinning.

"You're his world, Mike. The foundation." She pointed to Jason through the glass. "Does he react to fires? Has he seen one yet?"

Mike shook his head. "I have a fireplace in the living room, but I haven't given any thought to using it. Friends I visit knew not to light a fire in theirs when Jason was there." Ruby and Emma thought of that on their own. No need to remind the two of them. "He responded to a siren a few days ago. An ambulance. It was faint out where we live, but he ran to the window to look outside. I followed him and assured him it had nothing to do with us."

Gloria stared at Jason, seemingly gathering her thoughts. "He ran toward the sound?"

"He did. I was surprised he didn't run into his room or become agitated." Then Mike remembered. "But he had a bad nightmare that night." And long. "It took me a while to settle him down. Once it's over, he sleeps peacefully and it's like the torment, whatever the images are, never happened."

Gloria's face turned serious. "That's distressing for you, I know, but when I look at his drawings and the felt-board pictures, I see the two stories merging somehow. He's integrating his losses with the security of his life with you."

"It's not that different when we're older, is it?" Mike asked, thinking out loud more than expecting an answer. "I mean, everything that happens can be abbreviated into a story."

"True, but with a traumatized child," Gloria explained, "we hope we can coax the adjustment to the stories without leaving the raw pain behind or push the memories so deep they're triggered without warning."

Mike leaned against the wall. "Man, I sure understand triggers, not in the way Jason does, but the trauma is there all the same."

Gloria intensified her gaze, obviously expecting him to answer. "You probably don't remember this, or perhaps you didn't live here twenty years ago, but my mother was killed in a crash on the highway."

"I'm a relative newcomer, so I wouldn't know anything about that."

As Mike filled in the details of his mom's death, Gloria's expression registered surprise only when he brought Ruby and her dad into the story. "It was the night before graduation and the police came down to the covered bridge to find us. They took us to the hospital together and we learned what happened. The whole of it. And she and I never spoke to each other again until a few months ago, when we ran into each other here in town."

"Two traumatic losses in the space of an hour. That's a big deal."

It had taken him years to look at it that way. "At the time, I had to throw all my energy into my dad. He was destroyed."

"I'm glad you told me about this," Gloria said. "What happened to you is terrible, but I think it's helped you cope with Jason. You're doing a great job."

"Thanks." His voice, hoarse with emotion, caught him off guard. He quickly cleared his throat.

Gloria squeezed his arm. "You can take

him home now. Just keep doing what you're doing."

Frustrating as that was, it would have to be enough. At least for now. When he met Jason at the door to the playroom, he gave him an extra tight hug.

"We're off to Clayton to get supplies," Mike told him. "We're getting low on oatmeal and ice cream."

An hour later, still feeling good about Gloria's words, Mike pushed his loaded cart through the exit doors of the supermarket. He settled Jason in his car seat before unloading the groceries. When he closed the trunk he glanced across the street and took a quick breath of surprise.

Ruby was coming through the door of the Chinese restaurant carrying a large shopping bag. Wearing jeans and a purple blazer, she hurried off as if she had someplace to be and might be running late. But then, even as a young girl she'd walked with purpose in her step.

He started to call her name, but held back. What would he do after she waved back? Would her face light up? Probably. It always did. The smiles she offered him were bright. It was like old times. Would she be happy to see Jason? Of course. He hadn't mentioned it to Ruby, but he'd seen Ruby hug Jason. From halfway across the meeting room, he couldn't have missed the sweet way Jason snuggled in her arms. Jason had put the prescription pad and stethoscope on his shelf in his room. Mike had seen where he'd written HUG on the pad. That night Jason made room for Toto in the crowd of stuffed animals on the bed. Jason would always connect those things to Ruby.

It would be so easy, Mike thought, *to collect Emma and all have dinner at the lake house.* He'd pick up carryout food for him and Jason. No problem.

But no matter the time or place, if he did reach out to her, she'd only, eventually, pull away.

Later, at home, Mike caught himself again mulling over what it would be like if Ruby settled permanently in Bluestone River. He'd inevitably run into her at the bakery, or the library, or the hairdresser next door to his office. They'd shop in the same stores and say hello to the same people. And not be together.

When Mike finished putting the groceries away, he said, "Hot dogs coming up, Jason. With mustard and relish—the works."

The amused smile on Jason's face brought him back to what was really important.

I'm letting you off the hook, Ruby.

CHAPTER TWELVE

RUBY MET EMMA in the waiting room of the medical center.

"I'm a medical wonder, Rubes. The doctor even said so. And I feel it." Emma thrust her fists over her head. "See? I've got energy to burn today and that means I don't want to go home right now."

This was a new Emma, or maybe the old Emma was back. "You want to get some lunch?"

"Nah, not hungry—yet. Besides, Brenda left us plenty of food." She counted on her fingers as she listed, "Quiche, and baked chicken. Half a ham…"

"Good point," Ruby said, thinking of her waistline. "Brenda is the reason I have to run extra miles every day."

Emma clapped her palms together. "Which is how you discovered the back road to Mike's. See? Things have a strange way of happening at the right time. You've made a positive difference for the town already."

"We'll see," she said, allowing a note of skepticism into her voice. "So, where do you want to go?"

Emma couldn't make up her mind, but they had time to make a decision on the way home. It took them through farms and new housing developments on what was once farmland. As they approached the town, more wooded land took up the spaces between the vast acres of fields. With Emma's help, she and Mike had located the owners of all the other pieces of land needed to connect the trails.

"I'm looking at the town through different eyes now," Emma said. "I've been focused solely on getting better for the last couple of years, but now…" She laughed. "Do you know I'd forgotten all about the money for the kids' Halloween party? My accountant takes care of all of that."

"How easily that rolls off your tongue," Ruby teased. "You have to admit it's fun not to have to think about it every year. It's like it's running on autopilot."

"I do admit that. But since my fall and

then Neil dying, I've been in a desert. No fresh ideas. Until now. I want to do more good things for my hometown. Projects that make a real difference."

Ruby patted Emma's knee. "I know, Em. I was just joshing you a little."

"Hey, Rubes. Have you been by your old house? "

Sensing what was coming, she said, "No. I've kind of avoided going there. I'm not sure I want to deal with the memories."

"Come on, let's go have a look," Emma urged.

"Okay, you twisted my arm."

Ruby's house was easy to spot on the street. It was the only ranch style house on a block of two-story homes.

"Oh, Rubes, we had such good times here." Emma opened the car door, and climbed out. Awkwardly, but on her own. She took a few steps to the side and craned her neck. "I wonder if the picnic table is still there. Your dad was the king of burgers."

Ruby laughed. "He wàs. And you were always one of his favorite guests—you were easy to impress. You also appreciated his corny humor." It wasn't until the summer before senior year that her parents thought it was okay for Mike and sometimes Neil to be invited over to spend time with the whole family. Her dad had been careful about maintaining his principal-student distance. Senior year everything got a little looser and Mike was almost like family.

Staring at the house now, Ruby put her hand over her stomach, as if that could stop the churning. When her father wasn't being jovial and friendly to Mike and Neil, he was apparently sneaking away to meet Mike's mom. Post-accident, Ruby's mother had hired a private detective and discovered that the affair had been going on for at least a year. So much for fun times.

Ruby distracted herself by waving to the older woman who was on the porch next door. Mrs. Kovich. Ruby had to laugh. Her neighbor had seemed so old when Ruby was young.

"Can I help you?" Mrs. Kovich asked.

Addressing her by name, Ruby introduced herself. "You probably don't remember me or my family. We moved away twenty years ago."

"Of course, I remember you, Ruby. You

still have such pretty hair. Your daddy taught over at the high school until he got a better job somewhere else. Are you here visiting?"

"She's here helping me," Emma said, stepping forward. "I just had some surgery. I remember you, too, Mrs. Kovich. I spent a lot of time here. I'm Emma O'Connell. I still live in town."

"Oh, that's right. You two girls were always going off on your bikes." Mrs. Kovich chuckled. "And you had some handsome boys around. You kids were always so respectful. I sure appreciated that."

Talking with Mrs. Kovich made Ruby light-headed from the rush of images coming at her. She tried to listen to Emma and Mrs. Kovich chatting, but all she could hear was her dad joking with a neighbor about being outnumbered. "Surrounded by women," he'd said on a sigh. Then her mom would chide him playfully until he admitted he loved every minute of it.

There were the times her dad drove to the resort to drop her off and pick her up on rainy days. He and Ellen would make small talk, always cordial, with Ellen warning them about getting home safely.

Ruby smiled thinking about how popular her dad was with the kids. Maybe because he always seemed to know the right thing to say or do at exactly the right time. He was like that at home with his daughters, too. Her dad celebrated her top grades, but didn't criticize the ones that fell short. If she needed help with a chemistry test, he calmed her fears and stepped up to help her. He swore a hot drink that tasted suspiciously like sweet lemonade was his secret concoction to treat a cold. He'd mix up a batch at the first sign of a sniffle. Generous with compliments, he was the first to console her when she didn't make the softball team.

Now, standing in front of the house she grew up in, all that fell away. The memory of her dad at the kitchen table with his newspaper talking about graduation was sweeter than it had ever been before.

Pretending she was going to have a look at the backyard, Ruby left Emma's side and went to the fence fighting back tears. Grief over the loss, yes, but her heart overflowed with something else. *Love*. For all his flaws, and the huge betrayal, Timothy Driscoll was a great dad. She needed to say that. Out loud. To Mike. Because the same was true of his mom.

She swallowed hard and went to find Emma, who leaned heavily on her cane. "I better get you home."

"I still wear out too fast," Emma said to Mrs. Kovich.

"You two sure turned into lovely women. You take care of yourselves now. So nice you're back in town." She smiled warmly. "I hope you stay."

Ruby thanked her and she and Emma returned to the car.

Emma stared out the passenger-side window. "You really are leaving in a few weeks, aren't you? You've made up your mind."

"You've got a house cleaner, Em, a shopper and when it snows, a guy will show up to plow your driveway."

Emma shrugged. "None of that matters. This isn't about me being ready. It's about what's going on with you. You haven't finished with the trail project. The council meeting is next week."

Right. Emma and Mike were going to

present her idea. "I'll still go. I won't be gone that soon. It feels good to have my hands in this." She'd about made up her mind to look for freelance grant-writing work. Safe work. She was confident about that skill.

"What about Mrs. Kovich? She hopes you'll stay. And she doesn't remember anything about any scandal." Emma grinned.

"She was sweet, wasn't she?" Ruby came to a four-way stop sign and took a deep breath as she pressed her foot on the brake. "I just know in my heart, Em, I can't stay much longer."

Emma turned to face her. "What makes you think so? Tell me,"

Ruby started across the intersection, glad for the need to focus on the road and avoid Emma's gaze. "I told you about Jason becoming way too attached to me, and to Peach. I'm so…so myself with that little boy. I haven't heard him say one word, but it feels… Oh, Em, he could be mine. But he isn't."

The air around her seemed charged. "I haven't said that out loud. But Jason sees me interact with Mike. How we tease and joke. I've already crossed a line into risky territory. If Jason doesn't have the wrong idea already, he soon will."

"Or, he'll have the right one," Emma said, getting huffy. "Poor you. Talking and laughing with Mike. And everything is pleasant. How terrible."

"Quit twisting my words. You know what I mean. I can't stay." She hadn't confided to Emma that she had this same argument with herself every night.

"You must think men like Mike come along every day." Emma snapped her fingers. "Just like that."

Ruby groaned. "No, I don't." Like she needed that reminder.

"I'll say it again, Rubes, every woman I've ever known wants a guy to look at her the way he looks at you."

Ruby's face heated up and beads of sweat formed on her hairline. She wasn't angry with Emma, just surprised she'd erupt so fast. Was it frustration? Anger? Maybe both. "But what felt real a lifetime ago might be nothing more than a wispy fantasy now."

"If you take off again, you'll never know. You'll have to live with that."

Ruby drove across River Street, conscious of Mike's office a block away. No doubt he was working, planning his life, thinking about Jason. He sure wasn't spending his time wringing his hands over what might have been.

They walked into the house in silence, but Ruby was shaky, almost weak from the trip to the house and Em's sharp words in the car. "Listen, Em, I don't want anything, especially not Mike, to come between us."

"No, Rubes, Mike won't ever come between us. Nothing will," Emma said, her conviction clear. "But I admit it's frustrating. I'm worried about you for your sake. I don't want you to miss out on happiness if it's right there, close enough to touch."

Ruby watched Emma get settled on the couch. Then she went to her bathroom and splashed cold water on her face, relieved to be alone. The bedroom was as familiar now as any place she'd ever lived. She had everything she needed, from her computer and tablet on the desk, to her writing journal and favorite slippers and hand lotion.

Ruby opened her email and saw a newsy note from her mother. Full of talk about her starting as a receptionist at a retirement complex nearby. She'd had a series of part-time jobs since moving to Florida. She liked to work—up to a point. She pinched pennies so she wouldn't have to find what she called a serious job.

She read the final line of her mom's email: The invitation to stay with me is always open. Just say the word.

She hit Reply and wrote a quick paragraph on Emma's recovery, the weather, and the final lines: Emma will be fully mobile again soon and she has a housekeeper. We're doing as we please at this point. I expect to be ready to drive to Florida... Hands poised in the air, something blocked Ruby from typing those final words. The vision of Jason and Mike at the house on the lake loomed warm and full of love. Laughter, too. Lots of laughter.

She lowered her hands and slumped in the chair. Her dream seemed so possible when the sweet memories took center stage. Still, she knew her limits. If she and Mike ended up like Emma and Neil, it would destroy her. And it would be unforgivable to do that to a vulnerable child who'd already suffered huge losses in his six years. She snapped her attention back to the real world and watched her fingers finish the sentence: ...likely in early December, but definitely before Christmas. She hit the send button before she could change her mind.

"There, I did it," she said to Peach, who'd followed her into the bedroom and sat by her feet. "We'll be on the move again."

Later, she and Emma shared leftovers for dinner, an invisible tension still disturbing the air between them. Finally, Emma looked up from her empty plate. "Okay, I'm going to apologize for my tone. I can't live with bad feelings between us."

"Well, me, neither," Ruby agreed, smiling.

"*But* I want to finish what was on my mind." Emma raised her hands in surrender. "Promise. I'll only say it once."

"I have a feeling you might have already said it, but..." She gestured to Emma to go ahead and speak her mind. Ruby pushed away the plate and set her elbows on the table. This was obviously important to Emma. "Okay...shoot."

Emma nodded, but sent her a scolding

grin. "Do you remember the big poster boards we had in that special workshop we took? The one about having a vision for the future."

"Sure I do. Vision boards. It was my dad's idea. He brought in the motivational speaker and we did those collages with all our heart's desires and goals shown in pictures—to make our life map more real." Ruby flapped her hand in the air. "Sending us on our way with a concept for what we wanted our future to look like."

They'd been told to gather photographs and magazines to find and cut out relevant images that meant something to them. She and Emma had signed up along with about a dozen of their classmates. Mike came, but not Neil, who already knew he'd be working in the family auto business.

"Oh, Emma, I know where you're going with this."

"Okay, okay, then stay with me, Rubes."

"Yes, Mike's collage had pictures of a curly-haired little boy and a little girl with red hair he cut out of a magazine. Mine had a picture of twins. And, *ha, ha, ha*—everybody laughed." She folded her arms across her chest, surprised by how much that had hurt. Nothing was funny a month later when things turned bitter and ugly.

Emma reached out and put her hand over hers. "It was amusing at the time because even as eighteen-year-olds you both included each other and a family on your vision boards. Rubes, is it possible *you're* afraid of becoming attached to Jason?" Emma paused. "It's not only the other way around. I'm just going to say it. He's right there, a child to love as your own."

Ruby got to her feet and let Peach out to the yard. She watched the dog through the door, not wanting to look at Emma. "You act like Mike doesn't have a say," she whispered.

"It might be what Mike wants. He's been trying to get closer to you since the minute he saw you in the park. You know it's true. You're the one running away."

Ruby shook her head. Emma meant well. But it didn't change the risk of another big failure in her life, and this time, hurting not just teenagers, but a vulnerable little boy. She knew that for sure.

RUBY'S BURNING LEG muscles finally shouted an order to stop. Not having Peach with her, she'd sprinted the last mile along the river, her mind preoccupied with the trail proposal. She thought of it as a legacy. Maybe a tribute to Emma and Mike's commitment to this pretty little town that had grown on her, too, and helped her sort out her life. Or get a start on it, anyway. One good thing had happened—she'd started running longer distances again and pushing herself to cut her time per mile. She might even sign up for a five or ten K race when she got back to Florida.

She cooled down by strolling to the edge of the playground, and leaned over to rest her hands on her thighs to stretch her back. When she finally straightened up, there was Mike, leaning against the bridge, with an amused smile. He looked ready to tease her about something.

"Isn't staring at an out-of-breath sweaty woman against the law?" she hollered. "If it isn't, it ought to be." More to the point, why was he there? As if on cue, her body started tingling, first her shoulders and down her arms. Her legs would soon follow, if they weren't too tired from her run.

"I came down on a whim to look for you." He came closer, but still kept several feet of space between them. "You mentioned you've been running more and using the trails."

"I left Peach at home so I could do sprints." She slipped off her headband and shook out her hair.

Grinning, he cocked his head. "Uh, do you need to go home and dry off or something?"

"Well, sure, but it's not an emergency." She waited for him to explain himself, but when he didn't, she said, "Why were you looking for me?"

"Because I wanted to see you," he responded, as if that was obvious. "Also, I'm really here because I don't feel right about the way things are between us."

She let her head drop back and looked at the sky. "Mike, there isn't any *us*." Her own lie made her wince.

"Oh, right," he scoffed. "In any case I'd like to put *us* on the table."

She laughed. Of course she did. He wasn't

angry with her. Just exasperated. Besides, this conversation was inevitable. She glanced at the bridge. Their big talk, the closure they never had, well, maybe it had to be here at the bridge. Where else? Sighing, Ruby folded her arms across her chest. "I'm listening."

He pointed at her crossed arms. "Sure you are. But if that's the best I can get, I'll take it." He rubbed the back of his neck and caught a quick look at the bridge. "Ever since I saw you here in this park I've wanted—needed—to talk about what happened to us."

Ruby lowered her gaze, as if something on the ground demanded her attention. She couldn't argue with that, nor would she run. Not this time. She stole a glance at him now and saw a man's eyes and a mature, deep love, not a boy's innocent first love.

"When I woke up this morning, my feet hit the floor and I knew I wasn't letting one more day come and go without talking to you. We've been dancing around everything. You think I hated you, and I believe you abandoned me. Or, really, *us*."

"*You* let me run away without even trying to find me. But, Mike, so what? That's all in the past. We've moved on."

He put out his arm and, without touching her, steered her closer to the gravel shoulder at the start of the bridge. "In the past, huh? In twenty years, through college and law school, my job at a prized firm, closing down the resort, my dad's death, learning I have a son, *I've never moved on*." He stopped long enough to take in a breath. "And I don't think you have, either."

"It's not like we had some misunderstanding, Mike. What happened to us was permanent. We each lost a parent—and each other—in the same instant."

Mike's head jerked back, as if startled. "What?"

"I was surprised by what you said. I was talking with Gloria and she said almost the same thing in the same words. Like a double trauma." He braced his hand on the side of the bridge. She stepped a couple of feet closer, but kept her distance. A safe distance. But her rapid heartbeat didn't know it.

Mike thrust his arms toward her, across the gulf between them. "I blamed your dad, Ruby. I did. I admit it. I hated him for kill-ing my mom. That's what I believed at the time."

Ruby nodded. Right. That was the problem. "I blamed my dad, too, at least until we found out the other driver had been drinking so much he could barely stand up. And your dad blamed my dad." She raised her chin and made herself meet his eye.

"Twenty years ago."

"And it's a fact that won't disappear." Ruby shook her head. "You said even the mayor acted funny when she saw you."

"Who cares what she thinks. I sure don't and I can't imagine you do," Mike said. "I do care that you understand I'm not some kid blaming your father for what happened to my mother anymore. If I did that I'd become my dad. Bitterness turned him into an old man way before the years did."

Ruby listened as Mike filled in all the blanks. It wasn't until law school that Mike felt okay about leaving his dad alone during the week to run the resort. By the time Mike took the job in Ohio, the resort was beyond outdated. "Finally, rather than do any work on it, he decided to sign most of the property over to what would become the sanctuary and move closer to me. But he was as miserable in Cincinnati as he'd been here. It had nothing to do with geography.

"When my dad couldn't take care of himself, let alone the business, it was easy to blame your dad for everything." He smiled sadly.

"You could have asked Neil where I went. Or, Emma, obviously. They always knew where I was." She kicked the stones in front of her, stirring up gravel dust and coating her running shoes.

Mike grimaced. "After their wedding, I rarely saw Neil and Emma. I'd tried to put it all behind me. I sure couldn't allow myself to contact you."

"Why?"

"Same reasons you didn't contact me. I was mad, confused, hurt."

Mike kept his arm braced on the bridge, but shifted his gaze to the water rushing over the rocks below. Ruby's gaze followed. Without the sun to give the rocks their bluish cast, they were just ordinary stones under gray water.

"For what it's worth, Ruby, I've accepted who my parents were and I can live with it. My mom loved my dad. I know she did. And I know he loved her, no matter what had happened. They were human. Just like your dad was. And humans make mistakes sometimes. It doesn't mean we love anyone less."

Ruby closed her eyes against the image of her dad and Ellen. She wanted to believe what Mike was saying was true.

Ruby's body had cooled down from the run, leaving her cold in the chilly breeze, even in a sweatshirt. She rubbed her arms to warm them and glanced up at the darkening sky.

"I'm sorry, Rubes. You're cold. It looks like it's about to dump rain on us now." He took off his jacket and handed it to her. "Let's duck under the bridge. I won't keep you much longer."

The first drops of rain hit the roof of the bridge at the same time they were sheltered under it. Ruby put Mike's jacket around her shoulders and let her mind drift back to the day she always thought of as her escape. She was on her way to Wisconsin, where she spent a summer numbly going through the motions at a resort. Hour after hour, mile after mile, the rain beat down on her car, but nothing was going to slow her down for long. All summer, she'd dutifully called her mother every few days to see how the packing for the Florida move was going. And Mike was afraid to leave his dad alone. "I wish you hadn't gone through that with your dad. That must have been so hard."

Mike reached for her hand and she let him take it. "I knew I'd grown up when I stopped thinking of your dad as the villain. My mom was an adult. She made her own choices. Like you said in my office, whatever happened between our parents had nothing to do with us."

Not exactly. "It wasn't supposed to. But it blew up in our faces, not theirs. That being said…" Ruby told Mike about visiting her childhood house. "I was thinking about how much fun my dad could be."

When Mike smiled he finally looked like himself again. "Your dad never acted like I was trying to get in good with him. I liked him a lot."

"I allowed myself to just say that he was a wonderful dad. I can say that and yet still be disappointed that he hurt my mother." The rawness of her words startled her.

Mike drew her in and she let her head rest on his shoulder. "That's not such a shock. They broke promises. They were reckless."

Ruby let out a guttural sound of frustration. "Exactly." A long moment passed before she spoke again.

"Can we forgive each other *our* mistakes? Can we accept that we were kids?"

"Oh, yeah." Mike released her, but held on to her hand. "That's the reason I had to talk to you. To finish what we started in my office. You're going to leave, Ruby. I get that now. I'm letting you off the hook."

Since she hadn't seen that coming, her expression apparently showed she was lost in their conversation.

"I'm not going to keep pretending that will change," he said. "So, Ruby, I'm going to do something I've never done before. Accept that we were young and had no control over what the adults did."

Even in this tender moment, she couldn't resist joking like they used to. "But Mike, we were such *great* kids."

"And modest." His laugh was tender. "Really, Ruby, I couldn't let you leave again without talking about this. You'll get yourself a great job—when you're ready. I hope you give yourself plenty of time."

She nodded to show she understood.

He drew her to him and kissed the top of her head, letting his mouth linger there. She remembered that he'd always liked the feel of her hair against his skin.

As they waited for the rain to let up, he told her about Jason's progress in therapy. His drawings and the house he built and the balloons sent up as a symbolic way of sending sadness and fear away. "Does this sound familiar?" he asked. "The kinds of activities, the behavior, I mean."

"I've seen counselors do things like that in a kids' healing program I set up," she said. "All kinds of games and role-playing to bring emotions to the surface and build inner strength. Based on what I see of him, Jason's obviously responding well."

Ruby smiled to herself. If Mike had wanted to clear the air between them, he'd succeeded. She could leave in a few weeks without feeling like she was running again.

"Any sign of him talking?" Call it intuition, but she still felt certain it wouldn't be long.

Mike answered with a quick no. "I keep hoping, though."

"I suppose everyone involved tells you to stay patient," Ruby said, mentally walking in Mike's shoes.

"Oh, yeah, but I'm not good at patience."

She chuckled. Kind of like her.

"I wish I could offer some words of wisdom about your Jason. He's such a wonderful kid. Fun and sharp. Kind, too."

"It's meant a lot to me that you care about him."

"He's easy to like." She deliberately avoided saying Jason was easy to love because Emma's words about Ruby becoming attached to Jason rushed back. She would miss the boy more than she wanted to admit.

When the rain stopped, she accepted Mike's offer of a lift home. They pulled into Emma's driveway, but before Ruby could get out of the car, Mike grabbed her hand. "Friends? I mean, I want to see you when you come around to visit Emma."

This was it, Ruby thought. Another way of saying *there really is no us*. She swallowed hard. "Of course, we were always friends, and that's what we are from here on out."

She hurried out of the car and up the stairs to the door without looking back.

CHAPTER THIRTEEN

MIKE BROKE WITH his new rule to wait outside the school for Jason to exit through the door surrounded by classmates. He wanted to tell Mrs. Cermak about Gloria's work with Jason and check in on the classroom. Usually, Jason had addition and subtraction worksheets in his hand and almost always a drawing or two. Sometimes, Mike's heart nearly broke in two at the sight of Jason alone in the midst of dozens of kids streaming down the walk.

But today, Mike stood outside the classroom and watched as Jason stooped to glance at the aquarium before he gave Mrs. Cermak a wave goodbye. She looked up and pointed to Mike and said something to Jason before coming out to the hallway.

"He'll be fine for a few minutes," Mrs. Cermak said, clearly amused. "If I'd known how much the kids would become attached to those fish, I'd have set up an aquarium long ago."

Mike's gaze landed on Jason, who was using his index finger to follow the movements of a blue-and-green fish as it darted back and forth. "Anything I should be aware of?" Mike asked, taking his gaze off Jason.

"Everything's fine," Mrs. Cermak said. "Here's a notice about the school-wide art show at the high school this Thursday. When we decided to have an art show, holding it the week before Thanksgiving seemed ideal. I'd like to hang two of Jason's pictures in the space allotted for my class."

"Really?" Mike squared his shoulders and chuckled. "Funny how that's making me feel all puffed up and proud."

"Like a good dad should," Mrs. Cermak teased. "I've held back some of the drawings the kids do and I'll choose the best of them." She glanced at Jason. "I think parents like the surprise of seeing their kids' drawings."

"So, I won't know ahead of time which ones you pick?"

With a sly smile she said, "Nope. I'm keeping you all in suspense. It makes it more fun."

"Okay, I won't sue and try to pry it out of you," Mike said, sure Mrs. Cermak would get his humor. "I do wonder, though, how long the silence will continue. What will it take to make that breakthrough? Like I told Gloria, I'm trying to take this a day at a time. Noting the small things and enjoying each one."

"I admit I'm curious what he'll have to say when the time comes," Mrs. Cermak said. "I hope he'll still want to draw. The trauma he's suffered aside, his drawings are mature beyond his years. He's got some natural artistic talent."

"Maybe he gets it from his mother," Mike said, then he quickly added, "And some from mine. I'll ask his grandparents about that."

She leaned in as if confiding a secret. "I told Jason he'd have a picture in the show, so he'll be eager to go."

Mike immediately thought of Ruby. Maybe she'd like to see it. Jason would get a kick out of having her there. "I haven't been inside the high school in a long time."

"No, I don't suppose you have." She called out to Jason, who came running.

"We'll see you at the high school, then," Mike said, looking down at Jason, "at *your* art show."

Responding with his usual smile, Jason half skipped, half ran down the hall. "What energy," Mike commented.

Mrs. Cermak's gaze followed Jason as he ran to the door. "He so often reminds me of you, Mike. I remember you, and there's something about your son..."

She didn't finish the thought, but Mike saw the earnestness in her face and stayed quiet while she gathered her thoughts.

"You were your own little person. Complete within yourself."

"I can't speak to what I was like," Mike said, suddenly self-conscious, "but Jason seems to do things deliberately, like lining up his animal collection at particular angles or arranging the crayons in the basket in neat piles." Thinking of his neat stacks of legal pads and law journals, he had to laugh. "I guess I relate to that. Even now as an adult."

"I'm not surprised," Mrs. Cermak said with a laugh. "See you at the show."

"FIRST THINGS FIRST," Mike said when he and Jason got home. "One peanut butter sandwich coming right up." When that was out of the way and Jason was methodically eating the sandwich one crust at a time, Mike called Ruby. It wouldn't feel right not to ask her to come to the art show with him, not after the interest she'd taken in Jason. If she felt obligated to say no in order to avoid him, then Mike would have to accept that.

When she didn't pick up the call, he left a voice mail, explaining the art show coming up on Thursday. "Jason's going to have a couple of pictures in it, so I'm wondering if you'd come along with us. It's going to be at the high school. Let me know. Bye."

The hours passed. She didn't call him back, but around ten o'clock, a text came in: sounds fun—what time?

Short and to-the-point. Pangs of regret took over his thoughts. But as he reminded himself, settling things with Ruby had been his idea.

"HOW DO I LOOK?" Ruby asked, doing a half turn one way and then the other.

"Wonderful," Emma said. "Black heels are great with the dress."

"An extravagance. But for some reason I don't care."

Emma flashed an impish grin. "I wouldn't care, either, if I had a date with a really great guy."

"Date? It's not a date. I told you what Mike and I decided."

"Then what would you call it, Rubes?" Emma laughed as she spoke. "A little get-together with a friend."

"It's a kids' art show, his little boy's pictures are in it. He just wants company."

Emma dismissed that idea with a flick of her hand. "I don't care what he says. He wants you."

Ruby's stomach did a little dance at the sound of those words. They might be true, but they didn't matter. Did they?

"Anyway, you look good. You can wear that shade of deep, dark green better than anyone I know."

She'd pulled out a casual wraparound dress in dark green, perfect with black heels and the bronze-and-garnet earrings. She let her hair hang loose and brush her shoulders.

"Okay, I admit it. I like how I look tonight." She made a stern face and added, "For the kids' art show."

Emma laughed. "Have it your way. Now get out of here."

"I'm on my way." She grabbed her purple raincoat and handbag and hurried to her car.

Ruby had downplayed how much she was looking forward to being with Mike and Jason. She hadn't seen Mike since the town-council meeting, where she'd watched Mike and Emma successfully clear the first hurdle of the trail project. His client, Maggie, had designed a detailed poster showing the trails and landmarks. Emma had guaranteed to cover any overages in spending, and Mike negotiated permission from all the connected property owners and made the case for this modest project. Mike's hairdresser client, Georgia Greer, spoke up for it, and in the end, all but Jim Kellerman voted for it.

The outcome bolstered Mike's faith in Bluestone River's future. "I believe in this little town," he'd said to the group of project supporters.

Now, on the way to the art show, she

passed the skeletal remains of the shut-down food-processing plant. It hurt to see those buildings decay. Though she was planning on leaving, she hoped her trail idea would be her tiny contribution to boost tourism. And Maggie had reminded them that local people would use the trail and visit the sanctuary more often, too.

If she'd been planning to stick around, Ruby would jump in and find funding for other special events and projects the town. So many ideas were on the table, from craft fairs to sports tournaments to a colorful flea market in the spring and fall. Emma said a couple of people had suggested grander holiday festivals meant for local people to enjoy, but that also might attract visitors. Ruby would help write grants no matter where she lived. Emma couldn't be expected to pay for every innovation.

"Relax, Bluestone River isn't your project," she murmured under her breath when she'd parked the car. She took in the familiar sights. The tree-lined drive to the high school. The stadium standing off in the distance. And the gaslight-style lights on the edges of the parking lot.

Anxiety about being in the high school had gnawed at her all day. Now it was intensifying. She took a deep breath to reassure herself, but she didn't shut off the engine.

"WE CAN COUNT on Ruby to be on time," Mike said to Jason as he checked his phone for the time. "We're early." He'd stood under the lights at the entrance, so Ruby could find them easily. Why was he so jittery? It almost felt like prom night and he should have a corsage for her. At his side, Jason was taking two jumps forward to see if he could cross a whole square of sidewalk. He didn't seem nervous at all. Good.

Jason spotted her first and waved. She waved back, smiling happily. "Wow, Jason, you look so grown up in your blazer and tie."

"What about me?" Mike teased. "I've got a tie, too. Do I look as good as Jason?"

"You're both heartbreakers." Ruby said.

"And you're a knockout. But that goes without saying." Glancing down at Jason, he said, "So, let's go inside and see what's what?"

A hint of apprehension clouded Ruby's

face. Mike didn't know whether to note it or let it go. Finally, he decided it was better to acknowledge what was hanging in the air. "It's going to seem strange to go inside, isn't it?"

"I know perfectly well nothing dangerous is lurking inside that building. But I keep thinking about my dad in his office, walking the halls." With a wistful expression, she added, "You know how he used to take the time to stop and talk to all the kids."

"I remember it like it was yesterday," Mike said. "We were lucky. And of all the good teachers and coaches we dealt with as kids, he was the most interested in us."

"He could have been a motivational speaker, my dad." She glanced down at Jason. "And you're quite the artist."

She was ready, Mike thought. He led the way up the stairs and opened the front door. "The grade-school kids' work is in the gym."

Ruby cupped her ear. "I can hear it."

The school was buzzing with conversation and laughter piercing the air. "Check out those kids," Mike said, pointing to a group of older teens. "They have that studied bored look."

"I suppose we were the same at that age."

"You're probably right," Mike responded. "But did we pretend to be that cool and detached?" As a teenager, his priorities were Ruby, basketball and history. If he hadn't gone into law, Mike saw himself bringing history alive for kids.

In the gym, parents and kids were crowded around sections of corkboard and easels. A couple of glass tables held pieces of sculpture and pottery. Most of the walls were covered with artwork.

"Whoa, what an extravaganza." Ruby twirled for emphasis. She grinned at Jason. "It's a dazzling display of color."

I could watch her all day long. Stay, Ruby. Please.

"I don't know what to look at first."

"Well, I do." Mike took Jason's hand, getting hold of himself to focus on his son. "Let's find the pictures from your class? Do you see any of yours?"

Jason pointed ahead, not to a section of wall, but to Mrs. Cermak, who was standing alone near her class's display. "Okay, let's go say hello. Did I tell you, she was Ruby's teacher, too? We were in the same classes all through school."

Ruby smiled. Maybe a little nervously, Mike observed. "Mrs. Cermak has been a real rock for me."

Ruby took a breath and put her hand over her chest. "I know. This is my stuff coming up. Has nothing to do with her."

Mrs. Cermak's face lit up in surprise when she saw them walking toward her. She greeted Jason first, but then greeted Ruby with a lilt in her voice. "It's such fun to see my former students all grown up. And looking beautiful and handsome." She patted Ruby's shoulder. "Mike mentioned you were visiting to help Emma O'Connell. I remember her, too."

"Emma had surgery, but she's almost completely recovered now. I couldn't miss a chance to see Jason's drawings." Ruby spoke fast and fidgeted with her necklace. "I happened to see a couple of them on the fridge in his house."

"I tape every one of his drawings up somewhere," Mike said.

"Well, I told Mike that we grade-school

teachers decided to keep the choice of drawings for the show between ourselves and our students. That way, the parents will be surprised. I'm betting you will be." Mrs. Cermak looked over Mike's shoulder. "Oops, I have to catch someone before she leaves. Enjoy!"

"That was a bit suspicious," Ruby observed.

Mike agreed. He brushed aside his curiosity when Jason tugged at the sleeve of his blazer and led him to the wall. When they got closer, Mike recognized the scene in the first of Jason's drawings. He drew himself with three other kids and one adult with curly blond hair huddled under the covered bridge in the rain. "Oh, that's the day you got caught in the rain with Heather."

"Heather said Jason had to be coaxed to get under the bridge to avoid getting soaked," Mike explained to Ruby, who'd come alongside him. "Seems he likes being out in the rain."

"Very nice, Jason," Ruby said.

Mike took a couple of steps to the side to get a look at the picture next to it. Ruby's stuttered inhale caught his attention. He could barely breathe himself.

The noise in the room receded as a hush fell over him. And Ruby, who'd put a hand over her mouth in awe.

"So this is what Mrs. Cermak meant when she said I'd be surprised," he whispered. It was all there, complete in the picture. Mike, with curly hair and a big smile on his face, was in the front yard with Jason in front of him, and Peach at his side. The orange oval body with a round head and ears, four legs and a long tail left no room for doubt. The third person jumped off the page. A figure with red hair stood close to Mike, her head coming up to his shoulder. Like real life. Jason had even added the huge maple with golden leaves and the black tire swing he liked so much.

Ruby smoothed her hand over the top of Jason's head. "What a fine-looking Peach you drew. And you and your dad are so handsome."

Was her voice shaky or was that his imagination? Mike stole a glance at her, but she was pointing to the maple and the swing and then back to the bridge in the other drawing.

"You did such a good job with the details and your gray slashes look just like rain."

Mike scanned the room for Mrs. Cermak. She likely hadn't known who the third person was when Jason made the drawing, but one look at Ruby solved that mystery. Staring at the picture, Ruby's warning came back to him. *Too late, Rubes, Jason is already attached to you.* The longer Mike stared at the drawing, the more obviously it matched what he and Ruby had wanted for themselves. Dreamed of. Planned for.

So much for letting her off the hook.

He was convinced Ruby had seen it the same way, but rather than staring at it, she herded Jason down the row to look at his classmates' pieces. Mike busied himself by taking shots of the drawings with his phone, stepping back to widen the angle to encompass a large section. He turned away and took some shots of the room and the overhead sign: Bluestone River's Third Annual School Art Show.

When he turned around again, Jason and Ruby were gone, but he quickly spotted them at the long table set up with punch for the kids and coffee and tea for the adults. He hurried to join them.

Ruby scanned the room. "Did you get some good shots of everything?"

"I did." He tried to be as casual in his answer as she was with the question. "Hey, Jason, we'll put the photos in an album. That way, you'll always remember this art show."

"I didn't let him get cookies on his own," Ruby said, stepping back. "I told him he had to wait for you."

"Oh, these treats won't hurt him." Mike wrapped two peanut-butter cookies in a napkin and gave them to Jason.

"Do you recognize anyone else?" Ruby asked in a soft voice.

"Are you afraid someone will see you... see us?" He held up his hands as if warding off her response. "I'm sorry. That came out all wrong."

"No problem. It's okay. Really. But I was only assuming some of our classmates might have kids here. That's all."

Of course, that was logical. "So far, the person I see most often is the mayor. In fact, I see her across the room now. Maybe we should roam around a little and try to avoid her."

Ruby's smile was full of mischief. "Or, we could goad her and let her see us. Maybe this time she'll come right out and ask what makes us think we have the right to be here. I mean, Mike, no one else's families *ever* caused a minute of scandal in Bluestone River. Ours were the *only* ones."

He let out a frustrated growl. "Don't look now, but she's heading our way." He forced his expression to seem welcoming.

Ruby didn't respond but turned and smiled at the approaching mayor.

"We meet again, Mike." Kristine smiled.

"You're doing your mayor thing, I see," he said.

"And, Ruby, nice to see you again. You keep turning up. I didn't get a chance to tell you how much I liked your trail idea. Thanks to Mike it went right through." A puckish smile crossed her face. "But, last time I bumped into you, you had one foot out of town."

"I still do. December. I'll be gone in December."

"Unless Emma and I can talk her into

staying a few more weeks," Mike said, his jaw tightening. Something in the almost hostile way Kristine cut her eyes back to Ruby struck a nerve. "We both wish she'd decide to stay."

As if the conversation had nothing to do with her, Ruby turned her attention to Jason and remarked again about how great his drawing was.

Kristine kept her surprised eyes on Mike. "I can't imagine why she'd want to do that, Mike. I'm *still* surprised to see you around town."

Mike squared his shoulders and stood a little taller. "Why wouldn't I come back? Or Ruby? We were raised here, just like you."

"I only meant..." She pressed her lips together and clasped her hands.

"What?" Mike challenged.

Kristine looked helplessly at Ruby, as if expecting her to help get out of the mess she'd created for herself. Ruby lifted her chin and stared back.

Obviously flustered, Kristine said, "Oh, come on, you two. You know exactly what I mean. Your family problems became a big deal in this little place. It all took place in public for everyone to see."

"So?" Mike widened his stance and crossed his arms.

Kristine gave him a sharp look. "When your dad sold the resort, the lake was all that was left of the Abbots in this town. And the Driscolls were long gone by then. You all ran away."

Mike narrowed his eyes. "I expected more from you, Kristine. You were a year behind us, but we all went to school together. You knew Ruby, you knew me." He shook his head in disgust.

"Apparently, Kristine, a hideous tragedy to us is an unforgettable scandal to you." Ruby tapped her mouth as if surprised by her own words.

Kristine met her gaze, but quickly looked away. Mike offered Ruby a faint smile of solidarity and added, "And it changed everything."

"Okay, okay. Suit yourselves," Kristine said dismissively. "But a lot of us did stick around and have witnessed the place shrinking around us. You've seen the ruins of the

Riverside Foods plant. You've seen the empty storefronts."

"None of that is my fault," Mike said. "Or Ruby's. Our parents didn't cause it. So, what's your point?"

Her eyes flashed with anger, over what Mike still couldn't figure out. "You're outsiders now. You don't deal with the everyday troubles, like trying to find enough money to clear snow off the roads, or repair some crumbling sidewalks. Ruby comes up with an idea to expand the trail and now she's the big hero?" Kristine made a half turn and stepped away. "Don't be surprised if not everyone opens their arms to welcome you back."

"That's small, Kristine."

"Maybe so, Mike, maybe so." Kristine quickly headed toward a small cluster of people.

Ruby steered Jason to his side. Mike immediately crouched down. "I'm so impressed with you, buddy. Time to go home."

"I should be heading out, too," Ruby said, "but I'm happy I got to see your art show, Jason. Thanks for inviting me. You should be so proud of yourself."

Mike waited until they were outside before inviting her back to the house for coffee or a glass of wine.

Ruby's eyebrows shot up. "Oh, thanks, but I really should get back to Em. I need to let Peach out."

She bent down and cupped Jason's cheek with her palm. "I'm very proud to know you."

After a quick goodbye, he and Jason were standing right where they had seen her arriving that evening. Now they waved goodbye.

"Okay, Jason, let's go. It's been a big night. It's almost time to get into bed and read a story." He said the words in an upbeat tone, but was distracted by watching the taillights of Ruby's car follow other vehicles down the drive and out to the street.

Mike couldn't muster the energy to keep up cheerful one-sided patter with Jason on the way home. Soon enough, they were at the lake and it took only a few minutes to give Jason a quick shower and sit next to him on the bed to start the first of the two bedtime stories. "This one *again*," he teased, opening the book about an astronaut a long way from home. When they were done, Jason immediately handed him the second book. Mike laughed and ran his fingers through Jason's brown curls. "You don't waste a minute, buddy."

He started the first page of the story, this one about some city kids, when the knocking sound came from the kitchen door. "Who could that be?" he said to Jason. "You stay here. I'll go see."

Ruby...let it be Ruby.

He went down the hall and around the corner into the kitchen. He looked through the glass. *Yes, Ruby.* Simply seeing her lips turning up in a shy smile triggered a happy buzz zipping through his body and leaving him nearly without words.

"Can a woman change her mind?" Ruby asked when he opened the door and stepped back to let her in.

"Always. You're just in time to come and join us for the second story of the night. After that, you can tell me what changed your mind. I know my coffee is good, but..."

Ruby grinned. "I could wait here. I don't want to interfere with Jason's bedtime."

"You won't. He'll be happy to see you." He paused. "Like he always is."

Mike led the way to his old room, where Jason was thumbing through the book, probably reading it himself. Silence couldn't hide the fact that Jason read pretty well. "No fair, you're getting ahead."

"Hi, Jason. Your dad said it was okay for me join you for your story. Hope that's okay."

Jason's private little smile for Ruby always went straight to Mike's heart. And from the sweet expression on Ruby's face it did the same for her. She pulled out the kids' chair from the desk, but Mike pointed with his chin to the foot of the bed. "There's plenty of room for you."

With the light dim in the room, Mike read the new story about kids in a big apartment building camping out in the living room. They imagined themselves in the wilderness with the lamp turning into an eagle and the chair a grizzly. By the time the kids in the story had scared themselves with their imaginations, Jason had nodded off.

Mike closed the book, but stayed put until Jason's breathing was regular and his body limp. He eased off the bed and put the blanket around his shoulders. Ruby went into the hall and Mike kissed Jason's forehead.

Mike pulled the kitchen pocket door closed before joining Ruby on the window seat, where they could see the moonlight reflected on the rippling surface of the lake. Sometimes it was like glass, a still-life painting, but the light wind that night ruffled the surface.

"Quite a sight, isn't it?" he asked, nodding to the window. "What'll it be, coffee or red wine?"

"Wine sounds good," she said.

"While I open the bottle, you can tell me why you changed your mind." He took out two glasses and the corkscrew and lifted a bottle from the wine rack his dad made for his mom one Christmas.

She let out a light laugh. "Oh, such a hard question. I'm not even sure."

"Try, please." The words caught in his throat as the buzz in his body came rushing back.

"It's all mixed up with these feelings I have about what's good for Jason. For his sake, I shouldn't be here. I should leave right away."

He opened his mouth to interrupt to argue a different case, but her raised palm stopped him cold.

"Then, Kristine riled me up. Oooh, she made me so mad. She all but said there's nothing for you here in town. And the way she talked, *I* most certainly should get out of Bluestone River." Her voice rose with each word. "It shifted something in me about what happened to us." Her forehead wrinkled in a deep frown. "Not our parents, Mike, but us."

Finally, Mike thought, feeling all his muscles letting go. He poured them each a glass of wine, then sat on the opposite side of the window seat and handed her a glass. He had the urge to propose a toast.

"I have this sort vague and fleeting anger at my mom," Ruby said. "She convinced me that we wouldn't be welcome in town. She thought her friends would abandon her. A few years ago she admitted they tried to support her, but she rejected them."

"Doesn't that make sense in a way? She was embarrassed." Mike pointed down. "My dad didn't leave the house because my mom humiliated him. His word."

"Kristine knows you're a leader, Mike. She probably senses you're a rival. Something like that."

Mike laughed. "I'm a big threat to her. Me and my growing law firm. I didn't get a chance to tell you, but I may have a third client."

"Hey, see? I knew this would work." She looked down into the glass of wine. "Tonight I made a resolution. I'm not going to act like I need to slink around my hometown as if I did something wrong."

This was the crossroad. A second chance was one thing, but if he let her walk away again, he'd never get a third chance.

"Then don't go, Ruby. I love you. I've always loved you. *Stay.* For me. For us."

She groaned. "Mike…c'mon. You can't mean—"

"You bet I mean it." He put his glass on the island counter and moved closer so he could pick up her hand. "How much longer are we going to let our parents steal what was ours?" he demanded. "I know what I said the other day. And it's true. No more blame. I was prepared to give you up once and for all. But I don't want to. And I don't think you want that, either."

She closed her eyes, as if blocking out what he'd said.

"I'm not backing down. Your dad and my mom had an affair for reasons we don't know, and may never understand." He ran his index finger down her cheek. "Can we agree on that?"

She tilted her head the flirtatious way he remembered so well. "I'll stipulate to that."

"See? We're halfway there." He took the glass out of her hand and rested her palm against his cheek. "Do you love me, Ruby?"

"Mike, you know I do."

"Okay, that took care of the second half. That's it. We settled the hard part. We were robbed. And now we've agreed not to blame ourselves or each other for what happened. But, Ruby, let's take another step. Maybe reasons to be apart made sense a long time ago. But not anymore. We love each other."

Ruby put up a hand to stop him. "Love is fine, but we don't know a relationship would *ever* work out between us."

"Do you remember this?" he asked, lean-

ing in and kissing her lightly. "I never forgot. Never." He kissed her again and again,
deepening each kiss as he smoothed his fingers over her wet cheeks. He buried his face
in her hair and tightened his embrace. *Never
let go, never again.* Suddenly, she raised
her head and took his face in her hands and
kissed him as if twenty years had vanished.

"You haven't left me alone for twenty
years, Mike. You've lived in my heart all
this time." She pulled away and gulped back
tears. "This is so risky. Jason...nothing is
more important. He's precious. *Vulnerable.*"
She wiped away more tears, but she managed a smile.

"It was always so sweet between us, Ruby.
Now I see you with Jason. Of course, he's
attached to you. But aren't you attached to
him?"

Ruby nodded and then looked into his
eyes. "Can't fool you. I'm putty in your son's
hands." She chuckled. "Like Peach is. She
adores the little boy who's never said a word
to her."

He leaned in and kissed again, and then
again. "Who needs words when we can
share kisses like these? All the years drop

away. When I kiss you I'm like a kid crazy in love. Only now I'm an adult man in love."

She traced her finger along his jaw, her face tender, thoughtful. "But what about Jason?"

"What about him? He loves you. That's why we were worried, you and I both, about him becoming attached. If we're together, it's good news." As if reading her mind, he added, "He'll speak when he's ready. Meanwhile, he's gaining more confidence and reaching out more and more."

"But...still, he's troubled."

"And you're not up for a challenge?" He pulled his head back. "Since when?"

She stared out the window, no longer tearful, but still looking perplexed, uncertain.

Drawing her into his arms, he whispered, "Maybe it's too soon to talk about this, but we could have a child of our own. We always planned to. Think of it. We can still have the life we wanted." He laughed. "I'm sure Jason wouldn't mind adding a baby to his drawing."

"Oh, Mike, we had our strategies, our goals..."

"You don't have to finish that sentence,

Rubes." His voice was filled with frustration over the past. He pointed out the window. "Look out there, Ruby. It's the same Bluestone River moonlight we chased in the rowboat when we went out as far as we could to hide from my parents and steal a few kisses."

She laughed. "Or, even better on moonless nights when it was too dark to be seen." He wrapped his arms around her and breathed in the scent of her hair. "What do you say? Let's give it a try."

Silence.

"We should admit how we feel and—"

Suddenly, piercing shrieks startled Mike. He ran to open the kitchen door and hurried down the hall. "I'm coming, Jason, I'm coming." The sound of the crying was matched by Jason's thrashing, caught among the blanket and sheets. Inconsolable at first, Jason took a while to calm down, but Mike was patient. It just took time. He gathered him up in his arms and started rocking him back and forth, back and forth.

CHAPTER FOURTEEN

RUBY FOUGHT THE impulse to go after Mike and stayed behind in the kitchen. Mike knew what to do. She wanted so badly to say yes to a life with Mike. Maybe even a baby. All their teenage passion rushed back. It hadn't ever left them.

What do you say? Let's give it a try. Huh? His words haunted her. She couldn't afford to give it a try. That's what Neil and Emma did. They wasted years trying. It was only a few days ago that she and Mike had agreed to move on...alone.

She tiptoed down the hall to the doorway of Jason's room. With his back to her, Mike was murmuring soothing words. "You're okay, you're okay. I'm here."

She closed her eyes. It thrilled her to whisper about living in each other's hearts for two decades. And reminisce over moonlight and share kisses that seemed as familiar as her face in the mirror. She was a puddle of emotion watching Mike comfort his son. He'd had Jason for only a short while, and so quickly become a really great dad.

Jason's picture of the three of them and Peach reflected not just what he saw, but what he wanted. Ruby was sure of it.

As she looked on, though, talk about their feelings for each other could sound so perfect in the moment. With Jason to consider, they had no room to get it wrong. She didn't believe it would happen, but it was possible Jason would live in his silence for years to come. He'd need his dad. Ruby couldn't continue letting this child count on a family that would never match his fantasy.

Ruby mulled over what had compelled her to turn her car around and head to Mike's. She and Mike talked a good game about closure and letting each other off the hook. Right. And one look at a child's drawing stripped away the facade. Who were they kidding?

Still…this was too fast, too driven by what they wanted to be true. She—and he—needed time to be sure. Ruby found the pad of paper and the pen on the counter and wrote:

> I'm not running away. This isn't me avoiding anything. But please, think about what you want, not just for you, but for Jason. Meet me at the bridge in the morning. Love, Ruby.

She moved it to the center of the island, where he couldn't miss it. She went quietly to the door and let herself out.

RUBY ARRIVED FIRST on the cold, gray morning and leaned against the railing on the park side of the bridge. She wore her purple raincoat since dark clouds hung heavy in the sky. It was the perfect day to wear her favorite color.

Over breakfast, she'd told Emma what happened the previous night, from the minute she met Mike at the school to leaving his house and coming home by herself. She'd left Emma nearly speechless—both happy and apprehensive about what would happen now. *Just like me.*

She'd slept off and on, mostly restless and

eager to see the sun rise. In between dozing off for a few minutes she read through her journal and looked at the list of possible jobs she'd flagged on her computer. The jobs were all over the country, some that a second look told her were a bad fit. When she'd arrived, she'd been badly shaken by failure. And burnout. The years of work in crisis and trauma and dealing with that last school board had taken their toll. Like Emma had said about her surgery, time itself was healing.

And so is he.

Mike's car came down the unpaved road and pulled onto the shoulder. When he got out of the car, he smiled. With a purposeful stride, he crossed the bridge and headed straight to her. He gathered her in his arms and kissed her. She held tight to him, relieved he'd understood. When he broke the kiss, she pulled his head down to her and kissed him again. Finally, they paused, and he whispered, "I'm so glad to see you. Why did you leave?"

"It's going to sound trivial, but it's not. Last night you said, 'Let's give it a try.'" She lowered her gaze. "We can't afford to try. We need to succeed for all our sakes. I know you didn't mean it that way, but it startled me."

Mike knocked the heel of his hand against his head. "I can't believe that was my big proposal. That's what I thought I was doing."

"Really?" Ruby snorted a laugh.

She was teasing, and he was almost certainly aware of that.

"I can do better." He chuckled and turned red. "Just give me a minute to come up with a line or two a little more romantic than 'let's give it a try.'"

She let go of one of his hands and put her hand in the center of his chest. "Not yet.

"Mike, we have everything. We love each other. But we have a complicated history—"

"I thought we settled that." His voice sounded anxious. "We had that talk."

"And we let each other go. We said as much. Did everything change because of a child's drawing? You were speechless. I was thrown and had to walk away or I would have burst into tears."

"If I'd seen Jason's drawing, that talk we had would have been much different. I had argued against what I knew we could have together. Instead, I decided to accept that you were leaving. I couldn't let you go until you knew how I felt. No more blame, no more anger. And you gave the same back to me. I didn't love you any less that day than I do right now."

Her heart knew that all along. "I've been cautious. I was afraid of people like Kristine." She pointed to herself. "Me. Afraid of someone like that?"

"You pretty much handled her attitude when you reminded her that what happened was a tragedy." Mike tightened his mouth.

"I get that now. But, there's Jason. I left your house because I wanted you to have time to think that through."

Mike laughed. "Ya wanna know what I think. I think you'll be a wonderful mom to my son. He'll be ours, just like any child we might have." Mike wrapped his arms around her and whispered, "So, will you marry me? As soon as possible? Right here on this bridge?"

"Much better," Ruby said, nodding. "Yes, yes and yes. But how soon is as soon as possible?"

"Oh, I don't know. Tomorrow? Or, next weekend? How about Christmas?"

"Nope. This will be your first real Christmas with Jason. A time you—we—will start the traditions you want. No water parks this year." Ruby felt bubbly inside over the idea that popped up. "I got it. A new life for a New Year. How about New Year's Eve?"

Mike pretended to groan about how far away that was as he counted the weeks on his fingers. "Not too bad. Okay, December 31st. A great wedding anniversary."

She took Mike's hand and pulled him onto the bridge. "Do you remember where we put our initials?"

"I was so sure of us, I skipped the initials phase. I carved our names, remember?" Mike pointed to a corner and they crouched down. "See? There's the heart you painted. It was bright, but it's sort of faded now."

"Magenta. I'll get the paint. Why don't we carve our wedding date under the heart?"

He put his arm around her. "Great idea. We'll come back and fix it up."

Ruby traced their names with her finger. "I haven't stopped here to look at our heart in all this time. Too many memories about the day we painted it. The fun we had."

"I remember lots of kissing," Mike said. "I've avoided stopping inside the bridge, too. It always seemed better not to take too many trips to the past. But that's over now."

"Well, then kiss me. Right here. In our special spot." Ruby stood and opened her arms and welcomed Mike's cool lips pressed on her face and her neck, holding her closer and closer with every kiss.

They were locked in an embrace when a sudden noise above them captured their attention. Ruby let out a hoot. "Listen to that racket. It's rain. We used to get caught in the rain down here all the time."

"Do you have to be anywhere soon?" he asked.

"Nope. How about you?"

He put his cheek on the top of her head. "Not until this afternoon—that's still hours away."

"Aw, too bad. Seems we'll have to stay here a while."

Mike grabbed her hands and kissed the palm of one and then the other. "I guess we'll have to think up things to do."

"Like plan our wedding," Ruby suggested.

"In a few minutes. First, more of these." He leaned over and kissed her. And kissed her again.

CHAPTER FIFTEEN

RUBY SMOOTHED HER finger along the wood frame. Jason's drawing of the family now hung on the kitchen wall. "This is the one, Em," she said proudly. "The picture that changed everything."

Emma gazed at them—Mike, Ruby, Jason and Peach. "Amazing. He created the picture of his life *now*."

"It's a little daunting. A lot to live up to," Ruby stated. It was a fact. "The glow of all this happiness won't stop the bumps ahead. Mike and I have a lot to learn about working together to make sure Jason heals."

"Yep, but you're not kids floating on clouds. The two of you have your feet on the ground." Emma's smile was smug and amused. "I *love* being right. It took a while, but your dreams are coming true."

"I can hardly believe it myself."

"Believe what?" Mike asked, coming into the kitchen from the pantry with a large pot.

"That it's already Thanksgiving." Ruby sniffed the air. "Smells like a turkey is roasting in here."

"Jason and I have been busy this morning." He glanced fondly at Jason, who climbed on the chair at the table and rested on knees so he could watch everything going on. "I told him we were making a family tradition. Thanksgiving at our lake, with turkey and cranberries and pumpkin pie."

Ruby waved to the carryalls on the table. "Cranberries and pie, coming right up."

"Were you planning to cook potatoes for the whole neighborhood in that pot?" Emma said, making her way to the table. "Or maybe can applesauce?"

"I bought a ton of potatoes, so we'll have leftovers." Mike grinned at Jason. "I'll make you my dad's famous potato pancakes."

"And I'll make shepherd's pie." Emma wiggled the fingers of both hands. "Let the peeling begin. I think I can do that sitting down." Emma slipped into the chair at the table, but earlier she'd walked easily from the car to the house with her cane, looking fit and standing tall.

"Is shepherd's pie one of your specialties, Em?" Mike asked.

Ruby snorted.

"Uh, not exactly. I've never made it. Or even thought about it." Emma lifted one shoulder dismissively. "But who says I can't give it a try? Ruby and I can both read a recipe as well as the next person. Right, Rubes?"

"I'm sure we could if we tried." Laughing along with Mike, Ruby left the food prep to the others for the moment and wandered over to the row of windows that looked out on the lake and the tire swing hanging from the giant maple in the front yard. All the fall finery was gone now, but it would be back next year. *And I'll be here to see it.*

As Ruby watched the ducks paddling across the quiet lake, she stayed in the present and enjoyed the kitchen filled with the aromas of the holiday. Her favorite one. And her first Thanksgiving with Mike and the little boy she'd taken into her heart. Her mind jumped ahead to Christmas and then New Year's Eve, their wedding day. From there it was an easy leap to Easter and the Fourth of July and another fall and another and another and to more Thanksgivings on the lake.

She glanced at the table, where Emma and Mike were working on the potatoes and chatting about dinner. Peach sat next to Jason as if awaiting further orders. "C'mon, Jason, Peach. Let's go outside and throw the stick around."

"Now?" Mike asked quizzically.

"We'll work off a little energy. Kids get antsy waiting for a big holiday dinner. We'll come back in with plenty of time to make the pie and set the table. Everything else is done, or almost done."

"You're right." Mike signaled to Jason.

Jason slid off the chair and ran past her to the mudroom. "It's a pretty warm day for late November. Peach will head for the water—she likes being wet," Ruby said. "This will probably be the last day for a dip this year. We'll make sure we dry her off before we let her back in the house."

Confident at playing the throw-and-fetch game with Peach, Jason didn't wait for Ruby to direct the action. He scrambled around the ground until he found the perfect stick. Ruby laughed to herself at the way Peach's tail swished as she danced on her paws and jumped in anticipation of the stick flying through the air.

"A boy and his dog," Ruby murmured. Peach was *their* dog now, but in a way, Ruby knew she'd be Jason's dog more than hers. He'd soon be old enough to help take care of her. She'd probably want to sleep in his room. Ruby was so happy. Thanks to Peach, they were off to a strong start, she and Jason. She was truly grateful for that. How unlikely it was that she'd had a dog in the first place. Not on the go—or on the run—Ruby.

Moving closer to the shore and Jason, she said, "Our Miss Peach sure has a ton of energy. I bet she'll take a snooze in the corner while we gobble up our turkey."

Jason looked at her and gave her his amused smile, his way of showing agreement. He liked certain words, too. *Snooze* was one of them. He seemed to pay attention when she and Mike talked about projects and strategies, sounding a lot like Mike's mom.

Looking at Jason running back and forth along the shore, she wouldn't have guessed he'd had a nightmare last night. Earlier, Mike had called and talked about Jason crying out in the night. After racing to his room, Mike had stood in the doorway watching the boy turning on his side and snuggling under the covers on his own. The nightmare ended without Mike's rocking and reassuring words. That was the second time that happened. More signs of progress.

Peach dropped the stick in front of Jason and shook the water off her coat. Jason might as well have stood under a shower. "Okay, Jason, when you get that wet it's time to go inside. Maybe we can come out again later if it's still light out."

Hearing her name, Peach ran to her. Then Ruby held out her hand and Jason slipped his into it and, with Peach leading the way, they all went inside. Ruby took one end of a huge towel and gave Jason the other end and together they rubbed Peach's coat until she was damp but not dripping.

"Just in time," Emma said to Jason as she was preparing the cranberries. "Won't be long now."

"My helper and I will set the table, Mike." Ruby opened the glass doors of the hutch."

"We're going to eat in the dining room," Mike said to Jason, gesturing to the large oak table. "It will be our first time not eating here in the kitchen."

"See? That shows you what a big deal Thanksgiving is," Ruby said, beaming at Jason.

"Do you want to use my mom's harvest china?" Mike glanced from Ruby to Emma.

Emma said nothing, but looked expectantly at Ruby. She and Mike hadn't figured out all the details about converting this house into a home of their own. They'd only agreed the house and lake were too beautiful to abandon. This decision over dishes probably wasn't going to be the first time she'd make choices about traditions Mike grew up with. She'd make this one easy.

Moving closer to Mike, she said, "They'll be other days to decide what to let go of and what to keep. Today, let's remember your mom by using these things she liked."

Mike reached out, drew her to him and planted a kiss on her forehead. "Thanks, Ruby."

"You're not touching those, are you?" Emma laughed as she swept her arm toward the long row of windows.

"Are you kidding?" Ruby said in perfect unison with Mike. "The windows stay."

In the time it took to set the table and put the pie in the oven, Mike and Emma got the turkey on the table with all the side dishes. Ruby looked for Peach and found her in the living room stretched out in front of the couch asleep, a satisfied expression on her face.

"She's snoozing, Jason," she said on the way to her seat at the oak table. "Just like I predicted."

Emma stretched her arms out, palms up. Ruby knew that gesture. She wanted everyone around the table to hold hands.

Jason stared at Emma as if wondering what was going to happen next on this day that wasn't just another day with Dad.

"Thanks for including me in this wonderful celebration," Emma said. "I have a lot to be thankful for this year myself."

Mike turned his attention to Jason and gave his fingers a quick squeeze. "And so do we. This is the start of our holidays, Jason.

Next is Christmas in a few weeks, and then a week after that it will be New Year's Eve, the day Ruby and I get married at the bridge. Then we'll all be a family."

"And we'll eat wedding cake at my house," Emma said, clapping her hands.

She and Mike both wanted a quiet afternoon wedding at the bridge and food at Emma's house. Mike asked Maggie's husband, a chaplain, to officiate and he chose Mrs. Cermak as his witness. Emma would be Ruby's.

Her sister, Dee, was eager to come to the wedding, but Ruby hadn't been certain her mom would be willing to make the trip. But her mom insisted she wouldn't miss the wedding for anything.

Even now, Ruby was jittery with impatience for the day to come. She'd already found some grant-writing work and was scouring community development foundations to find funding for Bluestone River projects. But she wasn't rushing to fill her days. She wanted to take it slow with Jason and let him get used to her as a stepmom and someone he could trust.

With the updates she and Mike planned to

make this house their own, for the first time in twenty years, she'd have a place to call home. And maybe, if they were really lucky, Jason would be a big brother to a new baby.

"Look at me carving a turkey." Mike chuckled as he picked up the carving knife and fork. "I'm turning into my dad."

"It's a very good look for you," Emma teased. "So manly."

"I agree," Ruby said, amused at Mike's cheeks turning pink. "Hey, Em, would you look at that. We've made the man blush."

"I know, I know." He put part of the drumstick on Jason's plate. "You get to eat that with your fingers. It's pretty big, but what you don't finish today will be there tomorrow."

Ruby passed bowls of potatoes and stuffing to Emma, but out of the corner of her eye Ruby watched Jason shifting his gaze from one adult to another, listening to the banter about the best turkey stuffing ever and Mike's opinion that Emma's homemade cranberries were far superior to canned.

When they relaxed over pie and coffee, Jason slid off his chair and ran into the living room to be with Peach.

"He needs to ask to be excused," Mike said when Jason was out of sight. "He's old enough now, but I can't exactly demand it."

Ruby didn't know what to say to that, but Mike hadn't expected an answer.

Instead, Mike tapped a knife against his glass. "Okay, you two. I have something to say. It's big."

"Like anything could be bigger than the news about you and Ruby," Emma said.

"Let's hear the guy out." Ruby rolled her hand in front of her. "We're listening."

"It's time to test myself." Mike's face brightened with a self-satisfied smile as he looked at Ruby. "I've been sitting on this idea until I'm sure it's what I want to do."

Ruby smiled. "Whatever it is, you look mighty pleased."

"Okay, here goes." In what Ruby named Mike's lawyerly voice he said, "I've made up my mind to run for mayor in the spring. Kristine said she's going to run for the state senate, so it's an open job. I looked at the pros and cons. Someone's got to be the mayor. Why not me?"

Ruby burst out laughing and clapped her

hands. "I knew it. I knew it. I had the feeling you've been mulling this over for weeks."

"Then you're okay with it?" Mike leaned in toward her. "I wouldn't do it if you objected."

She rose from her chair and kissed Mike's cheek. "Seriously? I'm more than okay. I'm thrilled."

"We're facing a lot. Plenty of changes afoot and…"

Ruby dismissed that concern with the swat of her hand. "Ever since you and Emma backed my idea to extend the trail, I've been looking for more things to take on." Starting with the farmer's market off River Street she'd been thinking about. To succeed as a summer evening event it would need to include more than produce vendors. Music and carryout food and maybe a tent with local artists showing their work. She was still researching community grants to cover startup costs.

"Great," he said. "I'll consider you and Emma my first two votes."

Emma cleared her throat. "Now that I'm more myself again, I can get involved, too. Spending the day out here at the lake is like a giant push to making the bird sanctuary live up to its promise."

Those words wrapped Ruby in a pleasant buzz of happiness and optimism. Home. She'd gone all over the country believing she was looking for home and ended up back in this little town that had nurtured her so well. Now it was her turn to put her sadness and tragedy behind her and help shape the future.

They began clearing the table and putting away food. "Why don't you take Peach and Jason outside for one last run around before it gets dark," Mike said.

"Then we should probably go, huh, Emma?" Ruby asked.

Emma nodded. "I don't like admitting it, but I'm wearing out."

Ruby went into the living room and asked Jason if he wanted to come outside with Peach while there was still enough light. "We'll keep her out of the water, though, so we stay dry."

Outside, the orange-and-pink sky tinting the lake also left the bare trees on the far shore looking like a twinkling fairyland.

Even the ducks paddling by were bathed in the changing light of the fading afternoon.

Ruby's chest ached with happiness. Tears pooled in her eyes watching this little boy she'd come to love so much. She glanced back at the house. Through the windows, she spotted Mike loading containers in a bag, laughing over something with Emma. She could count the weeks until she'd move her few things into the house as Mike's wife and Jason's stepmom. Her head told her the challenges would be huge, but her heart longed to take them on.

With Peach following, Jason ran to the tire swing and began working up momentum as the dog looked on. Lost in her own thoughts about Christmas, the sound of Mike's voice calling her startled her.

As Mike walked toward her, he told Jason it was time for Ruby to take Emma home.

"Come give me a hug, Jason," Ruby called.

Jason stayed in place. A disapproving look took over his face.

He probably didn't like the day coming to a close, Ruby thought, stepping into Mike's open arms. She gave him a quick kiss and with their arms around each other's waists, they started up the slope from the shore.

"Come on, Jason," Mike said. "Let's say goodbye."

"He's being stubborn, isn't he?" Ruby whispered.

Looking puzzled, Mike said, "I guess so."

"Let's go, Peach." Ruby gestured at Peach, who looked back at Jason, but dutifully made her way to Ruby's side.

"No," an unfamiliar voice shouted. "Don't *go*, Ruby."

She spun around. Mike took off in a shot for the swing.

"You're supposed to stay here with *us*, Ruby. Peach, too," Jason said, his voice quivering.

Mike lifted Jason off the swing and held him tight in his arms. His voice broke when he said, "You have no idea how much I've been wanting to hear you."

"Why is Ruby leaving?" Jason asked.

Ruby moved closer. "Oh, sweetie, I'm only going back to Emma's house for now. I'll see you tomorrow."

Jason wiggled out of his dad's hug and Mike put him down on his feet. "But *you* said Ruby was moving into *our* house. We're a *family*. Like in my picture. Peach, too."

"Oh, buddy, Ruby *is* coming to live with us. After Christmas when the New Year starts."

Ruby crouched in front of Jason. "We're going to have our wedding on New Year's Eve. Remember, I said it's going to be an extravaganza. And then we'll be a new family."

Ruby pointed back at Emma, who sat on the stairs watching. Ruby waved and Emma happily waved back. "I'm going to stay with Emma and we'll all have Christmas here together." She stroked Jason's cheek. "Will you promise me something?"

Jason looked wary, but nodded. "Okay." Then he turned his attention to the dog.

"Starting tomorrow, when I come back here to make leftover turkey sandwiches, will you tell me your favorite stories and talk to me about what you like best in school? And I'm sure Peach will like hearing you call her by name."

With a little shrug, he said, "I know."

"And I guess that's that." Laughing, Mike stood and put his arm around Ruby.

Dropping her head to let it rest on his shoulder, she closed her eyes and sighed with happiness. "I think that little voice is the best sound I've ever heard."

"Wait, wait, Ruby," Jason hollered. "I have something to ask you."

Her heart made a huge leap to her throat. "Oh? Well, okay," she said, trying not to burst into tears. "What is it?"

"Can we do *projects* when you come to live here?"

Ruby laughed, and put her finger on her lips pretending to think. "Hmm…we can manage some projects. What do you want to do first?"

"Take pictures with your phone," Jason said without having to think about it.

Mike chuckled. "Ruby's phone is special, huh?"

"We can take all the pictures you want," she said. "We'll think up all kinds of things to do."

Happy as she'd ever been, she turned to go.

"Wait, wait, Ruby. I've got one more thing to tell you," Jason said, looking like he was about to reveal a secret.

Mike looked on with his mouth hanging open. Curious now, Ruby said, "Okay, let's hear it."

"Do you know what the ducks are?" he asked.

Ruby narrowed her eyes and frowned. "Is this a riddle? I'm stumped."

"Daddy says they're *u-bi-qui-tous*." He laughed. "That means they're all over the place."

Mike laughed and ruffled Jason's hair. "You remembered I told you that?"

One of Mike's mom's favorite words. "Well, your daddy is right. I bet you know lots of fun words."

"And we'll hear them all, won't we?" Mike said, picking Jason up again. "We have to let them go now, Jason." His smile reached from ear to ear. "Love you, Ruby."

"Love you, too," she said, and then pointing to Jason, she added, "And I love you."

Jason beamed. "I love you, too."

"Thanks, Jason," Ruby said, tears rolling down your cheeks. "That means a lot to me."

After turning to give Mike and Jason one last smile and wave, Ruby slowly walked toward the driveway. "This may be the best day of my life—so far."

"You and Mike closed your circle," Emma said.

Against the odds, but we did it.

* * * * *

*Don't miss the next
Return to Bluestone River romance
from Virginia McCullough,
coming soon!*

*For more Heartwarming romances
from author Virginia McCullough,
please visit www.Harlequin.com today!*

THE FORTUNES OF TEXAS COLLECTION!

18 FREE BOOKS in all!

Treat yourself to the rich legacy of the Fortune and Mendoza clans in this remarkable 50-book collection. This collection is packed with cowboys, tycoons and Texas-sized romances!

YES! Please send me **The Fortunes of Texas Collection** in Larger Print. This collection begins with 3 FREE books and 2 FREE gifts in the first shipment. Along with my 3 free books, I'll also get the next 4 books from The Fortunes of Texas Collection, in LARGER PRINT, which I may either return and owe nothing, or keep for the low price of $5.24 U.S./$5.89 CDN each plus $2.99 for shipping and handling per shipment*. If I decide to continue, about once a month for 8 months I will get 6 or 7 more books but will only need to pay for 4. That means 2 or 3 books in every shipment will be FREE! If I decide to keep the entire collection, I'll have paid for only 32 books because 18 books are FREE! I understand that accepting the 3 free books and gifts places me under no obligation to buy anything. I can always return a shipment and cancel at any time. My free books and gifts are mine to keep no matter what I decide.

☐ 269 HCN 4622   ☐ 469 HCN 4622

Name (please print)

Address   Apt. #

City   State/Province   Zip/Postal Code

Mail to the Reader Service:
IN U.S.A.: P.O. Box 1341, Buffalo, N.Y. 14240-8531
IN CANADA: P.O. Box 603, Fort Erie, Ontario L2A 5X3

50BFT19R

Get 4 FREE REWARDS!

We'll send you 2 FREE Books plus 2 FREE Mystery Gifts.

FREE
Value Over
$20

Both the **Romance** and **Suspense** collections feature compelling novels written by many of today's best-selling authors.

YES! Please send me 2 FREE novels from the Essential Romance or Essential Suspense Collection and my 2 FREE gifts (gifts are worth about $10 retail). After receiving them, if I don't wish to receive any more books, I can return the shipping statement marked "cancel." If I don't cancel, I will receive 4 brand-new novels every month and be billed just $6.99 each in the U.S. or $7.24 each in Canada. That's a savings of at least 13% off the cover price. It's quite a bargain! Shipping and handling is just 50¢ per book in the U.S. and $1.25 per book in Canada.* I understand that accepting the 2 free books and gifts places me under no obligation to buy anything. I can always return a shipment and cancel at any time. The free books and gifts are mine to keep no matter what I decide.

Choose one: ☐ **Essential Romance**
(194/394 MDN GNNP)

☐ **Essential Suspense**
(191/391 MDN GNNP)

Name (please print)

Address   Apt. #

City   State/Province   Zip/Postal Code

> **Mail to the Reader Service:**
> **IN U.S.A.:** P.O. Box 1341, Buffalo, NY 14240-8531
> **IN CANADA:** P.O. Box 603, Fort Erie, Ontario L2A 5X3

Want to try 2 free books from another series? Call 1-800-873-8635 or visit www.ReaderService.com.

---

*Terms and prices subject to change without notice. Prices do not include sales taxes, which will be charged (if applicable) based on your state or country of residence. Canadian residents will be charged applicable taxes. Offer not valid in Quebec. This offer is limited to one order per household. Books received may not be as shown. Not valid for current subscribers to the Essential Romance or Essential Suspense Collection. All orders subject to approval. Credit or debit balances in a customer's account(s) may be offset by any other outstanding balance owed by or to the customer. Please allow 4 to 6 weeks for delivery. Offer available while quantities last.

Your Privacy—The Reader Service is committed to protecting your privacy. Our Privacy Policy is available online at www.ReaderService.com or upon request from the Reader Service. We make a portion of our mailing list available to reputable third parties that offer products we believe may interest you. If you prefer that we not exchange your name with third parties, or if you wish to clarify or modify your communication preferences, please visit us at www.ReaderService.com/consumerschoice or write to us at Reader Service Preference Service, P.O. Box 9062, Buffalo, NY 14240-9062. Include your complete name and address.

STRS19R3

HEARTWARMING™

Available September 3, 2019

#295 AFTER THE RODEO
Heroes of Shelter Creek • by Claire McEwen

Former bull rider Jace Hendricks needs biologist
Vivian Reed off his ranch, fast—or he risks losing custody of
his nieces and nephew. So why is Vivian's optimism winning
over the kids...and Jace?

#296 THE RANCHER'S FAMILY
The Hitching Post Hotel • by Barbara White Daille

Wes Daniels is fine on his own. He has his ranch and his
children—he doesn't need anything else. But the local
matchmaker has other plans! Now Wes is suspicious about
why Cara Leonetti keeps calling on him...

#297 SAFE IN HIS ARMS
Butterfly Harbor Stories • by Anna J. Stewart

Army vet Kendall Davidson has found the peace she's been
searching for until loud newcomers
Hunter MacBride and his niece arrive
with love and laughter to share, making
her question what kind of life she's truly
looking for.

#298 THEIR FOREVER HOME
by Syndi Powell

Can a popular home reno contest allow
Cassie Lowman and John Robison
their chance to shine and fall for each
other with so much—personally and
professionally—on the line?